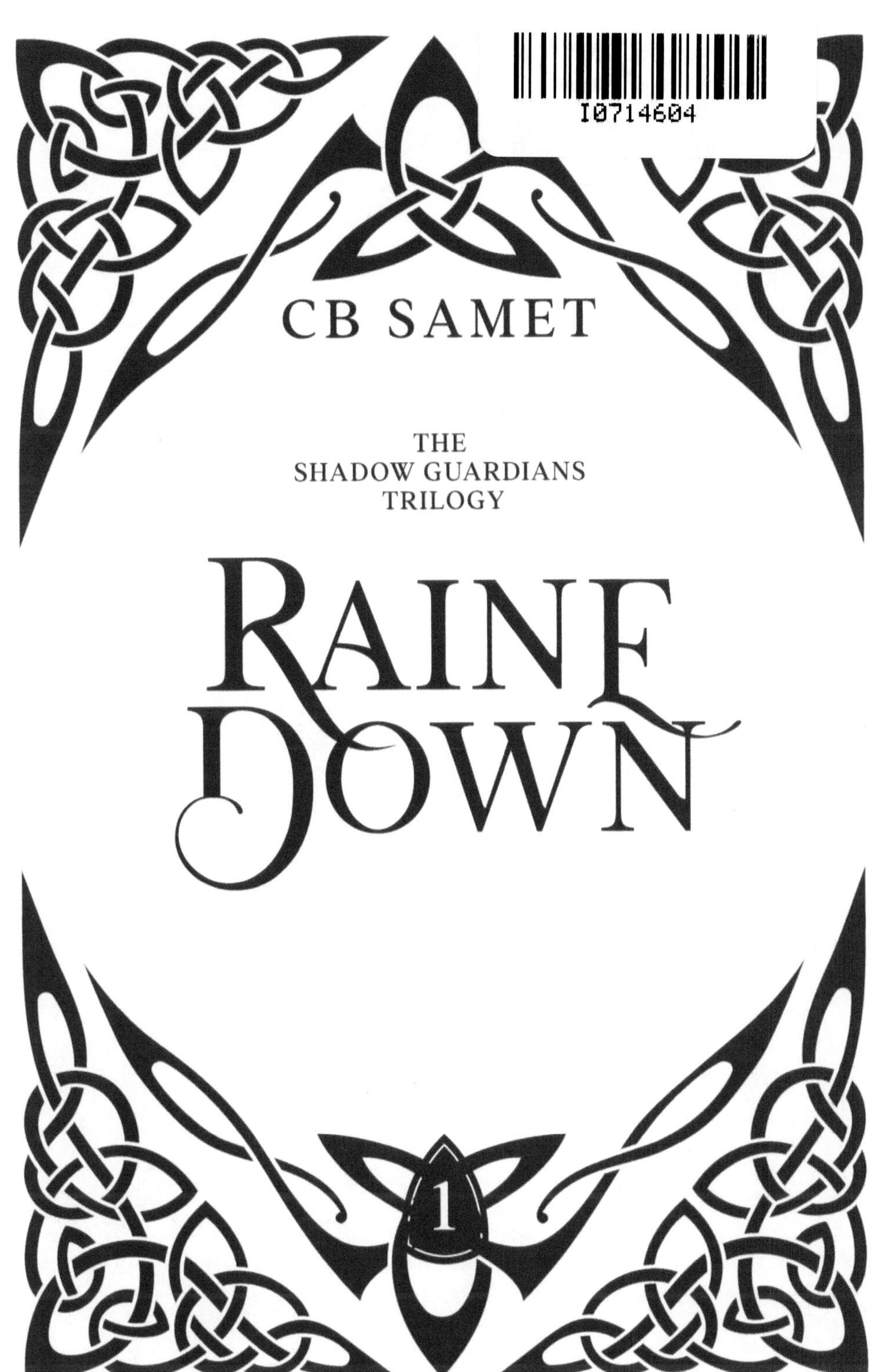

CB SAMET

THE
SHADOW GUARDIANS
TRILOGY

RAINE DOWN

1

RAINE DOWN

THE SHADOW GUARDIANS
BOOK ONE

CB SAMET

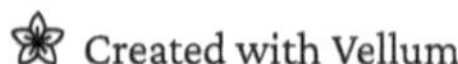 Created with Vellum

CHAPTER

ONE

Raine stalked quietly through the dark corridor on the second floor of the abandoned building, weapon drawn. The man she was pursuing had cornered himself here, and she would hunt him down like the snake he was.

Despite the adrenaline surging through her veins, she controlled her breathing and kept her heart rate steady. Her orders were to apprehend, but her employers wouldn't fault her for shooting a known killer. She doubted he would allow himself to be taken alive anyway. Given the chance, he certainly would kill her.

Gripping her Glock19 tighter, she reminded herself she had the element of surprise. She always had the element of surprise. It was one reason she was an effective Guardian.

She crept into a large rectangular space faintly lit by the glow of streetlights near the windows along one wall. By the indentations on the worn, carpeted floor, the room had formerly been heavily trodden upon by shoes and office chairs. The cubicles remaining were the skeleton of a once living, thriving office space. A few divider walls and shelves littered the room.

When Raine heard movement—the scrape of shoes along the

1

coarse fibers of the carpet—she took position, crouching in the shadows against one wall. Judging by the path he was taking, Jör would walk directly past her. He would have a knife, because that was his weapon of choice—a twelve-inch blade so sharp it could split skin like butter. He was deadly fast with the steel, but Raine had bullets.

And he would never see her coming.

Her plan was flawless.

"FBI! You're under arrest!" a male voice bellowed.

What in the name of Asgard?!

How was an FBI agent treading on her territory? Regardless of his job title, the man would be no match for Jör.

Raine eased up to her full height while still keeping in the shadows. She surveyed the scene. As Jör at her three o'clock wound toward the agent through cubicle dividers like a serpent through grass, the over-eager FBI agent stood at her nine o'clock with his weapon drawn, probably a Glock like hers.

The scene raised several dilemmas in her mind. She didn't have a clear shot on Jör, and if she fired she would give away her location. In addition, her gunfire would draw the attention of the FBI agent, who would then probably shoot at *her*. Meanwhile, if she did nothing, Jör would kill the agent. The man intruding on her hunt may be a moron, but she couldn't let him die.

By Odin's eye, she silently swore.

Moving quickly and quietly, she weaved her way toward the man. When she rounded a bookshelf, she saw Jör raising his silver blade to slice at the surprised FBI agent, who pivoted too slowly to readjust his aim.

Raine kicked the empty, dust-laden shelf to buy her a second of distraction as she lunged.

Leaping toward them, she raised her left arm in defense and fired her 9mm with her right. Jör's blade sunk into her left forearm, sending white hot pain up her elbow and into her shoulder.

Jör shrieked from the bullet wound and jerked his knife back out of her so fast she hadn't even landed on the floor yet.

Blinded by pain, she wasn't sure where her shot had landed. His abdomen? His leg?

Sturdy arms broke her fall.

"What the hell?" a deep voice reverberated through her ears.

She raised her gun, ready to shoot Jör again, knowing full well it would take more than one bullet to put him down.

A line of blood trailed along the carpet and around a cubicle, out of sight. At the far end of the room, a door opened and slammed shut.

Gone. He was gone.

Raine dropped her gun and clutched her wound as a wave of nausea swept over her. She couldn't follow now; she had to stop the bleeding. Cold sweat punched through her.

The FBI agent tugged off her scarf and began wrapping her arm with it. "That's a lot of blood. We've got to get you to a hospital."

"Just wrap it tight. We can't let Jör get away."

"It's a little late for that."

She turned her head and blinked at the FBI agent. He had a handsome face with strong cheekbones and a narrow nose. Intense green eyes filled with worry focused on her. His attractive features wouldn't save him from the tongue lashing she planned to give him at his monumental blunder in announcing his position to a lethal demon, but first the room needed to stop spinning.

WILL Decker holstered both of their guns. "Up you go."

He helped the woman to her feet as she cradled her left arm, now wrapped in a baby-blue rayon scarf. She was tall, probably five-eight, but still a half foot shorter than him.

How was she still conscious after enduring a knife plunging through her forearm? All the way through. He'd seen the silver tip come out the other side of her arm—a tip that'd had a direct trajectory toward Will's heart.

How had that man been so damn fast?

And how did this woman possess the prowess and gumption to put herself between him and a knife? He could still see her diving through the air, blonde ponytail trailing behind her. He wondered what organization she worked for that had trained her so well.

And despite a shot to the thigh, the criminal had bolted away, barely fazed and taking his deadly blade with him. Will was going to have nightmares about that knife.

The woman stumbled as if battling the urge to pass out. He needed her to stay coherent. She was slender but built of solid muscle. If she passed out, he'd have to sling her over his shoulder to get her down the stairs, which wouldn't be safe for either of them.

"What's your name?" Will asked, guiding her toward the stairwell exit.

"Raine." Her brown eyes fluttered, threatening to close.

"Rain."

"Rain with an e."

"Okay, Rain with an e. What organization do you work for?"

She blinked before she narrowed her eyes at him. "That's classified."

"Really? Classified? You're going to try that strategy with an FBI agent?"

They made their way down the steps together.

"I don't give a damn how good looking you are. You're the jackass who screwed up my catch." Beads of sweat formed on her forehead.

He blinked at her strange choice of words—an oddly timed compliment minced with insult. Was she delirious?

Her anger brought the redness back into her cheeks, which was a far sight better than how pale they'd been turning. Maybe keeping her angry would help her maintain consciousness until he could get her to a hospital.

At the bottom of the steps, she gestured to a jacket on the floor belonging to her. Will scooped it up, noting it was bulky and crinkly and understanding why she'd taken it off during her pursuit of the criminal.

"I had everything under control until you literally dove onto the scene," he said, knowing it was a complete lie. He'd almost died, and he should thank her. But sweetness wouldn't keep her lucid.

Raine scoffed. "You have no idea what that monster is capable of. You're a mouse to that snake."

The monster she referred to had certainly looked snake-like. His skin had a reddish hue with white flakes. Maybe some type of psoriasis or other skin disorder? The man had moved fast and deadly like a snake, too.

"A mouse?" Will huffed. "I don't know any six-two mice with a gun and a badge."

"Size and status has nothing to do with it. Did my bullet slow Jör down? No, it did not. Yours wouldn't have either."

Jör? She had a name for the serial killer. That was more than Will's files had, unless her organization had given him some kind of nickname. The FBI knew him as the serial killer Blade.

"And why don't bullets slow him down?" Will asked.

They reached the bottom of the stairs and exited the building. Will scanned the perimeter for threats but saw only dim streetlights, a watery moon, and a light drizzle of bone-chilling rain coating the deserted Chicago street.

"Classified," Raine said through gritted teeth.

"Okay, Agent Classified. What *can* you tell me?" He helped her into the passenger seat of his rented Lincoln Continental.

Because his was the only car in the vicinity, he guessed she'd taken a cab or rideshare here. As he leaned over to strap her in, he smelled the faint scent of lavender. A wayward strand of hair brushed his jaw.

After closing her door, he climbed into the driver's side.

"I can tell you that you drive an old man's car." She grimaced.

"Hey, these long legs need space," he fired back playfully,

masking his worry about how much blood she was losing underneath her scarf.

Damn, she was tough. An impalement wound like that, he suspected he would have been bawling like a baby.

"You need to drop your case against Jörmungandr and let me handle him." She cradled her arm.

"You and what army? Besides, I've been tracking this guy for three months. You and your classified-ass can take a backseat to my investigation." He kept his tone light; he wanted to irritate her and distract her from the pain, but he also wasn't going to simply drop his case.

"You're going to get yourself killed."

"Of the two of us, you're the one bleeding." He drove the car away from the curb and headed toward the highway.

"That's because—" She glared at him, but he grinned and winked in return. "Ugh. You're unbelievably annoying."

When she pursed her lips, he suspected she'd deduced he was intentionally provoking her.

In a more serious tone, he said, "Thank you for saving my life, Raine."

"Yeah, yeah." She looked out the window, one arm holding pressure over the bandaged wound.

"Now, I'll return the favor and get you to a hospital."

"No hospital." She laid her forehead against the glass of the passenger side door and closed her eyes.

He was definitely taking her to a hospital.

CHAPTER

TWO

Will glanced at Raine, who slept on the bed. A single bedside lamp cast a golden glow over the brown furniture. The air held mixed scents of vanilla and mothballs. The FBI safe house hadn't been properly ventilated in a while. At least it was warm with a roof.

After what Raine had been through, she was entitled to be sleepy. What was left of her blonde ponytail was in loose disarray around her oval face. Her gentle cheekbones looked peaceful, with soft cream-colored skin and a full set of pink lips. This angelic sleeping woman contrasted the fierce warrior she'd been while awake.

Who is she?

Will had patted down her pockets but found no source of identification. Her phone was password protected, requiring both a thumb read and a passcode entry. He had access to her thumb attached to her gorgeously fit, yet limp, body but didn't know her passcode.

He propped up pillows on his mattress, kicked off his shoes, and sat on the empty twin bed adjacent to hers. Exhaustion weighted his body down and tugged at his eyelids, but he wanted to stay awake long enough for Raine wake and him to know she was okay.

Raine stirred, then sat up and blinked at him. "Where the hell are we?"

He didn't like the way her tone suggested he'd brought her somewhere with dubious intentions. "FBI safe house." He tugged his badge out of his coat pocket and showed her his credentials. They usually seemed to set people at ease in his presence.

After looking at his badge, her gaze shifted to scanning the room. She relaxed with a sigh and said, "Thank you for not taking me to a hospital."

Will crossed his arms. "Oh, I took you to a hospital. The intake nurse pulled off your scarf, cut off your shirt sleeve, and asked me if this was some type of prank."

He waited for Raine to respond, but when she said nothing, he continued, "Because what lay beneath that blood-soaked garment? A scratch. The penetrating knife wound I saw—*I wrapped myself*—had completely vanished."

She frowned. "That's right. I remember leaving the hospital."

"After the nurse kicked us out of the ER in favor of people with actual medical emergencies, you had a moment of lucidness long enough to walk to the car and drink my entire twenty-ounce bottle of water before passing out again. Can you explain how a penetrating gash gushing with blood becomes a cat scratch?" Will asked.

She looked at her now completely healed forearm, rubbing long fingers against the skin.

"Raine?"

"I can't."

"Can't or won't?"

"Won't."

"Hmm. More classified information?" He glared at her.

"Yes."

"You want me to look the other way when confronted with a woman with superhuman healing? What about superhuman stealth, or did I honestly overlook you in that room before you dove in front of me?"

Her eyes went wide.

Well, he nailed that statement.

"Any other superhuman abilities I should know about?"

She arched an eyebrow at him. The expression sent a flare of delight through him, probably not what she'd intended.

He leveled his gaze at her. "I've seen two. Perhaps I should see the others."

When Raine blushed, Will couldn't help but chuckle. He thought maybe she planned to try to seduce him to get out of his questioning, but it seemed she was more modest than he'd initially judged. Good. Seduction was no superpower, just a deceitful tool.

She pushed to her feet. "Bathroom?"

"Directly across the hall."

He admired the way her tight-fitting burglar get up curved over a perfect ass. The black outfit was for theft, assassination... or yoga. He'd bet she was flexible, too.

Damn, he was a jerk. He had no business reducing the woman who'd saved his life to an object of physical desire.

She closed the bathroom door.

He'd been an FBI agent for ten years and seen the occasional superhuman feat, though nothing physics or recreational drugs couldn't explain. A potentially lethal wound healing itself defied everything.

Almost everything, he thought, twisting the dark ring on his right forth finger.

Tonight, he felt as if he'd entered some science fiction *Twilight Zone*. He needed answers from Raine but suspected they would lead to a rabbit hole of more questions.

He stood and walked to the door. "You can't hide in there forever," he called to her. "And there's no bathroom window escape route. My questions will still be here when you come out." His intonation crescendoed playfully at his last few words.

RAINE STARTLED at her appearance in the mirror. With her disheveled hair and mascara smeared eyes, she looked like a 1980s hard rock groupie. She pulled out her ponytail holder and tugged fingers through her snarls. The stab wound had drained her. She stroked a hand over her forearm; the healing was complete, and now the thing would ache and itch for a day.

Will wouldn't have survived the attack, but since Raine had used herself as a shield and he'd witnessed her healing abilities, unanswered questions lingered. The inquisitive FBI agent would have to live with his disappointment though. Raine wasn't authorized to share her genealogy with a standard human bloodline—known as sHBL in her organization—or hubble for short.

She checked her watch—midnight. If she slept here tonight, she could rest before skipping out on Will in the morning. She needed to report back to the Council of Mjölnir and explain her failure. She hadn't captured or neutralized Jör.

If she'd waited until the killer had attacked Will, she would have had a clean shot. But the point of her role as a Shadow Guardian was to protect hubbles. Besides, a good-looking man like Will was worth taking a knife for. She rubbed her throbbing arm and thought about how antagonistic he had been so far. Still, he had stayed with her when he could have dropped her at the ER and left her there.

Maybe he was worth it.

When she finished in the bathroom, she emerged and crawled back into the vacant bed.

"You're sleepy again?" Will stood in the doorway, arms crossed. He had trim brown hair, a clean-shaven face, and eyes more forest green and less intense than earlier.

She settled into the empty bed. Something in Will's demeanor made him trustworthy—worried about her safety, he had gone through the trouble of taking her to a hospital and then to a safe house to recover. Sure, he'd antagonized her, but more in a teasing and flirtatious manner rather than in a mean way.

Despite nearly being killed and then dragging her around bleeding in his car, he seemed unfazed. His relaxed expression and the perpetual curve of his lips suggested a casual amusement with the situation—or perhaps just life in general.

"Saving lives is exhausting." She placed a hand on her forehead in a melodramatic display. Truthfully, when her body healed itself, it consumed a great deal of energy.

Will snorted. "Well, since that ordeal is over. Telling me who and what you are and who you work for should be comparatively easy."

Oh, he's smooth. Or he at least he thinks he is.

"Classified."

"Keep singing that song, Raine. But your tune will change when you're sitting in the FBI office tomorrow." He kept his tone jovial.

"Am I under arrest?"

"I don't generally arrest people who save my life, but I will take you to the office and we'll get to the bottom of this." He grabbed the handle to the door and began to pull it closed, shutting himself out of the room.

"Then let's see what tomorrow holds." She closed her eyes.

RAINE SLEPT for a few hours and awoke around five am. The blue glow of the bedside clock was the only light. She closed her eyes and listened. Silence.

Slowly, she eased out of the covers and opened the bedroom door. Down the hallway, the house opened to a small living room and kitchen. Will slept on the couch. He hadn't taken the bed beside her nor the other bedroom she noticed. She suspected he wanted to position himself closest to the door. For their safety or to keep her pinned down?

She watched and listened to Will's rhythmic breathing. Smooth and even. She hadn't woken to the sound of a man breathing in a deep sleep in a long time.

Not for lack of want.

She'd been otherwise occupied, ridding the world of monsters, and when she wasn't on assignment, she was training. Where in her schedule could she fit a man? And how did she describe who and what she was to the average hubble?

She picked up her phone off the kitchen counter where it was charging.

Curiously thoughtful of him.

Lifting her coat off the back of the sofa by the tag, she walked to the door. She wouldn't put the garment on, as it would make too much noise—rayon brushing rayon.

When Will shifted, Raine froze in mid-step, keeping as stiff as a stork hunting fish.

He settled.

Her temples throbbed. The familiar dull ache started there but would soon move behind her right eye.

No, no, no.

She didn't have time for another migraine. Aside from the nausea and blinding pain, the episodes rendered her nonfunctional for hours—even up to days. She needed a cool, dark room. The longer she delayed in resting and giving in to the pain, the longer she would be incapacitated when she finally had solace.

Taking one last look at Will's handsome face, Raine left. She would never see him again, but she could take a mental image of him with her.

When she slipped out of the little house, cold air struck her face and her breath puffed in white wisps into the dark morning. She pulled her coat on and zipped it before tucking her hands in her pockets. She wished she still had her scarf, but she'd sacrificed it for a good cause. Despite healing abilities, she could still bleed to death if she lost too much blood before a wound was tamponaded.

The biting breeze of autumn in the Windy City snapped her thoughts away from the man she'd left sleeping on the sofa and back to the man she'd let get away.

If only her aim had been better, she would have slowed Jör down enough to make a second shot. Now, he was still at large, and another person might succumb to his brutality and join his long line of victims in the grave.

Jör hobbled back to his motel room, stiff from a throbbing pain in his leg and the freezing cold. He'd shredded his jacket and used it as a bandage to stem the bleeding until he had reached his room. He kept shivering and was barely able to unlock the door from his numb fingers and shaking hands.

He'd never been shot before, never been surprised and caught off guard like that. The pain that had started as blinding agony was now a throbbing misery. Other than maybe dousing it with peroxide to keep the wound clean, he didn't know how to care for a bullet wound. If pain was any indication, he suspected the bullet was still inside his leg. He would have to seek medical care. He didn't have time for delays, but an infection, poor healing, or lingering bullet could slow him down if he didn't get the projectile out and take some recovery time.

After closing the door behind him and bolting it, he cranked up the heat setting on the thermostat. The unit rattled and sputtered like a coal train. He sat heavily in the motel room chair.

Knowing Helen could tell him where to go for treatment, he pulled out his phone and dialed her number.

"Hello, my pet." Her voice was lovely and melodic, like her face with its high cheekbones, smooth lips, and creamy pale skin. Too long had he been on missions and deprived of the joy of seeing her.

"My queen," he said in return.

She had been his savior. He'd grown up knowing he was different from regular humans and picked on because of it. After years of being bullied for his skin condition and his lisp, Helen had shown him he had a purpose by her side. Rising to her cause was his pure and undeniable calling.

"Are you already finished with your next assignment?" she asked.

"I must humbly admit to a delay." He didn't know how they'd found him in that abandoned office space, much less how he'd almost been snared by two people. FBI, the man had called himself, and they seemed to have orchestrated their trap where the man was the bait and the woman lay in wait to shoot Jör down.

"I don't like delays," Helen said.

"The FBI laid a trap. I escaped, but they shot me. Can you tell me where to go to have my wound addressed off the record? I promise, my queen, I will return to my mission immediately thereafter."

A long pause stretched out over the mobile phone, and he felt small beads of sweat form along his forehead. He wiped the back of his hand across the moisture, dragging sweat and loose scales with it.

"I will have someone text you the name and address of a medical contact nearest you. Once you've been attended to, you must eliminate the evidence."

"Yes, my queen." Always get rid of the evidence.

She wasn't referring only to his blood-soaked clothes or the bullet. He must ensure those items were never found either, but she meant eliminating whoever treated him. He could leave no trails leading back to him. Just as he would never leave a trail leading back to Hel.

THREE

Will woke with a jolt. He'd slept hard, too hard, and he knew it the instant he was conscious. He stared at the spot where the now missing coat had lain. Bolting up, he took long strides down the hall and glimpsed in the bedroom, whose door lay open.

Empty.

Shit.

He scrubbed his hand across his face. Now he had no murderer and no one to answer his questions. So much for treating Raine with respect and not handcuffing her in hopes of bolstering her willingness to cooperate. Technically, he could have arrested her for carrying a concealed weapon, but he'd wanted to show some professional courtesy to the woman who saved his life.

And how had she snuck past him? He'd chosen the sofa in order to be nearest the door.

Will looked around the room before returning to the kitchen. She'd hadn't bothered to leave a note. Maybe no note was better. If she'd left one, he might have felt like she was mocking him—

sleeping through her escape *and* her note writing. Still, she'd escaped with her coat, and he hadn't even heard the puffy fabric crinkle.

He pulled out his phone and called his boss, Caroline Powell.

"Powell."

"Will here." He set to work making a pot of coffee. One good thing about the FBI safe houses—always guaranteed to have coffee.

"What's your status?"

"I had the suspect cornered last night, or maybe he had me cornered. In any case, he got away."

"Damn," Caroline swore. "Are you injured?"

She was right to ask. No one was reported to survive an encounter with the serial killer known as Blade.

"I'm not, but only because there was another operative on the scene." Will stood and stretched his long legs.

"Operative? Who? FBI?"

"Not FBI, and she refused to identify herself—name's Raine. That's all I've got." That and a photo of her sleeping face on his phone—strictly for identification purposes. And he'd lifted her fingerprints while she'd been sleeping in his car.

"Where is she now?"

Will paced. "I don't know. She snuck out of the bedroom this morning."

"You slept with her?"

"What? No. Why would you jump to that conclusion? We did not sleep together. She was injured, and I was going to bring her in for questioning after a night's rest at the safe house. But she got away."

"Why didn't you take her to the Chicago field office?" Caroline asked.

Will huffed out a sigh. "She saved my life, Caroline. She put her body between me and Jör's blade. I couldn't treat her like a perp after that. It was the middle of the night, and we both needed rest."

"Jör?"

"That's what she called him. Not Blade."

"So, you'll check hospitals for the woman? It sounds like she may have leads we very much need."

"She won't be there." She no longer needed a hospital—one of Raine's many mysteries, but he would keep what he'd witnessed of her healing abilities to himself. "You haven't heard of any other agencies working the Jör case, have you?"

"No. Get your report together. I want to read it. And get yourself in front of a sketch artist. You're the only person to have seen the serial killer and live to tell about it."

"Yes, ma'am."

"Will?"

"Yes?"

"Did you pick up any other leads on where Blade—or Jör—might go next?"

"No. I already asked local PD to spread the word to hospitals, since the woman hit him with a nonlethal shot, but I doubt he's sought public medical care."

Will had caught a lucky break when local PD reported spotting a suspicious man in the blocks near the abandoned building. Combined with Will's intuition, which had served him well on more than one FBI case in the past, he'd picked the correct building and floor where Jör had hidden.

Now that the killer had escaped, Will feared he wouldn't learn his next location until another victim surfaced.

RAINE COUNTED through pushups on the mat as sweat trickled down her face. She was halfway through her workout routine when Usha walked into the barn, letting in the cool, dry, Montana air with her.

Three days had passed since Jör had slipped through her grasp, and Raine waited for the Council's spies to find him again and send her back out. In the meantime, she trained and worked on target practice, sweating and panting through her frustration.

"Anything yet?" Raine asked between exertional breaths.

The elderly woman hobbled closer using her cane. "Nothing yet."

By appearances, no one would suspect Usha Bakshi, a withered five-foot woman with dark skin and wiry white hair, was the leader of the North American branch of the Shadow Guardians—not that anyone knew about the Shadow Guardians.

Operative word being *shadow*.

Raine finished her pushups and rolled onto her back, starting her sit-ups. She waited for her boss to speak. The woman, while pleasant, wouldn't have walked all the way to her barn for a casual visit.

"I've completed a background check on the young man you encountered—Special Agent Will Decker," she began.

Young man? Will was probably mid-thirties, maybe five years older than Raine. She supposed he would seem young to Usha, whom Raine suspected was about eighty.

"I want you to work with this man. He has an excellent reputation at the bureau, and he's the only one who's gotten as close as you have to Jör."

Raine stopped her sit-ups and felt her jaw come unhinged. Usha had never ordered her to work with an agent from a different organization, and she'd been working with the Council of Mjölnir as a Shadow Guardian for six years.

"How did you—?"

"I've already made arrangements with his superiors."

Raine shut her mouth. She didn't want to convey even the slightest disrespect to Usha. "What are my parameters in terms of what he's allowed to know about the Guardians and bloodlines? He saw me heal myself. He'll want answers."

The man was a walking fountain of curiosity, spewing questions one after another.

Usha stood hunched with one hand on the top of a wood carving of a horse's head decorating the end of her cane. "I read your report about his attempts to question you. For his own safety, this man needs to understand the bloodlines, as well as Jör's strengths and weaknesses. Special Agent Decker needs to know about the secret war and the Shadow Guardians' role in it, but not any members other than yourself. Since he saw you heal your injuries, he may be open to learning about the supernatural world."

Usha didn't have to worry about Raine talking about other members. She only knew a few and had met less. It wasn't as though a group of them hung out at the office water cooler, because there was no office. And there were no organizational holiday parties to meet-and-greet, as everyone worked in isolation.

There weren't holiday parties, were there? Surely, she hadn't been excluded from such gatherings. Sometimes she missed the social life she'd left behind when she became a Shadow Guardian.

Raine pushed to her feet. She also missed normal activities—things other thirty-somethings were doing, like working nine-to-five jobs, going to parties, having families, buying houses, and growing roots. But she'd answered a different calling and had no regrets. Evil lurked in the deep, dark shadows, and Raine had the power to stop it.

"When do I start?"

"You'll fly to Washington DC tomorrow."

WILL ADJUSTED his tie and pushed open the conference room door, where his boss stood waiting. The room had a six-seater oval table and mounted monitor for presentations. On one wall, several large windows overlooked a landscape of autumn colors. Frosted glass lined the hall wall.

Five days had passed, and he had no new leads on the serial killer. Fortunately, no new victims either. At least, not so far as they knew.

"Ma'am."

"Will." Caroline greeted him with a nod. She wore a fitted cream-colored suit and her dark brown hair in a bob. She'd called a meeting here, though, oddly, it was just the two of them. Usually, he came to her office for one-on-one discussions.

"In an effort to combine resources to find the serial killer, we will engage in interagency collaboration."

Will pursed his lips. Her declaration felt like she was dishing out punishment. He didn't want to share his case or have some other agency slow him down. 'Collaborations' meant more bureaucratic red tape.

"I'll let her fill you in on the details. Co-op-er-ate," Caroline added when Will started to open his mouth in protest. She turned and left the room, closing the door behind her.

"Unbelievable," he muttered. He always worked alone. He'd done some of his best work *alone.*

She who? No one else knew this case like he did—had studied the victims as in depth as he had. Was he just supposed to share all of that with a new person who'd elbowed her way into *his* case? To hell with th—

A woman stepped forward from the corner of the room where she hadn't been a moment ago. She wore navy slacks with a matching vest over a violet blouse. Her long blonde hair was pulled back in a smooth ponytail.

"Raine." He straightened as his heart skipped a few beats.

He'd thought she'd vanished forever, though he'd hoped he would encounter her somewhere again on his hunt for Jör. She was the one person who might actually be able to help him. Or was he helping her?

Hmm. They would need to establish some boundaries and parameters.

Will flashed her a smile. "Welcome to my team."

Raine arched an eyebrow. "Your team? Of one?"

"Now we're two," he said merrily, spreading his arms.

She shrugged. "If you want to call it your team so you can take the credit for whatever the outcome is, that's fine with me. I'm not here to battle for the alpha role. I'm here to stop a killer. I work for an organization called the Shadow Guardians, so you can infer by the name that we're not in it for the recognition."

Raine's matter-of-fact tone wasn't condescending, but Will felt schooled nonetheless. He'd been prepared to spar over a turf war, and she made him out to be the bully on the playground.

As far as recognition went, everyone at the FBI wanted it. Recognition was how promotions and careers were formed. There was nothing selfish in wanting recognition for having done the hard work and stopping the villian. He'd happily take the recognition.

Now that they'd established who received the credit, he needed to set the tone of their interactions moving forward. He took a seat and reclined back. "Then, we take down Jör as a team—share knowledge and resources. No one will order the other around. No one will keep secrets as it pertains to the case."

"I can agree to those terms, though you should know the danger of learning secrets."

Will cocked his head to one side.

She lowered her voice as she leaned forward. "Some of them you may decide later you don't want to know. But once you know them, there's no putting them back."

He arched an eyebrow. "Well, that was dramatic and cryptic. Let's start with your full name."

"Raine River Thoren." She straightened.

"And you've been with this secret group, the Shadow Guardians, for how long?"

"Six years. Although, the FBI knows the organization as the CoM. Short for Council of Mjölnir. The Shadow Guardians work under their authority."

He'd never heard of CoM and made a mental note to do a deeper dive to learn more about them.

He continued, "And before that, your family moved around a few years before settling in Texas. You have two sisters. You're the oldest child. No criminal record. College graduate with honors as a dual major in History and Criminal Justice—interesting combination." He gestured to an empty seat in the room.

"Do you also know my shoe size?" Raine's lips curved slightly as she lowered herself into the chair. She didn't seem surprised an FBI Investigator had checked her background.

"Dress size. I'm not really a foot fetish kind of guy."

She shook her head, but Will thought she was suppressing a smile.

"So, how did you manage the background check? Facial recognition?" she asked.

"I lifted your prints while you slept." He wouldn't tell her he had photographed her on his phone. He'd deleted the image once he had her full name and had run his background check.

"You're sounding less like an FBI agent and more like a stalker."

"I saw you heal yourself. I planned to track you down for answers. Fortunately, I don't have to. Now, your turn," Will said. He'd be disappointed if she hadn't researched him as well.

She crossed her arms. "You come from a long line of east coast lawyers, so I wonder if you're the black sheep who took a different path. You made a reputation for yourself solving the Binkley Case five years ago. You're thirty-three and never married—perhaps married to your work, or you have commitment issues."

Will let the last comment slide. "Tell me, Raine, when I first walked into this room, you weren't in here. How'd you do that?"

"Are you sure you didn't overlook me?"

He leaned forward as his mouth curved in a grin. "That could never happen."

A blush came over her cheeks.

Fascinating, he thought.

Whatever precise job description she had with this Shadow organization, she wasn't hardened, bitter, or desensitized because of it. And although she was beautiful, her behavior toward him suggested she didn't use her looks for career advancement. She wasn't trying to use her beauty to manipulate him.

"No secrets, Raine," he reminded her. He touched his thumb to the ring on his finger. Perhaps there would have to be some secrets between them, but he had specified no secrets as it pertained to the case.

"I have two gifts: my ability to heal—which does not make me invincible or immortal—and my ability for stealth. If I remain very still along walkways, walls, and corners, I become almost invisible."

"Almost?" he asked.

"If you saw me move into position, you'd still be able to find me. I'm not entirely invisible."

"Camouflage."

"Mentally suggestive camouflage."

Just two super-abilities? She was neglecting to list her magnetism as one of her powers; she possessed a calm energy about her, which, combined with her beauty, gave her some type of royal aura. He felt awed by her presence in a way that had him excited to be working together and to have an opportunity to get to know her better.

His mind flooded with questions—about Raine and about the case. Remarkably, she seemed patiently willing to answer them, unlike when they first met. Apparently she had been authorized to share her 'classified' information.

"And how did you acquire these abilities... gamma radiation? Fall into toxic waste?"

"I was born with them."

"The camouflage trick must've been hell on your parents."

Raine smiled, a glowing look that lit her face and made her features more stunning. "That one took time and training to develop. I wasn't a rogue toddler—at least, not in an abnormal way."

"But you and your organization know something about the origins of your abilities? And since there's an entire secret organization, I'm guessing you're not the only one with supernatural powers."

Raine stood. "Why don't I fill you in over lunch?"

FOUR

"Ragnarok happened. Asgard and the nine realms fell. Millions were wiped out—Asgardians, Frost Giants, Dark Elves, Light Elves, Dwarves, Vanir. Those who survived hid on earth and bloodlines mingled," Raine explained when the guacamole and chips arrived.

Will had driven them from the J Edgar Hoover FBI headquarters to Oyamel Cocina Mexicana in the Penn Quarter. The restaurant smelled of fresh salsa, cilantro, and lime. They had a seat in the corner, slightly apart from the busy lunch bustle.

Raine had rehearsed her introductory statement on the plane flight from Montana to DC, all the while wondering what Will's reaction would be. Would he be intrigued like he'd been about her ability to heal? Or would he discredit her all together, the way she'd always imagined every man would?

"Norse mythology?" Will bit down on a chip laden with guacamole and chewed as he blinked at her, looking like he was debating how much of what she explained he would actually believe.

She continued, "They weren't actual gods. Humans deified them

—as we tend to do with things we don't understand. But beings from the other realms had remarkable abilities."

"Which have mingled with our lowly genes?"

"The gene pool mixed, most of us think of it in a good way. Magic was diluted over thousands of years." Raine dipped a chip and took a bite—the flavors of lime and cilantro bursting in her mouth.

"And your bloodline is—don't tell me. Frost Giant? Just kidding. You're clearly a descendent of Thor with your blonde hair and perfect body."

Wasn't he charming? And unexpectedly relaxed as she discussed the supernatural. What rattled this man? Nothing she'd done or said so far.

"I do have some Asgardian genes. My mentor says I'm on my way to becoming a Valkyrie."

"Ah, Odin's warrior women. Makes sense."

"You know Norse Mythology?"

"I know the *Avenger* movies." He winked at her.

"Hmm." She frowned as she loaded another chip.

"So, *Valkyrie*. You discovered your origins and joined these Shadow Guardians to be a warrior for—what? America? Mankind?"

She swallowed her bite. "All of mankind." Probably because, in truth, she wanted most of all to protect her family. She took a sip of her water.

"That's a judicious undertaking. Have you always been an over-achiever?" He grinned.

Why was this man so easy to talk to? When Usha had first assigned Raine, she'd been determined to maintain a tight reserve. But damn, Will had charisma.

She cleared her throat. "I started having dreams at sixteen. I now suspect they were someone else's memories. They were apocalyptic dreams with people and places I didn't recognize. For the most part, I was a normal teenager."

"Cheerleader and gymnast. Winner of some state competitions. I'd say you had an above average teenage life."

She narrowed her eyes at him. Apparently, his background investigation of her extended into high school activities. She'd used the word normal to mean attending high school, socializing with friends, horseback riding with her sisters. It had been a simpler time, when she knew nothing about bloodlines and monsters in shadows.

His heated gaze had her wondering if he was imagining her in a short skirt holding pom-poms. She shifted her weight in her chair.

"Anyway," she continued, "once I learned there are dangerous creatures among us, I knew I wanted to do some type of law enforcement. When the Council of Mjölnir approached me, I accepted."

"Council of Mjölnir? CoM. You said they oversee the Shadow Guardians. And you accepted? Just like that?"

The waitress brought out their fish tacos—*Pescado Baja California.*

"Not just like that," Raine said when the waitress left. "One of my sisters was emotionally traumatized. She witnessed her fiancée murdered by a Dark Elf bloodline. When the council offered me a position and explained their role, I knew I wanted to be part of an organization to stop monsters like that."

She hadn't anticipated how isolating the work would be. Now that she was answering a barrage of questions, she wondered if a constant partner would be exhausting.

Will froze as he was lifting his taco to take a bite. "Do you kill them?" he asked in a low voice.

Raine shrugged. "Not always. But sometimes it's me or them." She began eating her entrée.

Will leaned back as his face paled and his easy demeanor faltered for the first time.

Is he judging me?

He obviously had an aversion to killing, which only meant he didn't understand the danger from the other bloodlines. A secret war was being waged, and both sides rarely took prisoners. When they did, it wasn't pretty. Death was a mercy.

She continued to eat and waited as Will processed her statement.

"How many people have you killed?" He glanced around as if ensuring he hadn't been overheard.

"Your mistake is in thinking of them as people."

"They're still people. Even if bloodlines were mixed, as you say, they're still people." His voice had grown an irritated edge.

"Is this going to pose a problem with us working together?"

"No, because you're going to swear to me right now that our objective is to catch the bad guy—justice, and not the vigilante type." He took an enormous bite out of his taco and chewed with no semblance of enjoying it.

"I swear to stop Jör by whatever means necessary."

"Raine—" Will began.

She leaned forward and lowered her voice. "I'm sure you've seen the photographs of what Jör has done to his victims. He's the worst type of sadist. No conscience whatsoever. If I'm given the option to kill him or let him escape for capture another day, I'm going to kill him. I've already let him get away and the next victim's blood is on my hands."

Will's brow furrowed. "You're talking about me. Saving me meant letting Jör escape."

"I didn't have a clean shot." She waved a dismissive hand as she leaned back in her seat. "My options were to protect you and try to injure him enough to slow him down or let him attack you."

"And while he was busy killing me, you would've been able to get your kill shot."

"Yes."

"Well, I appreciate your judgment call." Will rubbed his chin.

"Then perhaps you can trust me enough to make the right judgment call next time, too."

Will sighed, but with it returned his crooked grin. "We'll see. Can we at least agree that we will do our best to *capture* the villain?"

"I always do my best."

As he nodded, a dark flicker crossed his expression.

He doesn't trust me, Raine thought.

A lack of trust would make working together difficult, but she couldn't expect him to readily accept the secrets of the existence of otherworldly bloodlines. As someone sworn to uphold United States laws with no prior knowledge of the shadow war, of course he would oppose killing.

She set her napkin on the table beside her plate of finished tacos. If Will didn't trust her after she'd saved his life, perhaps nothing she could say would change that. Regardless, they were on this path and needed to work together.

WILL DROVE his spacious Red Chevy Impala with Raine in the passenger seat. A pregnant silence lingered between them.

He was still trying to process everything she'd told him about Ragnarok and bloodlines. Raine's abilities and the frightening serial killer Jörmungandr weren't irrefutable proof of this other world Raine claimed existed, but they were damn convincing.

Glancing at the ring on his right hand, he debated telling Raine about it, but he'd told no one. He had a little experience with bizarre events, though, and he wondered for the first time if the ring had a connection to Norse Mythology—the ring and his sometimes eerie intuition about people's whereabouts. Before he shared his secret, he needed to decide if he fully trusted this woman.

He gauged his gut feeling, like dipping litmus paper into liquid.

Nope.

She had killed people and was entirely too accepting of the concept. He understood her motivation, but that didn't justify her actions. He respected her perspective and certainly the value she would bring to their case, but respect and trust were too different animals.

Regardless, he could work with her on the case—provided he could stop envisioning her in his arms with her hair down; uninjured this time, but with the hint of playfulness that touched her eyes from time to time. He'd never mixed pleasure and work, but he had a sinking feeling he would be willing to make an exception for Raine. *If he could trust her.* She had the most delectable curves and full lips, and there was something about her he couldn't put his finger on that called to him.

She's your partner, jackass.

He wrung his hands on the steering wheel. He needed to get a grip on his libido, because it was disrespecting her.

Outside, splashes of autumn leaves dotted the highway. He was glad to be south of the chill of Chicago and liked that Virginia had all four seasons but rarely were any of them harsh.

"Where are we going?" she asked.

"My trailer where I keep files and brainstorm on Jör. I think better outside office walls. Do you have something similar? I'll show you mine if you show me yours." He wriggled his eyebrows.

"I don't," she said, matter-of-factly without acknowledging his flirtation.

Perhaps she had never mixed work with pleasure either. He needed to tone it down.

"You don't have a secret lair you work out of here or not at all?" he asked. According to his investigation of her, she had a PO Box in Montana, but he had no way of knowing if that was near a real home address.

"Not at all."

Raine's short answer suggested she was still prickly at his judgment of her taking lives. Whatever genetic variations might or might not exist, Will wouldn't condone murder. He wasn't judge, jury, and executioner. His oath was to support and defend against all enemies, not kill anyone.

He changed lanes to pass another car. "Well, do you have computer files on him or something to share?" he asked.

"I don't track him. The Council has people for that. They send me in when they find him."

"So, you're like the clean-up crew?"

"I guess."

"Don't you want to be part of the investigation?" he asked.

She bristled. "They send me on other assignments. It's not as though I'm going to the salon and having a pedicure while everyone else is working."

Now he'd insulted her again.

Smooth work, Will.

"Nor would I think you'd ever be idle," he said, placatingly. "But I'm sure you're not exercising your full potential if you're on the sidelines of the cognitive hunt preceding the physical one. I bet if you put those degrees of yours to work, you'll have valuable insight to add to the case."

Raine fell quiet, and Will let her contemplate his mixed complementary and motivational words.

"I want to see what I can contribute. That's why I'm here."

When Raine relaxed slightly, Will decided he liked how she seemed simultaneously in control of her emotions and not inclined to conceal them. He couldn't say the same for himself.

"You've been an FBI agent for a decade. Have you seriously never seen any supernatural activity?"

He shrugged. "I have an outstanding Spidey sense that's helped me solve cases. My gut instincts have given me an above average success rate in the Bureau, but I don't call it supernatural."

She regarded him with head cocked to one side as if trying to decide if his claim had significance.

"Does your family know what you do?" he asked.

She strummed her fingers on her thigh. "Do my parents know I work for a secret organization beholden to no government that tracks down supernatural killers? No."

"What do they think you do?"

"FBI," she answered.

Will choked out a cough, and the car swerved slightly. "Your parents thinks you work for the FBI?"

"It's safer for them if they don't know about the shadow war. I've even got a fake FBI badge."

"That's illegal. And why didn't you try to play that card on me back at the safe house when we first met?"

"With a badge and a suit, I can get cooperation from civilians. I can even sometimes fool local law enforcement. I can't deceive a real FBI agent. One question about protocols or division chiefs and you'd know I was a fraud."

"Okay." He rubbed his neck, keeping one hand on the steering wheel. "We need to lay some ground rules. Rule number one is we don't lie to each other."

"I haven't lied to you. And I thought rule number one was you take all the public credit when we take down Jör?"

"Truthfulness is the new number one. That includes you not claiming to be an FBI agent. Recognition can be number two."

"I thought no killing was number two?"

He shot a look at Raine, who was grinning, obviously enjoying getting a rise out of him. The woman was beautiful yet infuriating.

He gritted his teeth. "Number one—no killing. Number two—no lying. Number three—I get recognition." No one had ever mocked him this way, and he couldn't figure out how her playfulness simultaneously irritated and amused him.

"Got it. Any other rules?" she asked.

"I'm sure there will be," he grumbled. "We'll sort them out as they arise."

"What about your family? They don't have issues with you being the black sheep FBI agent?"

Will chuckled. "A houseful of liberal lawyers and I work for the government in law enforcement. You better believe they disapprove of my job. Your parents?"

Raine shook her head with a smile. "They're peace-loving, do-what-makes-you-happy, marijuana-smoking hippies."

Will barked out a laugh. "I'd like to see what family dinner looks like in that household."

"Okay."

Will opened his mouth and then closed it again. Had he just invited himself to meet Raine's parents? He didn't meet women's parents. Not ever. He rarely even dated a woman longer than a few weeks in order to prevent the formation of any attachments. In fact, consensual one-night stands were preferable. Meeting the parents was definitely sending the wrong message.

Except Raine and he weren't dating—they were partners. He would meet his partner's parents, which sounded like something a coworker might do.

He pulled into the gravel driveway and parked beside his trailer.

Raine exited the car and stretched as she looked around. "This is remote. You own this land?"

He nodded. "I want to build a cabin over there. I've almost saved enough money. Picture a large sitting room with a cozy fire in the winter. It'll have three bedrooms—the master will be big with a walk-in shower. My office will be large enough for a plump leather sofa and large desk."

A lot of space for one person, his younger brother had told him when Will had shared his plans. Will had ignored Walt's insinuation that deep-down, Will wanted to settle and have a family.

"I can picture that. You could build a barn and have some horses over there."

He scratched his head. "I suppose I could, but I'd be clueless as to what to do with a couple of horses."

"Most people ride them."

"I never have."

"Okay, then, how about a pool over there? My parents have a pool, and it made for a lot of good summer memories growing up." Her expression turned far away as if her mind was rummaging through those memories.

"A pool sounds nice." Except he wasn't picturing a pool; he was envisioning Raine in a bikini under the summer sun. He needed to get a grip on his hormones. Clearing his throat, he added, "I'm not sure I'd be home enough for the maintenance of a pool to make sense."

"True. I don't own a place at all because I work all over the country."

A slight sadness in her voice had him wondering if *she* wanted a place she could settle. He dismissed the urge to delve into too personal territory. Their agencies had thrown them together to work, not to get sidetracked with emotional bonding.

CHAPTER

FIVE

Raine surveyed the trailer with its mowed acre lawn and backdrop of woods atop rolling hills. The small structure was surrounded by sassafras, oak, birch, poplar, gum, sumac, maple, and Virginia creeper. The trees' leaves had changed color, creating a breathtaking vibrancy of reds and yellows. Will had picked a nice plot of land—cozy and quiet.

She followed him into the trailer. The small, rectangular space had a kitchenette, a sitting area converted into an office, and a bedroom. A bookshelf contained a complete series of Sherlock Holmes novels in leather hardbound form.

The place was tidy, and Raine wondered with amusement what set of rules Will held himself to that he would keep a tidy workspace only he saw—and wouldn't take out a loan like most people but instead save money to build his home.

"Coffee?" he offered.

"Yes, thanks."

Will fixed her a cup of coffee from a countertop instant machine. The logo on the mug read, "SMART, GOOD LOOKING, AND AN FBI AGENT. DOESN'T GET BETTER THAN THAT."

"Um?" She pointed at the words.

"Ugh." He grimaced like he hadn't paid attention to what mug he'd given her. "Yeah. Gag gift from my younger brother, Walt."

He turned and pointed to a wall. "Jör's victims and all the places the serial killer has struck." Pictures and notes were tacked in an orderly fashion to a cork board.

Raine blew on her coffee. She scrutinized the photos and notes—victims, locations, associations, and more on his wall of horrors. Will had worked hard to create this, and clearly took his job seriously.

She said, "It's fairly sobering to see so much death portrayed in one spot."

"Seven murders," he said dismally.

Raine shook her head. "Twelve."

"What?" His gaze snapped toward her.

"You're missing the five abroad. Jör doesn't limit his killing to the US."

"*Sonofabitch.*" Will ran a hand through his hair. "I'm missing a third of the victims. No wonder I can't find a pattern. Can you get those files?"

Raine set down her coffee, plucked her phone from her pocket, and sent a message. "Done. If I can access my email in the next thirty minutes, we'll have it."

"Done." Will sat in a chair and leaned back into his charismatic, carefree demeanor. "What shall we do to pass the time?"

Raine marveled at how easily he moved between serious and relaxed. Perhaps the quick transition came from a lifetime of disapproval and walking on eggshells around his family and he'd learned to turn the switch as a defense mechanism and a way to rapidly emotionally decompress.

Raine's parents had always been supportive, even when Raine had had her more social and promiscuous days through high school and college. Not until death reared its ugly head close to home, when her sister's fiancé had been shot and killed, had their family been disrupted. Five years later, Raine taken up her role as a Shadow

Guardian, leaving behind her days of fun and leisure. Memories of a happy, carefree youth sustained her. Maybe someday, when the world was safe again, she could indulge herself and find happiness. Someday might be a long time to wait.

"Tell me what you do for fun when you aren't hunting serial killers," Raine said.

Will glanced at a guitar along the wall beside the tiny sofa in the office. "I like to play. I was part of a band in college, and we did weekend gigs to earn spending money."

Raine tried to image Will's long body curled around a guitar playing *Brown-Eyed Girl*. "What happened to the band?" she asked.

"Life." Will shrugged. "We all got proper jobs, and most of the band members started families."

But not Will, Raine knew. He'd never settled, never had a family. Uninterested or emotionally incapable? Not that it mattered. His relationship patterns weren't relevant to them working together.

"Your turn." Will took a sip from his coffee cup. "What do you do for fun?"

"I used to ride horses. When I was growing up, our neighbors had horses, and they gave us girls an open invitation to mount whenever we wanted. Trail riding together with my sisters always felt like something special. Now, when I get the chance to hop in the saddle, the nostalgia puts me instantly at ease, recalling simpler times."

"Nostalgic. Yes. I like that. I agree. I feel the same way when I start strumming. Interesting how we both have to fall back to our youth to refer to a time when we used to have fun." His lips quirked as he arched an eyebrow.

"Perhaps I can listen to you play sometime." She took a sip of her coffee, not taking the bait to discuss a deeper topic.

"Perhaps we can take a ride sometime. I've heard there are horse trails through these mountains. That's if you can tolerate riding with an amateur."

"Sounds fun." Horseback riding did sound fun, but the small

trailer grew quiet and awkward. She'd known this man only a few brief hours, and they'd already planned a trail ride and dinner with her parents.

Perhaps he was simply one of those outgoing characters who became personal with everyone. Perhaps he was this engaging with all of his partners. Besides, these activities were necessary if they were going to build a foundation of trust, which she wanted whole-heartedly to do. They needed trust for this partnership to succeed.

If such easy conversation was part of normal coworker interactions, perhaps she should have a partner regularly. Working in isolation all these years had been lonely. Already she was bringing something of value to their collaboration—the missing victims.

Raine realized Will was studying her face. "I'd better check that email so we can get to work."

He grinned as he pushed to his feet. "I'll unlock my computer for you."

WILL PRINTED THE PHOTOS, demographic information, and death details of the victims he'd been missing. He carefully attached them, and his board now had twelve listed.

Twelve lives cut short.

He sank back into his chair, soaking in the enormity of it. When Will had been the closest to Jör of any law enforcement officer, he'd nearly become victim number thirteen. He would have died by the same knife, too. He and Raine needed to stop the psychopath.

As Will strummed fingers on his armchair, absorbing details, Raine sat on his couch, sipping coffee and clicking through screens on his laptop of information sent by her secret society. She had admitted this was the first time she'd had the privilege of reading the full files.

"They're all Vanir," Raine said in a tone of illuminated realization.

"What's that mean?"

"Vanaheim bloodline."

Will scrubbed a hand across his face. Was he really going to follow this case down a supernatural rabbit hole?

Follow all leads, his instinct told him. He had little else to go on, so he might as well start with mythology.

"Okay." He puffed out a breath of air. "I'm going to need a crash course in Norse history—*Cliff Notes* or *Nine Realms for Dummies*. Something along those lines."

Raine gave a slight grin as she set his laptop on the narrow oak coffee table. "Nine realms." She seemed a little too excited he was entertaining the idea there may be some role for Norse mythology in the motive for murder.

"I've heard of Asgard and Midgard," he said.

"Yes, Midgard is Earth and, presumably, the only planet that survived Ragnarok. Niflheim was the planet of fog and mist. And also where the well Hvergelmir, source of the eleven rivers of Norse mythology, resided. As well as the frozen rivers of Élivágar."

"And your name—Raine River Thoren—seems eerily parallel here."

"Yes. Raine and River are powerful names. And Thoren is technically son of Thor."

"Are you related?" he asked teasingly, knowing if she said she was related to an ancient mythological god, he would have to laugh her out of his trailer.

"I don't know. You're talking about millennia ago and DNA testing is only recent. The Council of Mjölnir can tell ancestry to broad bloodlines but not individuals."

"If your parents don't know your role in all of this," —and, heaven forbid, thought she was an actual FBI agent— "where did your first and middle names come from?"

"Even I don't know my role, exactly. Our last name was just passed along as last names are. My mom doesn't know about bloodlines. She once told me her daughters' names came to her in her dreams when she was pregnant with each of us. We always joked that she'd conjured them from her weed-smoking days, but there must've been something to those dreams, since here I am—fighting demons."

Here she was, in Will's trailer, trying to track a killer. And the more she talked, the more he felt a certain ease at her joining the case, which made about as much rational sense as her being a descendent of Thor.

And fighting demons? She really didn't see Jör as a human being, and Will knew this would become a problem. Lots of law enforcement officers referred to criminals as animals, but that didn't embolden them to think killing was acceptable. Mostly.

"Muspelheim," Raine continued, "was land of fire and lava. Home of the Fire Giants—including Sutr."

"Sutr? Why does that particular name sound familiar?"

"He was the Fire Giant who destroyed Asgard during Ragnarok. You probably remember him from the *Thor* movie."

"Ah. And is that bloodline still around?"

"Indeed. Fire Giants are still around." Raine's gaze turned sad and distant.

Will wanted to know the story behind that memory, but for now, he opted to concentrate their focus on his Nine Realms crash course.

"Next?" he prompted.

Her eyes focused back on him. "Jotunheim. Home to Jotuns—Frost Giants."

"I'm not sure what sounds worse—fire or frost."

"The Council claims Fire Giants are, but I've never met a Frost Giant to compare."

But she'd met a Fire Giant bloodline, Will deduced. It must have been unpleasant, to say the least. Worse than having a knife impaled in her arm? How many fights had this woman been in—and with only internal scars to show for them?

"So, Jör. He's not a Frost Giant?" Will asked.

"No. Jörmungandr is his full name. He's Midgard serpent bloodline."

"Hmm. Explains the snake-like movement and scaly skin."

"Yes. Then, another realm is Alfheim."

"Wait, don't tell me. It's where Alf is from. Alf?" he asked, her expression still blank. "The sitcom *A.L.F.*?"

"Never heard of it."

Will shook his head as doubt about the success of their partnership wormed into his mind. Pop culture references were a must, even if some of them were as outdated as A.L.F.

"Alfheim was home to the Light Elves. They were guardian angels and thought of as minor gods."

"And is that the origin of Valkyries?"

She shook her head. "Valkyries were the chosen warriors of Odin, and they could be from any realm so long as he deemed them worthy."

"A righteous leader who didn't discriminate based on origin. How very progressive of him." Will nodded in approval. "So who deemed you worthy? Who christened you a Valkyrie?"

She tensed before turning to look at his board of Jör's victims. "I'm not. Usha, my mentor, says it's something I'm meant for, but not yet ready. It's a rite of passage with three components. I have to wait until I'm ready."

"When will you be ready?"

"I don't know." She set down her now empty coffee mug with an air of finality to this line of questioning.

"Since there's a rite of passage, there must be some significance to making the transition," he pushed.

"I suppose so."

"Well, what three things do you need?"

"I haven't asked. I'm not even sure it's a title I feel I should aspire to attain."

Yeesh. Another sensitive subject. Interacting with this woman was like navigating land mines. And why did he have a desire to maneuver each of those, learn her secrets, and know her thoroughly?

He opened his mouth, thought better, and closed it again. He shook off the notion.

She shifted her weight and crossed her legs on the couch. "Look. I'm already an outcast—working in isolation for a secret organization. I don't know what it means to become a Valkyrie, but I can tell you I'm not ready to become more of an outcast."

"So... you trust this Council of Mjölnir's judgment? Usha's judgment?" He grimaced at the slightly challenging edge to his voice. He wasn't questioning her right to the title, but judging by her flash of irritation, she thought he was. He could accept her drawing the wrong conclusion—better that than she discern the truth about how irritated he was with himself at his level of interest in Raine personally.

"The Council keeps extensive genetic records. Apparently, they know something based on our genetic signatures."

Genetics. Will consider her words. If transitioning to a Valkyrie required a rite of passage, then he suspected the elevation in status had more to do with proving herself through honor or bravery. Apparently the All-Father's selection criteria rested more on valor than bloodlines. Genetics might earn her the right to attempt the rite of passage, but she would have to meet the three criteria to determine if she passed or failed.

He decided that was a conversation for another time. He'd been pushy and confrontational enough for their first day together. Since he was having trouble grasping the concept of the supernatural, he suspected his questioning, laced with doubt, would come off as an interrogation.

"Genetic signatures? You and your sisters?" he asked, veering away from the topic of Valkyries.

Raine nodded.

"But your sisters don't do what you do. And the Council knew what you were before you did?"

"Correct. My sisters don't know about the Council of Mjölnir, but we know about each others' powers. They know I fight evil bloodlines."

"Huh." More to that story, too.

"Svartalfheim," Raine said, continuing her Nine Realm debriefing, "was home to dwarves and Dark Elves. Helheim was home to the dishonorable dead."

"You saved Vanaheim for last."

"Since it's relevant to our victims."

"Whom the Council knew were Vanir because they keep bloodline records?"

"Extensive records. Vanaheim was home to the sorcerers, magicians, and prophets."

"So, Jör is killing off a skilled bloodline? Is there any way to find out which abilities the victims possessed, in case that helps with motive?"

Was he truly buying into all of this talk of Norse mythology? He supposed if it presented a pattern, the supernatural gave him some sort of lead he didn't otherwise have. Will didn't have to believe in the supernatural. If the killer did, that was motive enough to pursue this path.

"Not by Council records."

"Would the Council be able to tell us how many Vanir bloodline individuals are left in the world? I mean, if there's one left, we know who to protect."

"It won't be one. But, yes, they might know, and I'll ask."

"Okay. Next, we need to plan our interview trail." He rubbed his hands together.

"Interview trail?" she asked, her expression turning curiously puzzled.

"If the Council doesn't know what powers these victims had, then we need to interview family and friends and find out."

Raine looked at the board of victims as her eyes widened.

Will chuckled. "Welcome to the long, tedious work called *investigation*. It's what the 'I' in FBI stands for, after all."

CHAPTER

SIX

Raine finished a run on the hotel gym treadmill when her phone rang. She and Will planned to spend a few days reviewing their combined information. She'd opted to rent a car and stay in a hotel, driving back and forth to his trailer for long hours each day reviewing victims' backgrounds. After that grueling work, they planned to follow Will's outline to interview the victims' families one by one. Knowing the connection was Vanir bloodline, they hoped something new might emerge from a fresh interview with a new perspective.

She checked the caller ID.

"Hey, little sister."

"Hi, Raine. I was prepping Thunder for a trail ride and felt oddly nostalgic," Sky said.

Raine recalled Sky's favorite horse was a white gelding named Thunder. She swiped a towel across her face. "I miss our days of riding, too."

All three sisters riding together had been one of their favorite pastimes growing up. Life and supernatural forces had wedged time and space between the three of them. Interesting how Sky called to discuss their riding days the day after Raine felt her own nostalgia talking to Will. Coincidence, or were Sky's powers of perception at play?

"How's your shop doing?" Raine asked.

"Sales are good. Haven't missed a mortgage payment."

Raine had helped Sky move into her new house a year ago. It was a cute three-bedroom craftsman bungalow with a low-pitched roof and wide eave overhangs with exposed roof rafters. Tapered square columns framed the small porch. Sky had been thrilled, the purchase a marker of success in entry into adulthood and her entrepreneurial endeavors with her own herbal shop.

"How are Mom and Dad?" Raine asked.

"The usual. Happy playing bingo and volunteering at the rec center. When are you coming to visit?"

"Is that you just being curious or are you sensing something?"

"Bit of both."

"Visiting crossed my mind," Raine admitted. "I'm working on a new case, and we'll need to interview people. One of them is outside the Houston area, so not too far from you."

"We?" Sky asked.

"I have a partner this time."

"That's cool. I bet a partner will keep you from getting lonely with all that travel. I'm sure what you do can be isolating."

Although Raine had shared with Sky that she worked for an organization to eliminate murderous bloodlines, Sky knew nothing of the Council of Mjölnir. Her sister knew about the bloodlines because all three of them had grown up with the same dreams—dreams about when Ragnarok happened. They also all shared the ability to heal themselves.

"Yes, so far I like it. My partner probably thinks I'm crazy because I spent most of yesterday explaining bloodlines to him."

"Awkward. Did he believe you?"

"I have a feeling Will Decker has seen just enough of the bizarre in his line of work to not outright dismiss me as crazy, but he still has his reservations." Raine could have told her about healing herself, witnessed by Will, but she didn't want her family knowing just how dangerous her work could be. Although with Sky's gifts, perhaps she already had an inkling.

"Well, I hope it works out," Sky said.

Raine's phone chimed with an incoming call. She glanced at the screen. "Sky, this is—"

"Your boss. No worries. We'll chat more another time."

"Okay. I'll let you know when I'm coming to Texas and if I can visit the family while I'm there."

"Great! Bye."

Raine accepted the other call. "Usha."

"Is your assignment going well?"

"We've made progress already. All of Jör's victims are Vanir. The question is: why kill Vanir?" River fixed a cup of water from the hotel gym cooler and drank.

"Vanir can have a wide range of powers," Usha said.

Raine had received an email about how many people with Vanir bloodlines were in the Council's registry. Too many for a list to help her and Will isolate the next potential targets.

"We're interviewing victims' families in a few days to see what additional details we can uncover."

"The FBI agent is embracing your help?"

"I wouldn't call it embracing. Cautiously receptive is more accurate, especially since we found a pattern when previously the FBI had no link among victims other than the type of death. Special Agent Decker doesn't trust me, though. Fortunately, I think he recognizes there are supernatural forces at work, and he's willing to entertain an idea outside the realm of normal."

"You'll have to earn his trust."

Raine considered all of Will's rules and suppressed a chuckle. "I'll do my best."

"You sound hesitant."

"He's a lawman through and through. He has a no killing rule, and there is no way Jör is going down without a fight to the death."

"One problem at a time," Usha said calmly.

"Right." Step one, find the killer.

To do that, they needed to investigate what linked the victims beyond their Vanir bloodlines.

"You're fast and agile." Will blocked an elbow to his face, followed by Raine's roundhouse kick.

In two days, they would drive to their first interview. Today, Will spared with Raine. They practiced together at a local gym, wearing exercise clothing and protective headgear.

He wanted to know what she was capable of and where to remedy physical and mental weaknesses if they were going to be watching each other's backs. As they fought, he started to think he could actually learn a thing or two from her.

The FBI taught a hybrid martial arts of Krav Maga, mauy Thai, and ninjitsu. Standard hours' training was only a hundred, but Will had taken additional schooling and practiced on his own time to both improve his skill and provide cardiovascular exercise. Most of his work involved research and interviews, so he seldom used his skills outside of sparring. If Raine was right about Norse mythology and powerful adversaries, he might be putting his skills to use for a change. He might also need to learn from her since she seemed to have had more combat experience.

Raine was strong, but Will had her beat in the might department. Still, she would efficiently take down most men he knew. Jör, however, had superior speed rather than superior strength. With his speed and a wickedly sharp blade, he didn't need to overpower her.

"You're doing a good job of keeping me at a distance," Will told her.

He blocked a series of her blows. Longer arms gave him another advantage. She had the onerous task of trying to get inside his strike zone while simultaneously avoiding injury by being at the right distance from his offensive attacks and being too close to where he could overpower her in a wrestling move.

"You have excellent form as well," she said, a thin sheen of sweat forming over her bare skin. "But you have a tell."

"Oh, what is that?" He swung, but she ducked.

"You drop your shoulder slightly before you make a jab."

"I guess it's a good thing I don't spar with the villain before I take him down."

"I guess it is."

They continued with blows and kicks on the safety of the mat. Will was pleasantly surprised to find she was his equal in sparring. She'd been trained well. He felt like this was a partner who would truly have his back in any physical fight. Her agility combined with her sparring skill made her a great asset.

With that thought, his eyes briefly trailed to her backside—another asset—as she spun and kicked at him in her fitted outfit. With the momentary distraction, he'd nearly let her take his head off. He probably deserved to take a hit for his juvenile thoughts.

He ducked, taking a glancing blow to the padding around his jaw before dropping to the mat and lashing out a leg.

She predicted his move and jumped, but she couldn't dodge the second leg coming toward her. When it struck, she landed on the mat with a grunt and Will pounced.

She tried to take his momentum and fling him off of her, but he used the motion to tumble with her and landed her on her back once more. Relentless and with no apparent intention of surrendering, she tried to wriggle loose. If he didn't incorporate subduing maneuvers, she would be free of his grasp soon.

Using his weight and arms and leg muscles, he twisted around her and pinned her to the mat. He held his body tense as she struggled futility against his lock on her.

"Four years of high school wrestling, sweetheart. You won't get out of this one." He needed her to surrender soon or he would embarrass both of them by his body's masculine reaction to the friction of their embrace as she writhed in his full-body grasp.

Raine let out a huff before tapping twice on the mat in surrender. Will released his vice-like grip. They rolled apart and sat on the mat, both panting from the exertion.

"Okay, I concede. You pinned me." She took a few deep breaths, glaring at him. "But that won't help you against real bad guys. You're stuck in that position the same as they are. And when you loosen your hold, they'll be able to fight back. And eventually you will have to loosen your hold."

He shook his head in disagreement. "You recognized you'd lost and stopped squirming pretty quickly. Most people are going to fight that hold for several minutes and wear themselves out, so when I loosen my grip, they're a lot more fatigued than I am."

"Really, *sweetheart*?" She threw his term back at him laced with venom as she tore off her helmet. "Have you ever tried to wrap your body around a Fire Giant? No, you haven't. At least, I don't see the third degree burns to prove it."

He blinked at her, all gloating and condescension dissolving as he slid off his head gear. "You're right. I haven't. I'm not being receptive to your advice when you clearly have more experience fighting the supernatural than I do. Part of that is me trying to wrap my head around the supernatural and everything you claim we're up against."

Her expression softened.

He adjusted the helmet in his hand. "Of course, now that I have this kickass partner, I only need to pin the bad guy long enough for her to slap some cuffs on him."

"Right. Handcuffs." She drew out the word as if it was a foreign concept. "I probably need to get some of those."

Will pursed his lips. "Yes, you do. Because we are going to catch the villain. *Alive*."

CHAPTER

SEVEN

Raine drove her rental car with Will in the passenger seat. Their first interview was with victim number four's sister, Carla Noble. The victim had been Becky Noble, a fifty-year-old white accountant without so much as a parking ticket on her record. They'd chosen to interview Carla first since she lived in Virginia and her house was the closest to Will's property compared to the other victims' families, who were spread out across the world.

Raine parked on the curb and followed Will up the sidewalk. A fall breeze rustled through crepe myrtles, leaves brown with the changing seasons. The subdivision was row upon row of similarly cozy two-story homes with tidy lawns and little piles of raked leaves.

"I'll take the lead," Will said. "If you think of a question to ask, you can. But please avoid the supernatural. I really don't want the FBI losing all credibility."

"Rule number eight hundred and seventy-two: don't allude to the paranormal." She recalled him mentioning one of his rules was 'don't embarrass the bureau.'

He shot her a scowl, but she deflected it with a smile and a shrug. Like Will, Raine had dressed in navy slacks and a pressed white button-down shirt under a blazer. For a little differentiation and style, she'd added a striped button-down vest.

He wore the suit well, his handsome features reminding her of working together in the close quarters of his trailer or the feel of his body pressed against hers on the sparring mat. At the time, she'd seen his complete lean and sinuously muscular form through his bike shorts and snug t-shirt.

'*Four years of high school wrestling, sweetheart. You won't get out of this one.*' His smug words infuriated her as much as the strange desire she'd had for him *not* to let her go.

Shaking off the memory, she focused on the present. This was her first interview as an investigative agent, and she needed to keep her focus on the task at hand.

Keep your head in the game.

Will straightened his thin tie, rang the doorbell, and withdrew his badge. She reached for her cred-pack in her jacket pocket, but Will shook his head.

"The less you flash your fake badge, the fewer times you're breaking the law."

She let go of her jacket and dropped her hands to her sides, shooting Will a you're-too-cute look. At the end of the day, in a battle of good versus evil, how much did the minutia of his rules matter? But perhaps they mattered tremendously. Perhaps those rules were the very thing separating good from evil.

A stout woman in her late fifties answered the door. She had short dark hair and spectacles dangling from around her neck. Raine could see the similarities in the round face and small nose; this was Becky's sister.

"Carla Noble? I'm Special Agent Will Decker. This is Raine Thoren. Thank you for agreeing to meet with us."

Carla gave a sad, defeated nod. "You can come inside, Agent Decker."

"Call me Will."

"Will."

They followed Carla into her house as she gestured them inside. "I thought the FBI had given up, so it surprised me to get your call. It's been over a year since Becky's death."

Will straightened. "We haven't given up, Miss Noble."

"Must mean there are more victims." She led them to the living room and motioned for them to take a seat.

The living room had two beige two-seater couches and a recliner all angled toward a wall-mounted flat screen TV. Through a large window on one wall, Raine could see the neighbor's backyard abutting hers. She'd grown up on a large enough plot of land in Texas that neighbors weren't visible from the back porch. She wondered if Carla enjoyed Friday night neighborhood block parties or Bunco.

"Sadly, yes, but that also means more clues," Will told Carla.

He sat, but Raine didn't follow suit. Instead, she walked to the built-in shelves along one wall and studied the photographs. There were five—all family photos of Carla and her husband and children. One was of Carla and Becky in a park on a spring day.

"Lemonade?" Carla offered, gesturing to an already prepared pitcher and glasses on the coffee table.

Will accepted, but Raine politely declined.

After Will had a drink in hand, Carla brought out a cardboard box. "These are the same personal effects I showed the last investigator. What happened to him, anyway? He was another nice young man—very eager."

Will set his drink down on the coffee table. "Special Agent Gentry died in the line of duty."

Raine glanced back at Will. She hadn't heard about this prior agent's demise and wondered if Jör had eliminated him.

"That's dreadful." Carla sat in a lounge chair, face drooping.

Raine eased onto the couch next to Will and quietly riffled through Becky's effects on a table beside the sofa. A lifetime reduced to a small box after an untimely death. Raine didn't collect many things, but even she had more than one box.

As she listened to Will ask questions about Becky, Raine looked for anything related to Norse mythology or the magic of Vanir. She came across a wooden music box engraved with Yggdrasill—the acclaimed tree that once connected the nine realms. She ran a hand along the engraving.

"She loved that box."

Raine looked up to see Carla watching her hold the box.

"Did she know the origin of this tree?" Raine asked.

"I'm not sure about that, but she loved symbols."

Raine opened the box. "Symbols specific to any religion, sects, or beliefs?"

Carla shrugged. "It was a hobby. I never paid much attention."

A six-legged horse figurine was inside, but no music played. Raine turned the knob at the base to wind the music, but still it wouldn't play. When she lifted the small board the horse, Sleipnir, was attached to, she saw a key wedged in the gears. After she tugged it out, the music began playing.

Raine held up the key. "Do you know what this unlocks?"

"No. I've never seen it before." Carla shook her head. "But maybe it goes to something in her storage unit."

"Storage unit?" Will asked.

"Yes. The other agent suggested I keep all of Becky's possessions as long as the investigation was active. I don't have space here—or the heart for painful memories—so I keep it all in storage. I rented one of those nice climate controlled units."

"Can we see it?" Will asked.

"I'll give you the key so long as you return it."

Will thanked her. As he continued his interview questions, Raine finished looking through the belongings—photos, jewelry, and keepsakes. She suspected these particular effects either held meaning for Carla or Carla thought they held meaning for Becky. Nothing else appeared to reflect Norse mythology.

When they finished, Will thanked Carla before they left for the storage facility.

"'The game is afoot.'" He winked at Raine before sliding into the passenger seat.

Raine sensed Will's eagerness and wondered if he embraced this passion for investigative work with every case. His enthusiasm was infectious, making her more excited to see what they would uncover in the storage unit.

WILL HELD the two keys as he sat beside Raine, who drove them to the storage facility. He found he didn't mind being chauffeured by a partner as it meant he was free to think. One key opened the storage unit, and the other was a mystery. His mind churned through the conversation. Nothing supernatural had emerged about the single, reserved accountant, Becky Noble.

She enjoyed the local book club on Wednesday nights. Her only health issue was high blood pressure controlled with medication, but she also wasn't physically active.

Will turned the larger key over in his dexterous fingers, noting Raine's utter silence.

"Penny for your thoughts," he said.

"Agent Gentry was killed by Jör?"

"Yes."

"I'm sorry to hear that." She shifted in her seat. "I was also thinking about the crime scene photos. Becky was murdered in her home. And I remember the photos of the rooms looking messy. Carla's house was tidy in contrast."

Will considered the crime scene images. A cabinet door hanging by one hinge. A lamp knocked over. Clothes on the floor. He tried to recall from the report if the disturbances had resulted from a struggle.

"I don't think the disarray was from a fight," he said. "For one, no DNA contamination of any kind was found—no skin under her nails, no blood belonging to someone else. And second, because I've seen Jör in action now. A sedentary woman at the mercy of a lightning-fast killer like that wouldn't have had a chance to fight back."

"So Jör could have ransacked her place before or after he killed her."

"You think he was looking for something? And you think the hidden key could be related."

"You sound doubtful," she said.

He glanced out the window, watching the hills and forest and pasture land roll around them as they sped past. "If he wanted something from her, why not get the answer before killing her? She wasn't tortured. His precision killing with the knife wasn't any different from the others."

"Some of the other crime scenes were a mess. Some but not all."

Will continued to flip the keys between his fingers. "Some people weren't killed at home. When we get back, we can search the files and find out if the other victims had ransacked homes or offices."

"Maybe he didn't know what he was looking for. Or maybe he was removing anything that might connect the victims." Raine turned off the highway, following the car's GPS system to the storage unit facility.

Will frowned. Even after they'd added the international victims, no interactions or patterns had emerged. The only similarities were the type of death—a precision kill with a very sharp blade. That and Raine's claim that the victims all had a bloodline connection to Vanaheim. If Jör wanted something from his victims, why hadn't he tortured them?

He turned back to look at Raine. As she drove, she chewed her lip.

"Are you wondering if other victims had something in their possession related to their ancestry?" he asked.

"It's a possibility. But if the Council is right about the connection to Norse bloodlines, what are the chances Jör works alone?"

Will considered her words. "You're suggesting he's not a serial killer but an assassin?" The idea sent a chill down his spine. If he wasn't working alone, who did he work for, and was there more than one killer?

Raine didn't answer as she turned the car into the facility lot. The building was a stand-alone rectangular structure, which required a key code entry through a tall chain-linked fence. Security cameras were posted at the entrance and at every corner of the building.

She parked the car at the storage facility nearest Becky's unit, and they walked to her door number and unlocked it. Carla had stowed her sister's items carefully on shelves and labeled boxes.

"You want to split the room down the middle?" Will asked.

"Sure." Raine began opening a box filled with books. "But don't be offended if I search your half when I'm done with mine."

He smirked. "I like that you're fully embracing the investigative side, but I've been doing this a lot longer."

"But you don't know Norse symbolism. The engraving on the music box was the tree Yggdrasill. Knowing its significance clued me to take a deeper look."

Will lifted a book out of the box with a grin. "I can recognize Norse stuff." The book was entitled *Norse Mythology* by Neil Gaiman.

"Cute." Raine took the book and set it aside. "You know what I mean."

He did know what she meant, and he took no offense by it. He was doubtful they would find anything supernatural in a storage unit, but he didn't mind the company while he searched for more plausible clues than ancient mythological bloodlines. And he'd be checking the entire room himself as well.

After a few moments of rummaging, he opted for small talk. "So, Raine Thoren, son of Thor, what do you do to unwind after a case?"

"Train more."

He rifled through a box containing mostly tax records. "That doesn't fit the definition of unwinding."

He played his guitar, took long walks on his property, or hooked up with a woman. Did Raine date? Did she have a boyfriend?

None of his business, he admitted, though they'd spent several days together and she had mentioned no one.

"But it is stress relief," she was saying, "and after each fight, I see what else I need to work on."

After each fight. *Meaning after she killed someone?* he wondered grimly. This side of her would never sit well with him.

He moved to another storage container. "I've got a locked jewelry box here. Let's try the key you found. Oh, never mind, it looks like it was jimmied open and never repaired." Will ran a hand along the splintered oak wood.

Raine came over and inserted the key anyway. "It's a match. I wonder if Jör broke it open."

"If so, did he find what he was after?"

Hands brushing each other, they both sifted through the contents. The jewelry box contained an assortment of necklaces, bracelets, rings, and earrings. Separate carved out divisions were lined with purple velvet cloth, but the contents were all mixed and tangled.

Raine liberated a chain from bangles and held up the silver necklace. "This is gorgeous. Three rings. Three is an important symbol in Norse. There were three original beings. There were three sons of Bor, including Odin. Yggdrasil has three roots. The wolf, Fenrir, was bound by three chains. I could go on."

"I believe you could."

She chuckled.

"You also wear a necklace. A Celtic knot. Three points," he said.

She touched a hand to the pendant on her neck. "My mom gave all us sisters matching necklaces one year. Sometimes I see this symbol in my dreams—but only in a good way, like it brings a sense of peace and family."

Her fingers delicately moved along the silver symbol of Becky's necklace. Will took it from her hands and inspected it, fully aware his primary motivation was to touch Raine's hand again.

The contact sent warmth through him, and for a moment he

imagined fastening the necklace around her neck, his fingers brushing her bare skin. "Beautiful."

Annoyed with his husky tone and fantasizing, he dropped the trinket back in her hand and reached for a different piece of jewelry from the box. He would not get romantically entangled with his partner. They had a job and an obligation. Sleeping together when there was no leaving her behind the next morning would cause complications he didn't need.

He picked up a different trinket—a miniature brushed nickel of Thor's hammer with the chain linked through the handle end.

"Mjölnir," Raine mused.

Will weighed it in his hand. "Seems heavy for a necklace." He inspected the carvings before tugging apart the handle from the hammer head.

Raine tilted her head to one side. "Huh. It's a USB stick."

Will sheathed the device and dropped it in his pocket. "We'll look when we get back to the hotel. Could be nothing—an accountant keeping her client's data safe. Or it could be something."

"Could be the key to finding Jör, or who he's working for," Raine said hopefully.

And why, Will thought, surprising himself by actually considering the theory that Jör was a hired killer even as the thought soured his stomach.

Uncovering the truth wouldn't be as easy as finding all the answers on a jump drive, but he kept his negativity to himself during the remainder of their search.

EIGHT

That evening, Raine met Will in the hotel bar where he sat with his laptop open and two beers resting on a table. They'd had a long day of investigative work, from talking to Carla to digging through Becky's belongings at the storage unit. After agreeing to meet up for drinks at the hotel where Raine had been staying, she dropped him off at his trailer and they'd parted ways.

Raine had taken a few minutes to freshen up in her hotel room before their meeting. She was enjoying the detective part of partnering with Will, but, accustomed to working alone, she'd needed down time to recharge.

As she approached his table, she noted the Thor hammer USB was beside but not inserted into the laptop. He'd waited for her to unveil the clue, and the gesture felt as thoughtful as if he'd cooked a meal for her. Nonsense. Waiting to unveil clues together was probably something one colleague did for another—not an action based on mutual attraction.

Was it mutual?

Sometimes she thought so—in a glance or inadvertent brush of skin. They were playing a kind of dance with friendly jokes and polite respect for personal boundaries, getting to know each other little by little. The only way to be certain if attraction existed would be to make a move.

Not going to happen.

She would in no way, shape, or form jeopardize their working relationship.

With a cheerful smile, she sat beside him where she could see the monitor. "Shall we see what's on the flash drive?"

Will slid the glass of beer in front of her. "First, we toast." He raised his beer. "To our first successful interview."

She grabbed her glass. "Success as defined by…?"

"We gathered information, and you didn't shoot anyone."

She clinked her glass against his with a grin. "Cheers." As she drank the lager, the cool liquid felt like a divine finish to a long day.

He eyed her as she drank.

"What?" she asked, setting the glass back down.

"You like beer. I took a gamble that Raine Thoren, son of Thor, would like beer."

"You were correct."

After Will took a swig of his own beer, he inserted the USB drive into the laptop.

A row of text documents appeared. They had only past dates for names, as if tagged by the date Becky had typed them into the document. Raine scooted closer to Will as he randomly selected one to open.

The end shall come
Hell's will be done
Blood flows until war's won.

Will said nothing, leaning back and taking another drink. Raine followed suit, taking long, slow gulps and emptying half the glass.

"Wow. Maybe you are Thor's descendent." His tone held amusement.

He turned his gaze back to the laptop screen. "So, what do you make of this doom and gloom? A modern-day Nostradamus?"

"Becky must've been a prophet. Some Vanir have the gift of foresight."

"Oh, swell. You don't know if any of them are available to accompany me to the Super Bowl?"

Raine rolled her eyes but didn't conceal an admiring grin. "I'm no expert, but I don't think their premonitions are voluntary. What *would* be helpful is if one of these files predicted the victims. Then we could narrow down who to protect by who's still alive."

Will randomly selected another file.

Daughters of thee
By the faith of the tree
Face the demon she.

Three by three,
Sisters, Valkyrie,
Hell's wrath to free

"Three Valkyrie sisters?" He shot her a sideways glance.

"None of us are Valkyries."

He shrugged and crossed his arms. "I'm not sure Becky's notes are going to give us specific names or locations. This is all very vague stuff. I'll send it to Caroline and have the FBI team look at it."

"Let's make copies. You get one to the FBI for analysis, and I'll send one to the Council of Mjölnir. And we'll each keep one to study ourselves."

Will turned the ring on his finger, as he seemed to do when the topic of Norse mythology resurfaced. Obviously the idea of alien bloodlines was a tough pill for him to swallow, just like the fact that sometimes she had to kill demons.

He regarded her for a moment, probably debating sharing information with her. She kept her eyes fixed on him. Thus far, she had more than proven her willingness to cooperate, collaborate, and share.

Will turned back to the laptop, copied the files to it, ejected the USB, and re-sheathed it into the hammer head. He offered it to Raine.

Hesitantly, she accepted. "Just like that? No rules attached?"

He arched an eyebrow. "The rule is you share with me whatever your organization shares with you. *Partner*."

"Of course, *partner*." To quell the rising affection she felt at his words, she leaned back and finished her beer.

"Your first day on the streets investigating and you already found a clue."

"And you thought you were saddled with a rookie." She smiled.

"You're too good a fighter to be called a rookie. And, in all seriousness, I wouldn't have found this without you."

"Thanks. New York next?"

Will nodded. "New York next."

"Let's book the tickets for the day after tomorrow."

"What's happening tomorrow?" he asked.

"Tomorrow, I'm going to take you on a trail ride. We've worked four straight days. Ten hours a day."

Will raised his glass. "Yee-haw. Let's ride 'em, partner."

Raine blinked at him. "I don't even know what to say to that. I grew up in Texas, and I don't think those words in that terrible accent have ever come out of my mouth."

Will chuckled. "Come to think of it, you don't have much of an accent."

"My parents were transplants from up north. I was eight when we settled there. We girls never took to a Texas twang."

He pushed back from the table. "Rest tonight. Ride tomorrow. New York the day after that."

"Sleep tight, *partner*."

Back in her hotel room, Raine called Usha.

"Hello, Raine."

"I thought I should provide an update." Usually, she would call Usha to say if a mission was successful or unsuccessful. Since her partnership with Will was an ongoing investigation, she was in unfamiliar territory on when to give Usha updates to pass along to the Council of Mjölnir.

"One of the Vanir victims had the power of foresight. I have a USB of her premonitions. I'll send an encrypted copy to you. Will is going to send a copy to FBI analysts, too."

"How are things going with Agent Decker?"

"Better than expected," she said. Only two days had passed since she'd last talked to Usha, but she'd had more interaction with Will, and they worked well together. She and Will were fast becoming genuine partners. He included her in all aspects, even if he felt the need to reinforce his 'rules' from time to time.

"And his acceptance of the existence of otherworldly bloodlines?"

"Still skeptical acceptance without embracing the truth. Honestly, I think a main reason he accepts as much as he has so far is because he saw me heal myself." She unbuttoned her vest, slid it off, and hung it up in the closet.

"A wonder he accepts as much as he does. Perhaps Special Agent Will Decker is more than he reveals."

Raine froze. "You think he's not a hubble, not standard bloodline?"

"I will look into it."

Raine fell silent, thinking of how he'd bested her sparring and she'd never lost a fight to a hubble. Would Will have kept this from her after she'd openly divulged everything? He'd been the one to make the 'no secrets' rule. Growing irritated, she paced her hotel room.

"It is possible," Usha said gently, as if sensing Raine's distress through the long silence on the phone, "that he doesn't know what he is."

Raine wouldn't have known what she was without Usha. The woman had helped her make sense of her powers and dreams. How many mixed bloodlines had powers but didn't understand their etiology? Their heritage?

She thought about the ring on his finger and how Will seemed to turn it absentmindedly whenever they were discussing Norse mythology. "He might be hiding something."

"If he is, then it may be in the interest of self-preservation. You've trusted him this far. Trust him to open up to you when the time is right for him."

Although Raine saw the logic in Usha's words, it didn't eliminate the sting of Will not trusting her with all of his truth. Even if he didn't know what he was, she obviously had contacts to find out for him. She untied her boots and tugged them off.

When would he decide to trust her?

One day at a time.

"This is pleasant," Will commented.

Raine had found a trail twenty minutes from his trailer, so he was riding through the same beautiful woods near where he planned to build his home. The fall colors among peaks and valleys had been one of the most alluring factors of why he wanted to build here.

"You have officially passed horseback riding one-oh-one," Raine announced. "I know you memorized all the rules, so let's hear them."

He recited her teaching from when they'd saddled the horses.

"No sudden movement. Stay calm. Tighten the saddle a second time. Mount from the horse's left."

"You got it. Although, you're always calm. I can tell your horse is relaxed in your presence."

Will felt relaxed in Raine's presence, and she seemed at ease today. Brushing and preparing the horses had been the most casual he'd seen her. Tight blue jeans and cowboy boots fit her as deliciously as her black spandex pants the first day he'd met her. Fortunately for his hormones, her daily work clothes were slacks and a blazer, which mostly hid her curves—until she took off the blazer and showed her fitted vest.

"I'm enjoying the investigative side of this job," she said.

He smirked. "You say that now because the informant was cooperative." Becky's sister had led them right to important clues. "They won't always be that helpful."

"When they aren't, do we get to play good-cop bad-cop?"

The path widened, and he brought his horse alongside hers. The fall breeze tugged at the loose strands of her long blonde hair, making them wave around her face and neck.

He chuckled, hearing a slightly nervous edge to his laughter as he considered what atrocities she would commit as bad-cop. "That's not really a thing, except in the movies. The reality of interviewing family members, witnesses, and criminals is that the FBI wants a good rapport. Anyone treated right can become a valuable informant. Cooperation is the key to success, not intimidation."

He added, "And we both know I'd be the good-cop. I don't even want to think about how many laws you'd be willing to break being the bad-cop."

She scoffed. "I can play normal bad-cop—menacing and threatening—all teeth and no bite."

No bite? His mind wandered to a dark, intimate place with Raine. Alone, together, he didn't think he'd mind a little bite.

"Normal?" He shook his head. "The first day we met, I had to establish a 'no killing rule.' You are many things, Raine, but normal isn't one of them." He spoke the words playfully, but the way she turned her gaze forward and pressed her lips together suggested he'd struck a nerve. Maybe the once lanky teenage cheerleader had been normal, but she wasn't normal now.

"I happen to like you being not normal," he added lamely. He honestly liked how unconventional she was, but he didn't know how to say that without sounding like he was hitting on her.

And he wouldn't hit on his partner no matter how her legs straddling the horse conjured images of her straddling him.

"It's a little wider here. Do you want to run?" he asked.

"I don't think that's a good idea. You have to know how to rein a horse in before you gallop. If Merk there gets too excited, he could run you all the way back to the barn."

"I'm not the one riding the horse named Trigger."

She leaned over and stroked Trigger's neck. "You're a good boy, aren't you?"

His ears twitched.

"C'mon, coach," Will said. "Tell me what to do. Keep calm and what else?"

"Squeeze with your knees. Be gentle and smooth with the reins. If you're not in control, the horse will know it."

She leaned over to Merk, patted him, and whispered something in his ear.

"What are you, the Horse Whisperer?" He grinned.

"I've always had a special bond with horses."

"Is that a Valkyrie thing?" he asked.

"Maybe it is. Ready?" She took out slack in her reigns.

He copied her movements. "Ready."

They took the horses into a trot, followed by a gallop. Will found the loping smooth and exhilarating. He followed Raine's lead, who made the gallop of horse and rider look effortless. Meanwhile, he was pretty sure his thighs would hate him tomorrow.

When she slowed, he reigned in Merk beside Trigger.

"Well done!" She smiled, flushed cheeks illuminated her pink lips and rich, brown eyes.

"We have an extra night in New York after the interview and before our third interview in Houston. I was thinking we could have dinner with my family," he said, surprised by his own words.

"Oh?"

He swallowed. "Well, I haven't seen them in a while, and they've never met any of my partners. You're introducing me to your parents when we're in Houston, so it seems only fair. Besides, we're going to be close to where my parents live..." As his voice trailed off, Will became irritated at himself for his fumbling invitation.

This wasn't a date. This was collegial. Maybe if he'd been asking her on a date, his words would have flowed more eloquently. He never struggled with asking women on dates.

"Of course. It'll be fun," she said.

"It'll be something." The event would definitely not be fun. He already felt a twinge of regret at having extended the invitation when he considered the tense dynamics of his family.

He would need to let his parents know he was visiting with a guest. What had possessed him to invite Raine to his family's home?

He envisioned the dinner in his mind. She would meet them and see how dysfunctional they were. That disastrous event would then squash his whimsical delusions of a meaningful relationship with her, and he could get back to focusing on work.

CHAPTER

NINE

Raine listened to the loud thrumming of the plane as she watched the clouds zip by out the window. They were flying into La Guardia for their next interview.

She thought back to when she'd been recruited as a Shadow Guardian. After college, she'd wandered from job to job, unsure what to do with her life. After growing up in a world with only human contact, her eyes had been opened to the other world when the Dǫkkálfar had killed Storm's fiancé. Raine's childhood dreams suddenly made sense.

Nine realms.

One remained.

With each job, she spent her free time scouring Internet job boards for career inspiration. The idea of working nine to five in some commerce job and ignoring the world beyond humans made her feel hollow.

She'd looked down at the hand-written note she held as she stood outside the brownstone matching the address of the invitation. Something in the vagueness of the job offer within the unsolicited letter she'd received had intrigued her. The calligraphed words were scrawled on thick cotton paper embossed with a tree. No ordinary tree. Yggdrasil. The tree on the stationary had beckoned her as much as the invitation to learn about a job protecting the innocent.

She pocketed the letter and rang the doorbell. A small, frail-looking black woman opened the door. Raine placed her age in perhaps the late seventies.

"I'm Raine Thoren. I received an invitation to discuss a job offer."

"Right on time. I'm Usha Bakshi. Please come in." Usha stepped aside and Raine entered, following the woman from the foyer into a library with a sitting area.

They sat in chairs opposite each other with a table of pastries and hot tea between them. Usha poured two cups as Raine wondered how she'd been "on time" for hot tea when the invitation had only specified a day and location but not a time.

Steam from the cups floated into the air before dissipating. The fragrance smelled of orange spice.

Usha added two tablespoons of honey before stirring her beverage. She leaned back, cup in her hands. "I'm going to tell you a story about our ancestry and your destiny." She had then laid out the story about Ragnarok and the nine realms.

Raine listened quietly, sipping her tea.

"You have the powers of a warrior, if you harness them through hard work. I am part of an organization called the Council of Mjölnir. There are twelve leaders spread across the world. Among our duties are overseeing the Shadow Guardians, warriors who fight hostile bloodlines and protect each other and humans. We would like you to enlist in the Shadow Guardians and begin your training."

Raine sipped her tea again, stalling and trying to decide how much she believed of what the woman had said. "This is the part where you offer me the red pill or the blue?"

Usha smiled, a pitying expression that conveyed forgiveness for Raine's joke over a serious matter. She seemed to find no humor in Raine's quip.

"The truth is a jagged pill to swallow, but there's always a choice," Usha said solemnly. "I offer you a noble path as a protector of the weaker."

Raine envisioned the death of her sister's fiancé and the devastation Storm had faced. Her sister hadn't been the same since and had isolated herself from the family—from the world. Raine couldn't undo those events, but maybe she could spare someone else such pain.

"If I say yes?" she asked Usha.

"Then we start your training. You work only with me and the people I hire to teach you weapons and hand-to-hand combat. After your first successful mission, you meet the rest of the Council."

"There's a probation period?"

"Yes. Like any new job, we want to gauge your level of commitment. We have to guard our own identities from those who want to destroy us. Like any job, you receive a monthly wage. Travel is all expensed. The wage is modest compared to the work, which will be arduous, but we don't expect you to simply volunteer your time."

Raine had stared at her empty teacup. What would she fill her cup with—belief in the supernatural, which she could feel coursing through her veins like an animal waiting to be unleashed, or suppression of the discomfort of things outside what she considered her safe zone?

"I've given you much to consider," Usha said. "Think it over. I'll give you my contact number, and you let me know when you've decided."

"CAROLINE, you were right about teaming up with CoM. They had evidence Jör's murders are international. We may be able to find his pattern." Will paced his hotel room in Newark as he spoke to his boss. He'd already conveyed as much in his email when he'd sent Becky's file, but it bore repeating.

Though he wasn't about to tell her Raine's theory of ancient alien bloodlines.

He did squats in his hotel room, trying to loosen his aching muscles from yesterday's horseback riding. He was unbelievably stiff after sitting on the plane to New York and needed to get to the gym to work out the kinks. Raine was in a room down the hall, probably also giving her boss an update. Tomorrow was their interview with another victim's family member. The day after that would be dinner with his family. A strange urge had him wanting Raine to meet his family, despite knowing their propensity to bicker and incite awkwardness.

"It's going well then?" His boss's voice was uncharacteristically hesitant.

"Yes. We're making progress, I think."

"Fascinating."

"Fascinating? Why is that fascinating? I'm doing what you asked. I'm doing my job."

"I know. I'm not shocked by your work ethic, but you don't have a track record for interagency diplomacy. I wasn't sure the two of you would make it this long."

He frowned. "I would be offended, but there's a tone of admiration in your voice."

"Yes, well—"

"I didn't even hear this much awe when I brought in the Vertigo serial killer," he complained.

"First rule, special agent," she snapped.

"Don't embarrass the bureau," Will said through clenched teeth.

"Good. Keep working together and stop this maniac."

"Do you have any other information about this CoM organization?" he asked. He had done his own research and found nothing.

"Not that you're cleared for."

"I can work with an agent from their organization but I don't get to know more about it?"

"Knowing you, you'll learn what you need from your new partner."

Caroline wasn't wrong. Raine had opened up to Will quite naturally, but that didn't mean she had comprehensive knowledge about her own organization.

Council of Mjölnir.

Shadow Guardians.

Ancient bloodlines.

The bizarreness of it all was enough to make Will's head explode. And yet, as he twisted his ring, he wasn't completely without exposure to the supernatural.

Jör huddled near the clunky heater in his motel room as he reviewed his list of targets in order to select his next victim. He would travel south for warmer weather to soothe his aching bones.

After shutting his laptop, he redressed his bullet wound with clean bandages. His injury seemed to be healing slowly, though he didn't know the expected recovery time, so perhaps he was impatient. He wanted to ensure he wasn't compromised before undertaking his next assignment. Speed was his gift, and he couldn't afford pain and slowness to result in errors. Worse would be if more FBI agents ambushed him and he couldn't escape. He didn't understand how they'd found him last time, so caution was prudent.

Helen didn't tolerate mistakes and failures. Being caught by authorities would constitute a mistake. Not completing his kills would constitute a failure. His queen would have his head should either occur.

CHAPTER

TEN

"How's it possible ya haven't found the bastard yet?"

"Patrick, language," his mother scolded him.

Will sat at the kitchen table with Sean O'Donner's brother, Patrick. Sean had been one of Jör's earlier victims. His mother washed dishes rather than join them, and Will suspected her motions were the product of anxious agitation rather than needing to clean dishes the minute the FBI arrived at her home.

"I understand your frustration," Will said calmly. Patrick's anger wasn't personal so Will took no offense. The situation had to be maddening for families—not having justice for the loss of a loved one. "We're reviewing all the case files and talking to relatives again."

"Brilliant." Patrick sneered, tossing up his hands, as his shock of dark hair above a chiseled face wavered. "Our bloody tax dollars at work." He spoke in a sharp Irish accent, glancing at Raine, who moved around the adjacent living room looking at family photos.

She hadn't worn her blazer, and the vest over her shirt showed her narrow waist.

Will cleared his throat, drawing the young Irishman's attention back to him, both to keep him focused on the topic at hand and because he didn't like the way Patrick was eyeing his partner's backside. Will told himself his reaction to Patrick's roaming gaze was a protective flare in his partner's defense, not because he was jealous of another man mentally undressing Raine.

"We're also exploring supernatural possibilities," Will said, following a hunch and trying not to cringe at his own words.

Raine glanced at him, eyebrows raised.

"What?" Patrick snapped.

"Did Sean have any unusual abilities?" Will asked.

Even as Patrick scoffed, his mother stopped washing dishes.

Patrick leaned forward, his voice fuming. "Ya think my brother was killed because of super powers?"

"I'm saying the killer may have thought your brother had some abilities."

Patrick scoffed. "You people are unbelievable." He shook his head. "Graspin' at straws."

The mother, who'd been utterly still at the mention of the supernatural, snapped at her son, "Snuff it, Patrick." She walked over to the table and sat, drying her hands on a kitchen towel. After tucking strands of loose hair behind her ears, she smoothed the front of her peach-colored apron.

"Sean had an uncanny ability about some things," she said.

"Oh, for the love of St. Joseph," Patrick murmured.

Will kept quiet and maintained his gaze on Patrick and Sean's mother. He noticed his partner edge nearer to the kitchen to listen.

"Sean could always sense things—send the perfect birthday or Christmas gift. And he knew when family was in trouble. He would call when you needed cheering up. And that one time," she gestured at Patrick, "he called a tow truck before his brother even got a flat tire. Sean was three states away but knew his own brother would get a flat on his way to work."

Will felt a chill run down his spine, but he didn't hesitate to launch into a flurry of questions now that the victim's mother was engaged in the conversation.

After a half hour, he hadn't learned anything else of obvious value, but he and Raine left the house, having a least made the victim's mother feel heard and appreciated. The interview as a whole had furthered their investigation. Two victims. Both reportedly had premonitions or visions.

A pattern had emerged, and it made the hair on Will's neck stand on end.

RAINE SAT at the hotel bar table across from Will. They sipped on a dark stout with undertones of sweet espresso as they discussed the case and the interviews of the O'Donnor family. They had taken their blazers off, laid them on their chair backs, and left their guns in their rooms. Because they were the only people seated, they could talk openly. Faint jazz music floated out of surround sound speakers near the bar.

"We didn't get much to go on," she said.

"Well, they don't all have secret journals to uncover." Will ran a finger down the condensation along his glass.

"We learned he had some keen intuition ability. It confirms our Vanir theory."

He glanced up at her. "Did Jör really kill Sean because he could pick the perfect Christmas present?"

Was he purposefully playing devil's advocate, or was he just not ready to embrace the supernatural? Raine wondered.

There he went, twisting his ring again.

She decided to press past his glum mood. "What if the killer didn't know the extent of Sean's abilities?"

Will took a swig of his beer. "What do you mean?"

"What does the Council of Mjölnir know about these people? Not much. They know the victims are Vanir based on DNA samples. We don't have any documentation of what their actual abilities are unless they made it public somehow. Maybe Jör doesn't know either. What if all he knows is they're Vanir? Or, more specifically, they're the type of Vanir with the gift of seeing the future?"

"You mean he targets them because they *might* have some premonition ability without knowing if that magic is as powerful as telling the future or as harmless as predicting a loved one's desire for a cashmere scarf?"

"Exactly."

Will scrubbed a hand along his jaw, drawing Raine's attention to the five o'clock shadow he was developing around his full lips. She looked away and drank another gulp of beer.

"What's nagging me," he began, "is what you brought up earlier. What if Jör is an assassin and not a serial killer? When I first started accepting that maybe he was killing all Vanir, I could still rationalize that these murders were the work of a serial killer targeting certain people. But silencing fortune tellers is a real motive. And if he's working for someone, then who?"

"And why," she added.

"And are we up against one madman or many?"

THE NEXT DAY, they had breakfast at a Tops Diner, still mulling over the case. Raine could tell Will was a little morose and distracted. She wasn't sure if his mood resulted from solidifying their Vanir theory, the thought that their target was an assassin rather than a serial killer, or knowing they would have dinner with Will's family tomorrow night. She suspected the combination was affecting him, so she didn't push for him to share his feelings. After a lingering meal studded with bouts of picking at their food in silence, Will drove them back to the hotel.

"Hey, can we stop off at an ATM so I can get some cash?" Raine asked.

"Sure."

Using her phone, she pulled up the location of an ATM, and he took the exit. Most of her purchasing power came from debit and credit cards, but she found it handy to keep some cash on her. If someone witnessed a skirmish or there were property damages related to the work she did, people were often willing to exchange cash for silence rather than reporting it to the police, which would only create loose ends for Raine.

When they pulled in next to the machine, it had an OUT OF ORDER sign taped to the screen.

She glanced around their surroundings at the chain restaurants and convenience stores. "There's a bank across the street. I can use that ATM."

He drove over, but the branch didn't have an external ATM.

"I'll just run inside," she said.

When Will parked at the entrance, she opened her door to slip out of the car.

"Uh, gun," he said. He patted the passenger seat as though he expected her to set it down.

She looked from her holster to Will. "I have a badge if the security guard inside notices my gun."

"You know how I feel about your fake badge." He arched an eyebrow at her, turning her insides to mush.

To mask the attraction she felt, she huffed and feigned annoyance. "Fine." She didn't usually carry her gun in public anyway.

She took off her suit jacket and wriggled out of the holster. She slapped the gun, holster and all, into his hand. For good measure, she removed her credential pack and tossed it in the passenger seat as she got out.

After shutting the car door, she walked into the bank, past the guard, and stood in line behind three other people waiting to be served by a single teller. The other three stations didn't have bank staff. The walls held three mounted cameras, and the bank offices were situated off to the right. A large banner in one corner offered mortgages with competitively low interest rates.

She reached the teller counter and pulled out her phone with its small case for cards, ID, and cash.

A voice behind her boomed, "Nobody move!"

Another man shouted, "Everybody down on the floor!"

Raine smoothly returned her phone to her pocket and turned slowly around to see three armed men with grotesque facial features preparing to rob the bank.

ELEVEN

Will stuck Raine's gun into the glove compartment. Why the hell would she want to take her gun into the bank? Was she expecting to find an evil dwarf hiding out in there? Were there evil dwarves?

He pulled out his phone and checked football scores before sending a quick text to his friend, who lived in Hoboken. Will hoped to stop by for beers this evening.

One parking space over from him, a van backed in. When the side door slid open, three men wearing some type of warty monster masks and armed with various types of large guns filed out of the Ram box van and stormed into the bank.

Will's blood ran cold. "Well, shit."

He took inventory of the number of cars in the parking lot and tried to guesstimate how many people were inside the bank, including workers.

Including Raine.

He couldn't very enact a one man rescue mission. To make matters worse, as soon as authorities arrived, this debacle would morph into a hostage situation.

He stepped out of his car and noticed a woman crossing the parking lot with purse in hand, making a beeline for the bank.

Whipping out his credentials, he headed her off. "Federal agent, ma'am. There's a bank robbery in progress, and you need to clear this area." He kept his body between the van and the woman so the driver couldn't see her startled expression. "If you wouldn't mind also going ahead and calling 9-1-1. Give them the location, name of the bank, and tell them Special Agent Will Decker told you to call. Three armed men."

Will turned and casually walked to the front of his rental car. Since the robbers' van was facing the opposite direction, the driver wouldn't clearly see him. He leaned over the windshield and snapped off one wiper before sauntering behind the van, out of view of its large side mirrors.

He needed to take the getaway driver out of commission so he couldn't alert his friends inside the bank that they'd been discovered.

Crouching, he shuffled low to the ground as he worked his way quickly to the driver's side door. He grasped the windshield wiper at the narrow end while tugging back the broader base. As he stood, he released the end of the windshield wiper with the steel. It whipped forward like the snapping of a taut rubber band into the corner of the driver's side window. The glass shattered.

The man in the driver's seat screeched and reached for the gun on the dash between the seats, but Will was faster. Using the windshield wiper, he cracked the narrow end across the man's face, striking his left eye to blind him.

In a low voice, Will said, "FBI. You're under arrest. Hands on the wheel."

As the man cried out and reached for his face, Will opened the door and dragged him out of the van and around to the hood, out of view of the bank windows. Will hoped the men inside hadn't heard him break the window and snatch the driver away.

Despite the man's attempts to resist, Will forced him down face first, kicked his ankles to spread his legs, and began reading him his rights. He cuffed the driver and left him bent over the hood of the van, hurtling curse words at Will about his eye.

Sirens sang in the distance.

Damn. So much for the element of surprise.

Will took out his badge, ready to take an active role in whatever events would unfold next. Sweat broke out on the back of his neck and under his arms, his perspiration seemingly disproportionate to the cool fall weather and the exertion of taking down the criminal. Raine was inside that bank with three armed men and no gun of her own.

Yet, she'd been handling herself with bad guys long before they'd partnered up. He would have to trust she knew how to keep herself safe in this type of situation.

He let out a little chuckle. What he really should worry about was how much damage she was going to do to the three men inside the bank.

All joking aside, he honed in on his true worry. What would she allow to happen to herself to keep everyone else inside that bank safe? The first night he'd met her, she'd put her body between him and a gruesomely deadly blade. And she hadn't even known him. She would risk her life to save every single stranger inside those brick walls.

Despite the knot in his stomach, he tried to dismiss those dismal thoughts. Even though she possessed healing abilities, she'd clearly stated that she was mortal. One well-placed bullet and...

Two police cars came to a screeching halt, and Will held up his cred-pack while maintaining one hand on the cuffs of the driver. Damn, it would have been better if the police hadn't come in hot. They could have quietly secured the scene and nabbed the robbers when they climbed in their getaway vehicle, thinking they'd succeeded in robbing the bank.

Now it was a hostage situation.

Raine stood perfectly still. She didn't have the element of surprise and couldn't simply fade out of view.

Had the men realized they had simultaneously given contradictory orders? 'Freeze' and 'get on the floor.' No one seemed to know which command took precedence, since both men held guns.

"Customers on the floor!" one of them barked. "Face down! Bank workers, don't move."

Raine and the others in line complied. She rested her chin on the floor and made sure she was facing where she could see the counter, the back offices, and the entrance. When she glimpsed outside the door, she saw Will was no longer in his vehicle. Had he seen the men come inside? Was he calling the police?

Will. The man who'd made her leave her gun behind!

Not that she could whip it out and start firing against three men. Taking offensive action would risk the lives of too many people in this room, including the gunmen themselves. They weren't evil bloodlines, just common criminals. She had no reason to kill them, but she also wouldn't tolerate them hurting anyone.

They disarmed the security guard and began screaming at the teller to fill bags of cash, waving guns carelessly around.

Sirens sounded outside the building, and the robbers froze.

"What? How is that possible?" one of them demanded.

"Cops? Who called the fucking cops!" another screamed, sweeping his gun across the room as everyone cowered and whimpered.

"Lock the door," barked the third. He stalked over to the security guard and jabbed the toe of his boot into the man's side. "Get up, asshole, and lock the damn door."

The guard did as he was told.

"Oh, crap, man. Oh, crap." The man behind the counter, money bag in hand, paced.

"Keep your shit together," said the one by the door.

"I can't go back to jail, Brent. I can't."

"Hector," Brent, the tall leader, clearly giving the orders, snapped at him. "Take the guard and lock him in one of the offices."

"Which one?"

"I don't give a shit which one."

The smaller man, Hector, slunk away, nudging the guard with his shotgun.

"Everybody off the ground!" Brent roared. "Stand up. Line up along the glass doors and windows, ass and backs facing the cops."

Raine, the other three customers, the two tellers, and the bank manager complied. She would bide her time and wait for an opening.

WILL INTRODUCED himself to the first man out of his patrol car, Officer Bert. "This man was their getaway driver. That's their van." Will gestured toward the vehicle.

"FBI, huh? What are you doing here?" He motioned for another officer to take the cuffed man away.

"My partner needed to stop off at the bank for cash."

"You're saying there's an FBI agent on the inside?"

Ugh. Sure. Fine. "Yeah." Will pursed his lips.

When local law enforcement wrote their incident report, Raine Thoren would be listed as an FBI agent. However, if he'd told them his friend was in there, who was also a woman, they would think 'girlfriend.' FBI partner was better. They would think he could more calmly handle the crisis with his partner inside rather than a lover. And he was going to need to appear impartial in order to take the lead in negotiations the way he intended to.

The police cars kept piling up on the scene. The next man who approached had a bald head reflecting the sun as he squinted around, either severely bothered by the rays, straining to take in the entire scene, or some combination of the two. His name tag read Chief of Police Tim Clark.

Officer Bert spoke up. "Chief, this is Special Agent Will Decker with the FBI. Just happened to be at the bank and apprehended their getaway driver."

"What are we dealing with?" The Chief asked, nodding toward the bank. His approach was straightforward, and he didn't seem threatened by Will's presence, both of which Will appreciated.

"Three bank robbers. I watched them pour out of the van. There are at least four civilians inside. Probably one security guard. I'm not sure how many bank employees."

"Bert, you're the Incident Commander. You and Parker assign four men to cordon off this area. Run those van plates for me and give me a name of the owner of the vehicle. Could be stolen but let's find out who that guy is." He pointed toward the driver being put in the back of one of the squad cars. "Call Trish so she can start heading off the press and arrange for them to set up a location to conglomerate a safe distance away from here. I'll call SWAT, and they can set up a perimeter." He turned to Will. "Any experience with hostage negotiations?"

Never Split the Difference, Will thought of the expert FBI hostage negotiator's book he'd read a few years ago by Chris Voss. He'd also read *Stalling for Time* by Gary Noesner. "Some experience," he told the Chief, though Will had never before been the one to talk directly to the hostage takers. He had at least done his share of courses and calming angry law breakers.

"I don't. And I'd appreciate some help with that department."

"Yes, sir."

"Let's get you a number to call inside that bank."

Contrary to movies, which entertained audiences with overdramatized conflict, the FBI made efforts to be collegial with local law-enforcement. The idea was to work together for the best outcome of all involved. Will appreciated the Chief deferring to him for this part of the bullpen. He also understood police politics. If this whole fiasco went to shit and the bull got out of the pen, local law enforcement could blame it on the FBI and save face with the public.

Ugh. One horseback ride and he was making country idioms.

If taking the risk of public failure meant Will won first dibs on a conversation and nonviolent resolution with the bank robbers, he would gladly accept responsibility, even knowing there were elements out of his control, like how patient two dozen armed police would be once the SWAT team arrived.

He glanced at the bank entrance and saw the outline of figures standing against the glass. Whoever the ringleader was, he obviously had the intelligence to place bystanders between him and potential snipers.

CHAPTER

TWELVE

Brent paced near filled money bags on the floor against the teller counter. Raine's gaze trailed from him to the others in the bank with their terrified expressions.

A young man in his twenties looked like he was fresh from the gym and might cry at any moment. A woman in her sixties glared at the men as if they were traffic cops standing between her and home gardening. Another woman in a sundress sniffled quietly as she stared at her feet. The two tellers wore navy slacks and white shirts with red vests. They shook where they stood. The bank manager wore a skirt suit and two-inch pumps. Large sweat stains marred her shirt.

Brent came over to stand against the wall beside Raine and peered around her to look out the window. She contemplated making a move. She could disable the leader and perhaps convince the other two to surrender. Alternatively, the others could panic, start shooting, and the hostages would become casualties.

She clenched her fists at her side. The lead robber was so close, she could hear his heavy breathing echoing from inside his mask and smell his aftershave. Disarming him would be easy, but she couldn't take the risk of anyone else getting injured.

When the phone behind the counter rang, Brent jolted. "Watch them," he said to Hector. Walking behind the counter, he tugged off his rubbery mask and picked up the phone.

"What do you want?"

Raine listened intently to him talk, wondering who was on the other side of the phone.

"Hi, my name is Will. Who am I speaking with?" His tone was polite and spoken with a smile on his lips.

"I'm not telling you my fucking name," the man answering the phone replied.

"Okay, we can skip that part of the introduction." Easy and calm.

"You a cop?"

"I'm an FBI agent. Cops take it personally when you rob banks in their town, so it's better you and I talk and avoid them. I'm just outside the bank on the phone." Will, ear pods in place, paced thirty feet from the front doors. He made a little wave, although he couldn't see deep enough into the bank to tell if the man was looking at him.

"How can you and I resolve this situation?" Will asked.

"I'm taking all this money and leaving. If anybody tries to stop me, I start killing hostages."

"Killing hostages," Will echoed in an even tone.

"Yeah. Don't cross me."

"Let's talk about those people with you inside the bank. They're going to get tired standing there while we work out your situation. How about letting them sit?"

No response.

"If you're worried about moving them from the front, maybe have someone move chairs to the windows?"

"I don't care about them. What makes you think I'd do shit for them?"

"You don't care about them?" Will kept the smile in his voice.

"Of course not."

"They're your most precious commodity. They're keeping you safe in there and the cops away out here. Right now, they're worth more to you than all that cash."

The robber scoffed but didn't argue.

Will let the silence settle between them. There was no need to rush. Rushing caused errors and escalation. Criminals didn't think you cared when you were in a hurry.

"My van still in one piece?" the robber asked.

"I have a van out here, untouched, registered to a Brent Shaft."

Silence.

"I want a pizza delivery."

"I can do that, Brent. Tell me how many pizzas and what you want on them. How about we order enough for everyone? You a Coke or Pepsi kind of guy?"

Brent began rattling off the order, and Will noted the man had never corrected him using the name Brent.

After Will took his order, Brent hung up the phone. Will walked back to the command center, a trailer in the parking lot of the adjacent fast-food restaurant where Chief Clark stood over three deputies sitting in front of laptops.

"Pizza?" He arched an eyebrow at Will.

"You got the order?" Will knew the police were listening to their conversation.

"Yeah."

"Thanks. This ends with everybody walking out of that bank alive, which means we rush nothing. We force nothing. If they're holed up inside the building until dinner time and ask for fillets, we're going to make that happen too."

"We can plant bugs inside the pizza boxes," one officer suggested.

Will shook his head. "In Jacksonville, Florida 1971, a hijacked plane landed to refuel with plans to go to the Bahamas. Impatient FBI agents shot out the engine, after which the deranged gunman shot his hostages and then himself. The FBI learned from past mistakes, and hostage situations need to be handled with calm patience."

The Chief shrugged at his officer. "I like your enthusiasm, but seems like our FBI specialist is working hard to build rapport. We might damage that if we bug their pizza and the robbers discover it." He turned to Will. "How do you propose we get the pizza to them?"

"Brent will tell us exactly how he wants it delivered. Whatever he's comfortable with is what we'll do. We'll let him control everything that's safe for him to control. This is just a pizza delivery, not an opportunity to storm the building."

Will rolled his shoulders. "What's the head count inside?"

"Two tellers and the bank manager—that's per the other two employees on staff today who were gone to lunch at the time of infiltration. One security guard. At least three bank customers, including your partner."

Will nodded.

The Chief ran a tongue over his teeth. "We've got SWAT covering both entry points. There's a second floor of offices and a basement where the vault is."

"Tell them to find comfortable positions. We don't need to be in a hurry to save the day."

"The media are setting up camp too."

"They most certainly can wait."

Brent had a clean-shaven face heavily burdened with pock marks and the discolorations of sun damage. His eyes were calculating, but he appeared less on the verge of shooting someone after hanging up the phone.

Apparently, talk of pizza soothed his troubled soul.

Raine thought of the slight bluish tint to his otherwise white skin. She suspected he had some Frost Giant bloodline, but not much. Not enough to be considered a threat by the Council of Mjölnir. Many people had small mixes that were harmless. Obviously Brent wasn't harmless, but his actions were probably related more to nurture than nature. His life experiences as opposed to his genotype.

"What's the plan?" Hector asked, taking the cue from the other man and pulling off his mask. He raked his shirt sleeve across a sweaty brow as a wiry beard glistened with sweat.

"We're going to get them all chairs to sit in." Brent gestured to Raine and the others lined up against the window. "In exchange, the cops are going to deliver pizza to us."

"How are they going to get it inside?" Hector asked, voice rising in alarm. "We can't let them in or they'll start shooting."

"One of the hostages can fetch it." Brent started eyeing the row of them.

Raine maintained direct eye contact as everyone else looked at the floor. She'd be happy to collect the pizza. It would give her a chance to move and keep limber and also glimpse what the turmoil outside looked like.

The third robber started pushing chairs over toward the window for the hostages to sit on.

"You," Hector barked at Raine. "What's your name?"

"Raine."

"Okay, Raine, you're nominated. Come here." He motioned her toward him and away from the window.

In careful motions, she walked to him.

"Arms up."

She raised them. Again, she was so close she could easily overpower him, but she couldn't disarm his colleagues before they had a chance to hurt someone.

Patting her down, he found only her mobile phone in her back pocket, which he pulled out and set on the counter. She was glad she had neither a gun nor a badge. If she'd been carrying, she would have either been forced to take offensive action or allow herself to be locked away with the bank security guard.

Brent opened the phone case and inspected her driver's license. "Raine Thoren. Says here you live in Montana. You're a long way from home."

"I'm traveling." Slowly, she lowered her arms.

"Well, here's what your next trip looks like. This FBI guy is going to call us back when our pizza arrives. Gym jock over there is going to open the door for you. You are going to get the pizza and bring it back inside the bank. You run off or try to pull any stunts, and gym jock gets a bullet to the balls. You got that?"

"I get the pizza and bring it back. Nothing else."

Hector sniffed. "What do we do after we eat the pizza?"

"Eating the pizza is going to give me time to figure that part out."

"So, who delivers the pizza?" Officer Bert asked.

Chief Clark turned toward Will. "Seems our FBI agent is in the robbers' good graces. What do you say, Will?"

"No problem." He was hoping they would allow him to make the hand off in order to continue his relationship with the robbers, but didn't want an eager attitude to deter them.

"Officer, get this man some Kevlar, will you?"

"Sure thing, Chief."

Ten minutes later, the pizza arrived, and Will strapped into his Kevlar vest. Balancing the pizza boxes in one arm and holding the plastic bag of two-liter soda bottles in the other, he approached the front of the bank and stood waiting.

He avoided gazing around the perimeter at the many anxious

faces of law enforcement. If Brent was watching him, he didn't want to draw his attention to the plethora of armed men in uniform surrounding the building.

His heart leaped into his throat at the sight of Raine coming outside, but he kept his expression neutral. With a determined look, she took the pizzas and sodas. He tried to read her expression.

Was she scared? No.

Pissed? No.

Calm in the face of danger? Yes.

"Three robbers," she said.

He gave a slight nod. "No tricks. Pizza. Soda. Nothing more."

"I hope you got a meat lovers."

He blinked at her.

She turned and walked away, back into the bank as a man in exercise clothes held the door open.

Stomach in his throat, Will walked back to the trailer with Chief Clark.

Clark crossed his arms. "Now we wait."

"Now we wait," Will agreed.

"That was your partner?"

"Yeah."

"Doesn't look worse for wear."

"She's as tough as they come. Can you get word to all of your men that she's an agent? I'd hate for her to be wrestled to the ground when this is all over."

"No problem." The Chief motioned for his officer to make the announcement through their radios.

WILL HAD PLANNED to call at the thirty-minute mark, but Brent called him first. He was still inside the trailer.

"This is Will."

"The pizza's done."

"Great. I hope it was still warm. Are you ready to safely exit the bank?"

"No."

Will smiled. He was hoping for a 'no.' Being able to say 'no' would help Brent feel in control. A placating 'yes' would have been a promise Brent had no intention of keeping.

"Did the tellers and customers have any food and drink? They may need to use the restrooms in shifts in order to remain comfortable." Will made his suggestion amicably, hoping Brent would think of Will's words earlier: *They're your most precious commodity.* They were the barrier between Brent and bullets.

"You're right."

"Call me back when you're ready to talk some more." Will hung up the phone.

"That's it?" The SWAT leader sneered. Tucker had introduced himself earlier on as in charge of SWAT but had remained a quiet observer until now. "You took a call to tell him to let everyone take a bathroom break and you end it there?"

"Larry," the Chief began in a tone of caution.

"Well, shit, Carter. We're two hours in and we've talked about pizza and pissing."

"We're making progress," Will said, sliding his hands in his pockets to appear less confrontational.

"How? He just said he wasn't ready to surrender."

"He was establishing his control, which is fine. The moment Brent no longer feels in control is the moment he's a danger to everyone." He let that sink in before continuing. "Brent called me first this time, a sign he's reaching out for help. He also agreed to bathroom breaks for the hostages after having let them eat and drink, indicative that he's behaving like a rational human being."

These were all good signs that hopefully negotiations would end peaceably.

THIRTEEN

Brent hung up the phone, looking composed.

"What's happening?" Hector demanded.

"Durk, take them for bathroom breaks. One at a time."

Durk complied while Hector wiped sweat off his brow for the dozenth time and looked expectantly at Brent.

"What are we doing, Brent?"

Brent looked contemplatively at the hostages and the bank doors.

Raine saw the conflict in his expression—like he was considering walking out those doors but suspected Hector wouldn't agree to a path which led to jail since he'd been the most panicked about cops arriving.

They argued for several minutes. Brent suggested a peaceful end, and Hector was hearing nothing of it. Hector played on their child-hood friendship and unfulfilled promises Brent had evidently made.

At last, Brent frowned and slung a hand over Hector's shoulder, seeming to have made a decision. "I have an escape plan. I'll take care of you. Find me some tape, okay?"

Raine had a sinking feeling Brent's loyalty to Hector won out over a safe play to surrender.

Hector began rummaging through desk drawers as Durk continued to take the hostages, one at a time, to the bathroom. Raine declined so she could watch Brent's movements and try to discern his plan.

Hector produced a roll of black electrical tape and passed it off to Brent.

"Keep your guns on them." Brent gagged three of the bank customers and then put the warty monster masks over their head. "If you take these off before the cops do, I'll shoot you in the back."

He pulled aside Hector and Durk. "Here's how it's going to play. Those masked hostages are going to walk out front ahead of us. They are the distraction. Cops got to take them down, because they don't know if they're hostages or us. I'm going to put on the security guard's uniform. While the police are busy handling those three in masks, the three of us are going to go out the front door."

"Why can't we take the back door?" Hector protested.

"Our van is parked out front." He jangled the keys in Hector's face. "Then we all pile in the van. By the time they figure out what's happening, we'll be in the van with the engine fired up."

Brent turned and walked toward the back offices. "Watch them. I'll be back."

Ten minutes later, Brent emerged from the other room wearing the security guard's uniform, gun in hand. He pulled Durk and Hector aside, spoke to them, and then the two disappeared into a room.

Brent paced until the other men returned. He directed Raine and the bank employees to walk into the back room while Durk watched the other hostages.

They moved into the office, and Brent kept his gun trained on them as Hector secured their wrists with twist ties. Raine noted how all the robbers seemed to gain about thirty pounds around their midriff. She suspected they'd taped cash to themselves under their shirts.

While their scheme showed some ingenuity, it was a recipe for disaster. The police would have to know how many workers were at the bank and they would estimate the number of customers. They would know the sum of the people exiting the building did not total the number who'd been inside. Even if the robbers made it inside the van, they wouldn't get far in a lot surrounded by police. When they realized they were truly trapped, they might start shooting.

As soon as Brent and Hector left the room, the three women sat in resignation on the floor. Raine bent one knee up and brought her arms swiftly down, snapping the twist tie.

"No, what are you doing?" The bank manager asked. "You're going to get us all killed."

Raine crouched low and addressed them, making careful eye contact with everyone the way Will always did when interviewing victims' families. "I work with the FBI. Stay here until the police arrive, and you'll stay safe. When I close that door, you move the desk over here and barricade yourselves in. No moving it until the police knock."

There. She had told them she worked *with* the FBI and not *for* the FBI.

You're welcome, Will.

She left the office, closing the door, and pressed herself against the wall as she eased slowly down the hallway back toward the teller room. She would need to retrieve her phone from the counter on her way out.

WILL STOOD outside the bank and away from the confines of the Chief's trailer.

When his phone rang, he answered. "Will here."

"We're coming out," Brent said.

Will's throat constricted. The timing was too soon, and Brent's tone was filled with a dismal sort of resignation. Something was wrong.

"Okay. You want to come outside? Let's talk about how to do that safely."

"We're coming out. Don't shoot."

"Wait."

The call disconnected.

Shit. Shit.

What the hell is Brent planning?

He turned to look at the trailer where the Chief emerged. His smile turned to a frown when he saw Will's expression. Behind Clark, Tucker rushed out, barking something into his radio.

Will moved off to the side by one of the police cruisers with a sickening sensation in his gut. Every policeman in the vicinity had eyes and guns trained on the front of the building.

Seconds ticked by as his heart thumped.

The bank door slowly opened.

The three people in the lead were dressed in casual street clothes and wearing monster masks. Will's mind flashed back to the three robbers pouring out of the van. These three people with their arms raised were not those men. In fact, one was clearly an older woman based on her figure. Chief Clark's men were screaming for the by-standers to lie down on the ground and extend their arms.

The deception had Will on high alert with alarm bells ringing through his ears. Masking the hostages would cause a clever distraction, but to what point? Every person would be in handcuffs until the police sorted out the confusion.

The next group of three emerged. These were in stark contrast to the masked group. Two of the bank robbers came out with arms raised. Will recognized their blue jeans and boots. But where was the third?

Behind the two men, the bank security guard pointed a gun at their backs. "I got them! I got them both right here."

Both of them? Will knew there were three robbers, but Brent didn't know Will had seen them filing out of the van. Brent had never divulged the number in his group. Will hadn't thought to ask because he'd already known the answer.

But wouldn't the security guard know how many men had stormed into his bank?

Will's stomach clenched at how wrong the scene was. The row of people in masks lay on the ground as they were told. Will circled the perimeter slowly so as not to draw attention to himself, but he wanted a better look at the guard. The man's build was bulkier compared to any of the men he'd seen exit the van, but the entire scene wasn't sitting right with him.

Only a few seconds had passed since the robbers, arms raised, had emerged from the front of the bank, but they were still advancing forward and not dropping to the ground as ordered. The guard's eyes darted nervously left and right, sizing up the scene and seemingly too worried about the number of guns trained on him.

Will cautiously drew his weapon.

"Run!" the fake security guard screamed.

The two robbers spun and ran toward the van—the van that the SWAT team had disabled an hour ago. The simple solution would be to let the villains climb into their own van and fail to escape. But too much testosterone was flying free on the playing field to let a gunman think he got away.

There were also too many potential targets for friendly fire. Three by-standers lay on the ground with three police officers currently restraining them. Then, an unclear number of hostages were still inside the building, possibly near windows.

Brent—Will was certain he was posing as the security guard—raised his gun toward the nearest police officer, who was reaching for his weapon. Before the robber could pull the trigger, a blur of blonde appeared. Raine appeared from behind the van and kicked her foot up into Brent's wrist, displacing the trajectory of the gun toward the sky. She immediately followed that with a right hook to his jaw.

"Hold your fire! Hold your fire!" Will, terrified Raine would get shot if the cops started shooting, ran toward her. The officers might not yet have realized the man in the guard uniform was one of the robbers, not a friendly.

Brent stumbled backward. Before he could react, Raine unleashed a well-placed kick to his knee. When he crumbled to the ground, she stomped on the wrist of his hand holding the gun.

The robber screamed.

Will reached them, kicking the weapon aside as two of the police officers pounced on Brent. Raine blew a loose strand of hair out of her face as she smiled at Will, apparently pleased with her take down.

As he holstered his weapon, Will glanced around the scene to see that everyone had at least one police officer on them, including Brent's two co-conspirators. Police were entering the building to check on the other hostages.

He grabbed Raine by the elbow and hauled her out of the heavy foot traffic, under the shade of a tree in the bank parking lot. His heart was still pounding against his ribcage.

"What the hell was that?" he demanded.

Her expression went dark as she jerked her arm back. She shoved him out of her personal space he was intentionally crowding.

"Oh, *for the love of Frigg*! You are impossible!" she said, throwing her hands up in the air. "Nothing makes you happy. Did I call myself FBI? No. Did I kill anyone? No. Did I intervene at a critical point? Yes. Are you still mad at me because I broke some other rule of yours? Yes!"

He wanted to laugh, wanted to cry. He was furious with her for risking her life as a dozen men with itchy trigger fingers after half a day of hostage negotiations had pointed guns in her direction. Will hadn't made a rule about not acting recklessly because one, it seemed self-evident, and two, he didn't know he would get so bent out of shape over it.

Struggling with his emotions, he grabbed Raine by the shirt.

"What the—"

"Shut up." He pulled her into a fierce embrace. "Just shut up."

She stood motionless, letting him hug her with her arms stiff at her side.

With the feel of her safe in his arms, he finally found his words. "You scared me. I was afraid one or more of the dozen cops were going to pull the trigger. Either because your sudden appearance confused them or because they thought they had an opening on the robber."

"Okay."

"I'm sorry I yelled at you."

"Okay."

"And I shouldn't have told you to shut up. Are you okay?" He squeezed one last time before stepping back and running a hand through his hair to keep from touching her again—a hand to her cheek, a thumb over her pouting pink lip.

"No, I'm not. I was the hostage in there, and you treat me like this?"

"I'm sorry. I obviously suck at having a partner, and I'm a condescending ass. You intervened at a critical point. I was afraid for you. I overreacted."

She nodded, but her expression was still guarded.

"I need to go talk to the Chief. You need anything? They have a cooler of chilled water by the trailer. I'll grab you one."

"Sure, sounds good." She nodded, throat bobbing in a swallow.

After Raine gave her statement to the police, she waited for Will to wrap up with the Chief of Police.

Will drove his rental car back to the hotel while she stared out the window, trying to process his burst of emotion earlier. She'd thought he was mad at her for breaking one of his rules, easy to do when there were so damn many of them that keeping track was impossible.

He'd been angry because of the danger she was in, not because of an infracted rule. He cared about her, and something in those muddled feelings scared and angered him. She didn't like his anger, but at least she recognized it hadn't been directed at her. Despite her initial frustration at his outburst, those raw emotions and the way he struggled with them touched her.

"Your hostage skills with Brent were effective," she said, breaking the silence. "Every time he talked to you, you brought him to a calmer place."

"Thanks. Ideally, he would've actually surrendered instead of still thinking he was going to escape and not go to prison for armed robbery."

"You almost had him ready to surrender. One of the other men—either a close friend or brother—convinced him to risk his life to get away. Could they have gotten away in the van?"

"No. The SWAT team had disabled it. Brent would've killed some people before being shot to death himself. In fact, he was about to shoot that police officer when you intervened. You should know that the local police recognized you saved at least one of their own." Will stared ahead at the road, not making eye contact as he spoke.

She didn't know if his averted gaze was because he was exhausted or was still struggling with his emotions over the events.

He shifted in his seat as he flipped his turn signal and changed lanes. "Tomorrow, we'll take some downtime. We can meet back up in the evening to make the drive to my parents' house."

Downtime.

The word sounded more like 'separate time,' which was fine with Raine. She needed a little space, too. How would she have felt if roles had been reversed and Will had been inside the bank?

She wouldn't have had the skills to keep the hostage situation calm. She would've been worried about Will the entire time. What if all of those guns had been trained on him? She would've been terrified on his behalf as well. Yet, all of those feelings flowing through her at the thought of role reversal felt disproportionate for a simple partnership. Were Will's feelings disproportionate also? She couldn't tell.

She'd liked his embrace, more than she should have, even though she'd been too baffled and surprised to return it.

Yes, downtime sounded perfect.

FOURTEEN

By the time they reached the hotel, the evening sun had dipped below the horizon. Will parked at the hotel entrance. "I'm going to skip our usual evening beverage and hit the sack." Raine put a hand to one temple.

"No problem. Are you okay?"

"Yeah, just tired."

Part of him wanted to park the vehicle and see her up to her room. He wanted to tuck her into bed or some other overly sentimental shit after the day they'd had. But he refused to give in to irrational desires. She was tired and didn't need him acting any more overprotective than he already had. She was a badass who'd taken down a gunman and didn't need Will's doting affection.

"Goodnight, Will. I'll see you tomorrow." She exited the car.

Tomorrow they would have dinner with his family and the following day fly to Texas for their next interview, but tonight, Will would meet up with Coup, one of his prior band members and long-time friend. Will was in desperate need of some relaxing camaraderie.

Coup snuck Will into the man cave basement of his home, complete with a minibar and seventy-five-inch flat screen TV. His friend poured two mugs of his home-brewed beer and turned the football game on to mute.

Coup raised his glass, and Will obliged with a "cheers."

Will glimpsed the drum set in one corner as he followed Coup to the couch. "You still play?"

"Nah. The kids do, though. Danny is taking lessons."

"Drum lessons? How old is he now?"

"Ten."

"Wow. Ten. I remember the newborn photo you sent me like it was yesterday. You had more hair back then."

"Jackass." Coup scowled. "I remember you talking me into calmness when I was in full panic mode with Cindy in labor."

Will remembered the desperate call he'd gotten from Coup. The calm, collected cop had been in shambles over the delivery. Ten years later, he had two kids, a house in suburbia, and a receding hair line. But Coup was happy, a contentment with life Will didn't possess.

"Yeah. Where was I then? Seattle?"

"You told me you were out-of-town hunting some killer, but for all I know, you could have been three doors down sleeping with the neighbor. Anyway, time flies. Not for you, though. The immortal bachelor—Will Decker."

Will took a long drink of his beer, thinking of the day's harrowing events and the worry he'd had over Raine. "Yeah, I guess."

"You guess?" Coup's face screwed up in bewilderment. "Once a year you come to my house, we talk about getting the band back together, and you re-commit to another year of no commitment. This year I get a half-assed, 'I guess'?"

"I met this woman." Will set down his beer and settled back into the couch. He felt the urge to tell someone, and he sure as hell couldn't tell Raine.

"Oh? You meet a lot of women."

"But I got to know this one. We're working this case together—"

"Uh oh. Did you break your 'no sleeping with your co-workers' rule?"

"Not exactly. She's not FBI. We're just collaborating. But I find her fascinating. The more I know, the more I want to know about her. I enjoy spending time with her." And he cared about her more than he should.

He absently stared at the tight end sprinting down the field on the television screen, except all his mind registered was how much he wanted to hold Raine again like he had after the bank heist.

"This sounds deeper than any relationship you've ever had with a woman."

Will didn't care for the amused, slightly mocking tone in Coup's voice.

"It is. I tried a relationship once. Once."

Coup acknowledged the statement with a nod. Will had told him about the seductress he'd fallen in love with who'd turned out to be a liar, a cheat, and a thief. He hadn't bothered to form attachments after that.

"Well, how many dates have you been on?" Coup asked.

"That's just it. None. We've done activities together—horseback riding and sparring but all in the context that we're two partners hanging out."

"When you say sparring..."

"Fighting, not fornicating. I haven't slept with her."

"Are you losing your touch?"

"What? No. I haven't tried to sleep with her. I didn't want to jeopardize our working environment."

They made a good team, working the case together. His mind wandered to Raine with her golden hair, long legs, and smart mouth, mocking his rules. Breaking his rules. Making him want to break his own rules.

"Huh." Coup scratched his chin. "Have you slept with anyone else since meeting her?"

"Is that relevant?"

Coup snorted. "You're the bureau investigator. Isn't everything relevant?"

Will frowned. "I haven't slept with anyone since meeting her, but we've been busy on the case."

"And off the case?" Coup propped his feet up on the coffee table and shifted his tone to cop-questioning mode. "During any previous investigations, have you remained celibate because the work-load prevented sexual encounters?"

Will shifted his weight in his chair and tugged at his shirt collar. "No."

"And you said you didn't want to jeopardize your working rela-tionship. *Didn't*—past tense. So, now you do?"

"Yeah, I guess I do."

"You're worried about screwing this up!" Coup barked out an obnoxious laugh as he leaned forward and slapped a hand on his own leg. "Will Decker—charismatic ladies' man—who always stole all of our band groupies is nervous over a woman."

Will scowled at his friend and reached for the remote. He had every right to be nervous. He was contemplating a relationship with Raine, which was far more complex than his usual one-night stands.

Not to mention this entire world of Norse bloodlines opening before his eyes like an earthquake crevice of unimaginable depth. He had a right to be uncertain. If mockery was Coup's reaction, Will would rather watch the game. He raised the remote to press the UNMUTE button.

"Okay. Okay." Coup raised a hand in surrender. "You can at least understand the amusement of a mere mortal. I appreciate you seeking advice, or encouragement, or whatever the heck this is. Anyway, be your charming self and just see where it goes. Take her on a date—one that you establish ahead of time is a date. What does she like? You could buy her something."

Will grinned as he set the remote back down. He suspected Raine had little use for flowers and jewelry. She'd probably be most excited if he brought her the head of a Dark Elf, but that wouldn't happen.

A date and a gift. He could do that.

He settled back into the couch. "Tell me how the kids and the job are going."

RAINE RAN on the hotel treadmill at the guest gym, pushing images of Will's worried expression out of her mind. She'd never had a man look so filled with compassion that his emotions threatened to swallow her whole. She didn't want to derail their working relationship, especially if she was misinterpreting the situation. His reaction to seeing her after the bank heist could have been normal worry for a partner. She wouldn't know since she'd never had one.

Taking a deep breath, she focused on her run as she thought back to her early training.

Her guidance under Usha had been intense: exhausting cardiovascular workouts with running and gymnastics mixed with strength-training exercises. She'd pushed her body beyond the limits of anything she'd tried during high school sports. The duration was an unfamiliar experience for her as well. Such long days.

Usha's training facility was a ranch in rural Montana. Raine had stayed in the ranch house, rising at the break of dawn and training until dusk. She ate ravenously and slept soundly. Meals were spent in Usha's company, learning about her heritage and the powers of her ancestors. Months had passed in a blur of enrichment and exhaustion of mind, body, and soul.

Six months later, Raine had embarked on her first assignment. Someone was killing dwarves, and her mission had been to stop him.

She'd flown to Atlanta and rented a car to drive to Douglasville, Georgia. Council of Mjölnir intel had reported the man was holed up in a motel on the outskirts of town. Armed with a photo of her target and her Glock she'd had hours of practice on, she staked out the motel. She wanted confirmation her target was in the room, but she also needed to summon the nerve to kill another creature.

She had placed an inordinate amount of faith in the Council. What if they'd lied to her and she was just a hired killer for them? The weight of the gun in her holster felt unusually bulky and heavy. Her concerns about being deceived warred with her trust in Usha and desire to be part of the greater good. If this man—Sydney—was killing innocent dwarf bloodlines, he needed to be stopped.

At motion near the motel room door, Raine looked up from her spot, parked across the lot. The man exiting the room matched the photo.

She played the sequence of events in her mind. Approach with gun in hand behind her back. When she was thirty-feet away, aim and pull the trigger. Avoid witnesses. Get a blood sample.

She had envisioned all of those steps within the context of saving a life, but approaching and shooting this man in broad daylight as he walked to his car suddenly seemed like a monumental task she wasn't sure she had the stomach to execute. What's more, once she shot him, what should she do with the body? Usha said darker bloodlines decomposed rapidly, but what if she was wrong?

Blinking, Raine tried to imagine this man was the Dark Elf who'd killed her sister's fiancé. He wasn't, but maybe she could summon the fury to do her job. As righteous anger pumped through her blood, she gripped the steering wheel.

Nope.

She still couldn't find the resolve to strike here and now.

Sydney climbed into his car, oblivious to Raine's presence. Starting her engine, she gave him a few second's lead and then followed.

"RAINE!"

"Hey, Mom." Raine put her on speaker and towel dried her hair. After an hour and a half in the hotel gym, she'd taken a relaxing bath, followed by calling her mother.

"I'm so glad you called. I was telling your father just yesterday how I knew you'd be calling soon."

"I call every week, Mom," Raine said.

"Well, that's what your father said," she replied cheerfully, as though their statements supported her implication of a sixth sense rather than refuted it.

"I'm coming into town in a few days."

"Oh, that's wonderful! How long will you be in town? We'll make up the guest room."

"Just a few days for a work trip." She debated taking the guest room or not. Staying at home would give her more time with her family, but she would miss out on those post-interview re-cap hotel bar evenings with Will. As confused as she was by his behavior, perhaps a little space would be a good thing. "I can stay with you."

"Oh, good. If you're here until the weekend, you can come to Betty Sue's son's wedding."

Raine chuckled. "I'm definitely not crashing a wedding while I'm there."

"You might meet an eligible young man."

"You know that pressure only works on Sky, right?"

"Well, a mother can hope."

"Work trip. Three days max, Mom. But I have a partner coming with me. I'd like to introduce him."

Her tall, dark, handsome, athletic, morally incorruptible, compassionate partner with a set of delectably kissable lips... who was off-limits.

"Oh, yes, wonderful. We'll have him over for dinner. Will he be staying with us?"

"No. He'll get a hotel room."

Her mother gave a disappointed *tsk*. "Tell him to stay at Martha's bed-and-breakfast. We want to support local."

"I'll tell him."

Poor Will did not need excessive exposure to her family. She loved them, but they could be overwhelming. Also, her goal was keeping her distance from him, not spending the night under the same roof with him while her mother probably made not-so-subtle hints about them both being close in age and single.

CHAPTER

FIFTEEN

Raine stared out the window as Will drove them from their hotel to his parent's house. The hum of noise outside the vehicle was a conglomeration of honking and rumbling engines. As they drove north into the countryside, the noise faded.

"It's not too late," he began. "You can back out of dinner with my family. They have a propensity to bicker and incite awkwardness."

Raine smiled. "Not on your life. I must meet all of them."

"Don't say I didn't warn you."

She wore slacks and a blue blazer to meet Will's family. He had assured her the gathering was relaxed attire, but she felt she ought to look the part of an FBI partner. In an effort to seem more casual, she wore her hair down instead of in a ponytail or bun. Both of them would leave their guns locked in the rental car.

Although Will teased, she suspected part of him wanted her to meet his family. Yet, she noted his tight grip firmly on the wheel. His eyes were on the road ahead of him, but his focus was clearly elsewhere.

"You seem uncharacteristically tense," she said.

He'd been tense talking about the case this morning too, when they'd briefly met over hotel coffee, but the emotion seemed to have intensified since then. She wondered if the strain had to do with the bank robbery, all the paperwork he'd had to do because of it, or seeing his parents.

"I don't see my family much."

Which explains nothing, Raine thought.

He could see his family once a year and still be excited to do so. Instead, he looked like he was steeling himself to be waterboarded. Was he experiencing a normal level of dread, or was her presence amplifying it?

"I don't have to go," she offered.

He glanced at her and took her hand. "Oh, no you don't. I withdraw my offer to let you back out of this." After giving her a squeeze, he retracted his hand, eyes staying fixed on the road. "Having you there might be the only thing that saves me. They might behave themselves if you're there. I've never brought a wo—partner, a coworker for them to meet."

She looked down at where he'd touched her. They'd never held hands. The feel of his calloused palm and long fingers in hers generated a connection that had her wondering what the rest of him felt like.

Before she could ponder that further, he pulled onto the concrete driveway of a three-story red brick home sitting on a half-acre of manicured lawn. The circle drive had a decorative fountain in the middle, and spotlights bathed the grounds in a golden glow.

"Did you grow up here?"

"Home sweet home," he said without a trace of joy.

She kept a step behind him, noticing his rigid posture beneath a pair of pressed slacks, a button-down shirt, and his suit jacket.

So this was casual attire in the Decker household?

Or maybe Will felt he needed the barrier of his FBI outfit between him and his family.

He rang the doorbell—also oddly formal. At her house, the children knocked a few times while simultaneously pushing the door open and announcing their arrival like a celebrity stepping on the stage of a talk show.

A dark-haired man a few years younger than Will answered the door. "Will's here!" he called over his shoulder before giving Will a rough hug. "We've been missing you, man."

"Good to see you, Walt. This is my partner, Raine Thoren. Raine, my younger brother, Walt."

She shook his hand.

"Great to meet you." Walt seemed genuinely delighted.

As they entered, another tall man greeted them, this one stiffer, despite wearing jeans and a soft, gray sweater. He gave Will only a brisk handshake.

She blinked at the curt greeting. In her family, hugs were passed around at every gathering. She would even bet her mother would hug Will the first time they met.

"Winston, this is my partner, Raine. Raine, my older brother Winston."

"You're FBI?" Winston asked Raine, a hint of disbelief laced his voice, as if cross-examining her in a courtroom.

"You want to see my badge?" she grinned, hoping to lighten Will's mood, but he didn't crack a smile.

Walt playfully punched Winston on the shoulder. "What the hell kind of question is that? She's a guest, not taking the witness stand."

"I'm merely surprised the FBI would give Will a female partner. I'd have thought he'd slept his way through half the Bureau by now."

Will took a menacing step forward. "Show some respect to my partner."

Winston, unfazed by Will's show of aggression, looked around him at Raine. "I hold you in the highest respect, Special Agent Thoren, to be both an agent and to put up with my brother."

"Thank you, Winston. We get along fine. And the sex is just a bonus."

As Winston turned a crimson shade, Walt barked out a laugh. Will gaped at her.

"Company?" An older man emerged from the kitchen, wiping his hands on a dishtowel, and looked at each of his sons, probably trying to make sense of their vastly different expressions.

Will cleared his throat. "Dad, this is my partner, Raine Thoren."

She extended a hand. "Nice to meet you, Mr. Decker."

He accepted her hand while giving her the once over. Raine suspected Winston got his 'charming' personality from his father.

As if finally remembering his manners, Will's father smiled. "Call me Tom."

When they ventured deeper into the large home, Raine met the matriarch of the family. Ilene was a petite five foot two and looked like a midget among the tall men. She smiled warmly, seemingly oblivious to the tension between Will and his father and Will and his brother.

"I've missed you so much." Ilene gave Will a fierce hug.

Finally, a hugger, Raine thought. Will introduced her to her mother, who smiled politely and greeted her.

"Please, everyone, have a seat." Ilene gestured to the dining room. "The food is ready."

Raine sat beside Will and across from Winston and Walt. Ilene and Tom sat at the ends of the rectangular table in the formal dining room. The burgundy tablecloth complemented heavy drapes over a large window.

Ilene passed Raine the platter of pork chops. "When Tom told me Will was bringing a woman over to meet the family, well, I thought hell had frozen over." She gave an adorable, high-pitched, mousy chuckle. "Then, Tom clarified Will was bringing his *work partner,* who happened to be a woman. I think he worded it the way he did for effect."

Raine took a pork chop and passed the plate, accepting a bowel of mashed potatoes. "Will's never brought a woman to meet the family?"

"Will doesn't exactly *date,*" Walt cheerfully grinned.

"Unless one-night stands count as dating. Then, he's a prolific dater." Winston stabbed a pork chop before adding it to his plate.

"Politeness at the table," Ilene chided. "We all have our strengths. Will has charisma. He could always woo the women."

"We thought he'd make an excellent lawyer with his charm," Tom added. "Instead..."

When his voice trailed, Raine suspected he'd stopped himself from saying anything derogatory about an FBI career choice since their guest was supposedly FBI.

"Instead," Raine began, "he makes a good FBI agent because he's excellent with people. Interviewing victim's families and contacts is an art. Will's good at it." Raine cut into her pork chop and took a bite.

The Decker family hesitated before resuming filling their plates.

Tom gave a forced smile. "We're all sure Will is a very competent FBI agent."

"You're right about that!" Raine smiled, infusing her words with her buoyant cheerleader voice she hadn't used in years. "Top of his class. Diffused a hostage situation yesterday involving armed bank robbers. And he was hand-picked to track down a serial killer." Technically, she believed they were after an assassin, but Jör was still a deadly adversary.

"What?" Ilene gasped. "A serial killer?"

"Mom, I can't talk about that." Will bumped Raine's knee under the table.

"The last agent on the case didn't survive." Raine shook her head before taking another bite of the pork chop.

Tom's face paled.

"Raine—" Will began in a cautionary tone.

"Mmm. Mmm." She chewed and swallowed. "These are so good." She pointed her fork at her plate. "Don't worry. He'll be fine. He's already survived one attack."

Will's fork clinked forcefully against the plate. He dropped his napkin on the table and pushed his chair back. "Raine? A word?"

She blinked innocently up at him. His face was a mask of calm even as his steely green eyes burned with fury. Standing, she excused herself from the table and followed Will into the kitchen.

Once alone, he whirled on her so fast she had to stop abruptly to keep from bumping into him.

"I know you think you're helping, but you're not."

She'd never seen him so angry. This was worse than post-bank robbery, and she suspected his fury wouldn't end in a hug for her this time. Regardless, she stared back nose-to-nose without flinching. She wasn't afraid of him.

"I am, actually." She'd grown up in a happy household, and she couldn't stand the lack of unity she'd witnessed tonight. She would accept his anger at her if her actions pulled his family together.

"You're not," he insisted.

Her own anger flared. "Your family in the other room shows no respect for what you do—that you risk your life to help people."

"It's not that dramatic, Raine. Mostly I'm just investigating."

"And yet you nearly took a knife to the chest the day we met." Righteous rage on his behalf filled her tone.

"That—"

"You saved the lives of every person in that bank yesterday."

"R—"

"My point is that those people should treasure you, and they don't. My family may be ridiculous in many ways, but at the end of the day—or the end of our lives—not one of us will ever question if we were cherished. Storm saw her fiancé murdered in front of her. You don't think I'm aware how easy it would have been for the gunman to have fired one more bullet?" Realizing she let her voice pitch rise, she dropped it lower as she paced in a circle. "They're your family. They should treat you better."

Will's expression had softened somewhere during her rant. On an exhale, she eliminated the hot air filling her lungs and head. She rested a hand on the kitchen island when she realized the spot was already occupied by his.

When she began to pull away, he grasped it and held it. She

looked up to see him staring at their joined hands. When his eyes lifted to hers, his pupils were dilated.

"I'll keep my mouth shut if I'm upsetting you," she relented. Her intentions weren't to add to his pain.

He touched his other hand to her jaw and ran his thumb across her lips, causing her heart to thump forcefully with excitement. Mere inches separated them.

"No, I don't want to make you keep quiet."

Winston cleared his throat as he entered the kitchen. "Mom sent me to get the ice cream."

Will withdrew his hands from Raine as Winston walked to the freezer. He retrieved the ice cream and a stack of bowls before disappearing back to the dining room.

"Can we talk about this later?" Will asked Raine.

She nodded, though she wasn't sure what *this* he was referring to —his family or their undeniable, burgeoning chemistry.

CHAPTER

SIXTEEN

To Will's relief, the dinner conversation turned to sports, followed by politics, without ever cycling back to his FBI work.

He'd planned to coast through this meal like he had in the past, keeping the family interactions superficial as no one acknowledged the tension beneath the surface. Raine, though, had brought the conflict to a head.

They should cherish you.

He wanted to kiss the lips that uttered those words. No one had ever said such a thing to him.

When they finished eating, Walt and their father went into the library for cigars. Winston and Will set to work cleaning the kitchen.

His mom took Raine for a stroll through the garden in the backyard, probably to see her elaborate rose collection. The idea of the woman he liked spending time alone with his mother frayed his nerves.

"Serial killer?" Winston loaded leftovers into plastic containers.

Will washed dishes. "That's right." Close enough to the truth anyway, he thought.

"And Raine—your partner—is helping with that?"

"That's right."

"It doesn't bother you to sleep with your partner?"

"That's none of your damn business."

Would it bother him if he was? A relationship with someone he saw day in and day out would be a new endeavor for him. Part of him was interested in finding out what that layer of complexity would feel like.

"Hey, don't get touchy. She's the one who mentioned it."

"She only said that to prove a point that you were being rude in front of her. As always, you missed the point."

"So, you're not sleeping together?" He rolled the pork chops in tinfoil before putting them in the refrigerator.

"Again, none of your business."

"Did she turn down the irresistible Will Dick-her?" Winston asked.

"That nickname's been old a long time. Let it go." Will shoved the silverware into the dishwasher rack.

Winston loaded another storage container into the refrigerator. "Are you trying to keep work and relationships separate? Because that's not what I saw in the kitchen... judging by the *fuck-me* eyes she was giving you."

"Hey!" Will snapped, shaking a soapy ladle in his brother's direction. "Watch your mouth. That's my partner you're talking about."

"Oh, yeah? You didn't seem to care when you were screwing up my relationship."

"*Shit*, Winston. That was ten years ago. You're happily married now."

"You slept with Nicole."

Like he needed a reminder.

"I did you a favor," Will said flatly. "If not for me, she'd have slept with someone else."

"But it was you!"

As Winston started to lunge forward, Will braced for a fight. The key would be to humble his brother without outright hurting him.

"Whoa. Whoa. Whoa." Walt stepped between them.

At the kitchen threshold, Raine appeared, holding a red rose and standing beside his mother. They both looked surprised at the near eruption of a physical fight.

Will dried his hands on the dish towel and tossed it on the counter. "I'm so sick of this feud. We're leaving."

He kissed his mom's cheek goodbye. "Dinner was delicious. Thanks, Mom."

She stared at him, wide-eyed and sad, as he led Raine out of the house.

When the front door shut behind them, he said, "I'm sorry you had to witness all of that." He opened the passenger door and watched her slide inside the vehicle. He had never opened the car door for her but didn't stop to ponder his behavior.

"I'm not."

He climbed into the driver's side and started the engine.

She continued, "Part of learning about someone is learning their roots. You have some unresolved issues with your brother."

That's an understatement. Will drove in silence. Some of his roots were gnarled and ugly. Some of his roots were better off beneath the ground, where no one could see them—or trip over them.

He wasn't sure how much of the conversation with Winston Raine had overheard, but he felt the need to defend himself. "I didn't know Nicole was my brother's fiancé when I slept with her. We hooked up at a bar when our flight was delayed out of DC. Imagine my surprise later when I see her at our family dinner. I came clean with Winston, and he's never forgiven me."

They drove in silence for several minutes.

"Do people really do that?" she asked. "One-night stands with people they meet at bars?"

He shrugged. "Of course. Some people want the release without the commitment." He shifted his weight in the seat as he parked his car.

"That's what you prefer?"

"I guess so." He fiddled with the key ring.

She appeared to be contemplating his words as he exited the car. He followed her into the hotel and onto the elevator, watching the sway of her hips and her long blonde hair trailing down her back. She'd worn it down tonight, a look he rarely saw. He ached to grab hold of that hair and feel the silkiness between his fingers.

"You've never had a one-night stand?" he asked.

"No. Call it a fear of the unknown. I don't have any interest in being intimate with a stranger. What if I catch an STD? What if it sucks?"

After leaving the elevator, they reached her hotel room door.

"It never sucks with me," he said in a voice huskier than he'd intended.

She smirked, revealing one adorable dimple. "You mean no one's ever complained to your face. If they were truly one-night stands and you never saw them again, you don't know if there's room for improvement."

He leaned closer. "I don't suck."

"You don't unequivocally know that," she shot back, not moving away from him.

He leaned forward, toward those succulent lips which had been calling his name for days. He hesitated just millimeters away, giving her time to retreat. She didn't, but instead looked into his eyes like she wanted what he was offering.

He closed the gap and sealed his mouth to hers. To his surprised delight, she returned the kiss. Her lips were warm and her tongue inviting. His body zinged with primal hunger. She tasted like the red wine they'd had at dinner—dark cherry with a hint of cedar.

His rational mind tried to apply the brakes. He didn't want to take her to bed to prove he could or to simply satiate a carnal desire. He wanted so much more, even if he couldn't define what that was.

He wove his fingers in her hair. With his other hand, he cupped her butt and tilted her hips so he could rub his body against hers.

She made an enticing purring sound as she swiped her keycard and opened her hotel room door. He broke from the kiss to look into her dark eyes.

Her hungry gaze, disheveled hair, and alluring grin had him wanting to sweep her in his arms and carry her to bed. There were so many places he wanted to kiss and caress, so much pleasure he wanted to give her.

They should cherish you.

He wanted to show her he cherished her.

"I'm not a one-night stand, Will." Her voice was needy and breathless.

As her motions drew him closer to the threshold of her room, his legs locked in place. Her words threw a rock in the hormonal gears of his mind, bringing them to a stuttering halt.

He placed his hands on either side of the door and looked down, collecting his thought.

"Will?"

Raine was right. She was classy, smart, caring, and a hell of a fighter. She was no one's one-night stand—least of all his. She deserved better. She deserved a long-term relationship with love.

Long-term love.

The words in his mind cooled his lust and had him gulping air.

"Will?"

Could he give that to her? And was it fair to her to have sex with her when he didn't know the answer to that question? Was he actually considering a long-term relationship with a woman? With Raine?

Yes, he was.

"Decker?" Her voice hardened to a block of ice.

He looked up to see she'd retreated into her room, glaring at him with a mixture of pain and anger.

Not like this, he thought. She deserved better.

"Raine, I can't do this. I—"

The hotel room door shut in his face.

He glowered at the door as his temper flared. His intentions were to do right by her, but she hadn't let him explain. He sure as hell wouldn't stand and talk to a door.

He straightened, shoved his hands in his pockets, and spun on his heal. He needed a drink, and maybe he'd find someone who did want a one-night stand.

RAINE STARED AT THE DOOR, shocked by her own reaction. She'd never shut the door in a man's face. Well, there had been one time, but he'd been a Dark Elf trying to kill her.

She'd also never imagined turning a man away because he wanted a one-night stand and she didn't. What would have been so terrible about a one-night stand?

The future beyond them stopping Jör was uncertain. Unless she believed the Noble Prophecies, in which case the future was death, destruction, and agony. Until then, she wanted to work to discover who was behind ordering the killing of prophets. Will might go back to hunting actual serial killers for the FBI.

She didn't want a fling, but she struggled to define what she wanted. A chance at something more? But what chance did they have? They moved in different circles, like a Venn diagram, only overlapping for this case.

Will's hesitation had stung, but how could she be angry with him if she didn't know what she wanted either?

She opened the hotel door, but he was gone. Rightly so, she thought. He was a man of rules. And one of those rules was one-night stands only. Even his family knew that rule.

Well, she had her own rule: no one-night stands. On this, neither of them would yield. She wouldn't suspend her rule to appease him the way she had agreed to his 'no killing' rule for the duration of their case.

She closed the door and kicked off her shoes.

So, that was that then. She'd focus her pent-up sexual energy on solving the case. She had Becky Noble's bleak premonitions to finish sifting through.

But first, a phone consult seemed in order. Her younger sister, Sky, had a gift for understanding people and relationships. She might have insight on how to help Raine survive the next weeks in the presence of an attractive, charismatic man who was off limits.

She pulled her phone out from her pocket and speed-dialed Sky.

"Raine! How are you?"

Raine grinned into the phone at her sister's bubbly greeting. Sky—as the younger of the three sisters—certainly had the most buoyant personality.

"I'm good. I'm still working the case."

"Oh? How's it going?" Sky's tone was all intrigue, as if Raine was tracking a celebrity rather than a killer.

"Mostly tedious investigation, but I am adjusting to having a partner."

"Uh huh? You mentioned him. Do you not like your partner?"

"I—" Raine bit her lip, thinking of Will and how loaded that question was.

"Are you going to tell me you work better alone—because that sounds more like our other sister. Oh! You like him."

"Hey," Raine snapped.

Sky wasn't supposed to use her paranormal detection skills on family, though Raine understood what Sky gleaned wasn't always voluntary. Her power of perception wasn't as user-friendly as an on-off switch.

"Sorry," Sky said. "But that's why you called, right?"

"Yeah, I like him. We nearly just slept together."

"The fact that you're talking to me suggests things did not go as planned."

Raine flopped onto the bed. "None of this was planned."

"Well, did you put the brakes on or did he?"

"Kind of both." But for very different reasons.

"Except, if it didn't bother you, you wouldn't be calling me sounding distraught."

"Will is some type of self-proclaimed lifelong bachelor, according to his family—"

"You met his family?"

"As his partner not his girlfriend." She took her laptop off the hotel desk, pulled it out of its case, and tossed it on the bed.

"Are you his girlfriend?"

"No. And trust me, he was very clear I never will be."

I can't do this. The echo of his words bit into her self-esteem.

"Anyway, we had a moment. Well, I think we've had a few smoldering previews leading up to the moment. Then we shared an amazing kiss. We were almost inside my hotel room when he stopped."

"Just like that?" Sky asked.

"Um. I told him I wasn't a one-night stand."

Sky gasped. "And that turned him off?"

"You would've thought I'd said 'marry me' the way he shriveled and withdrew."

"What a jerk! If you said you're not a one-night stand, he ought to be like *'sign me up! I get to sleep with this woman more than once!'*"

Raine laughed at Sky's impersonation. "But I said I wasn't a one-night stand knowing he has this aversion to attachments."

"So, you're worried you struck a nerve?"

"Maybe severed a nerve, judging by how fast the moment fizzled."

"He should respect that you respect yourself enough to set boundaries. It sucks he wasn't willing to accept them. He's a fool for passing you up. As your partner, I'm guessing he knows what you are and what you're capable of?"

"Yeah."

"If he knows you're a kickass woman fighting evil and he's running from the possibility of a lasting relationship, he's a fool."

"Thanks."

Her sister's words offered some comfort, but Raine was still going to bed alone tonight. And the next. And the next.

"Ah," Sky began, "but you have to face him tomorrow and each subsequent day until you solve the case."

Raine paced the small hotel room. "I think we'll keep it professional. We're not vengeful juveniles. I mostly wanted to get your take on how dejected I should feel. You've had more relationships than me."

"Hey, watch your implication, sister. I can't help it if I glean the inner thoughts of my dates and it truncates our relationship. By default, I will have to go through many more men to find the right one. But to answer your question, it sounds like you knew what his parameters were. You had a choice: sleep with him and try to change his mind—much sneakier and riskier—or check up front and see if he was willing to reconsider his stance prior to copulation. Your plan didn't work out, but at least you're not left having slept with him and then facing rejection."

Silence settled for a moment as Raine digested Sky's words.

"Did you just use the word *copulation* in a sentence?" Raine asked.

"Don't miss my point." Sky continued, "By the way, if you were calling to get permission for a one-night stand, you're again talking to the wrong sister."

"I don't want that."

"Well, Will's still a fool. It's hard to know if he'll regret his choice to turn you down or appreciate you not trying to trap him with sex."

Regrets?

Raine didn't think Will was a man who spent much time with regret, though he had apologized for his behavior after the bank robbery.

"Okay. Good chat. I feel like I can face him tomorrow calmly. We dodged disaster. We could have jeopardized our working relationship but didn't."

"Yeah, that attitude is all fine and dandy until chemistry sizzles again. And if my perfectly practical sister Raine was hot and heavy with a non-boyfriend, then there must be some powerful, magnetic chemistry."

"Right. Chemistry." Raine deflated into the chair by the window as she envisioned Will's lips on her bare neck while he ran hands under her shirt. "What's the antidote for that?"

SEVENTEEN

Will knocked on Raine's door the next morning, carrying a peace offering in the form of coffee. He'd replayed last night's heavy petting, concluding with a door in his face, and realized how the situation probably appeared to her.

She had every right to be pissed at him, and he wanted to explain —as soon as he could articulate the words. For now, he hoped they could continue their symbiotic working relationship while he recovered from his hangover.

He sipped his own cup as he heard her shuffling in the room behind the closed door.

Last night, he'd planned to pick up a woman and forget about his attraction to Raine Thoren. No one slams a door in his face. He went to the busiest bar in Newark, but instead of finding someone he wanted a one-night stand with, he knew none of them would compare to Raine—her strength, determination, and personality. He ended up drinking alone.

He didn't know any of those women the way he knew Raine— her unguarded expressions, her devotion to this global mission of helping others, and the way she demanded he be cherished. He should have let them cherish each other last night, but his hesitation had driven a wedge between them.

As such, he was grumpy, sleep-deprived, sex-deprived, and in no shape to talk to Raine about the possibility of a relationship.

More importantly, they still had a killer to catch.

Raine appeared at the door. "Oh, coffee! Thanks." She took the cup and returned to her bag packing. "I went over the rest of the Noble Prophecies last night. Lots of doom and gloom in them." She zipped her bag shut and extended the handle. With coffee in one hand and luggage in the other, she stepped into the hallway and let the door shut.

"Ready." She smiled, facing forward with her gaze aiming toward the elevator down the hall.

"Is that what we're calling them?" Will asked.

"Well, Becky Noble wrote them. Anyway, she keeps harping on the number three."

Will listened to Raine's overly chipper voice while his hangover took deeper root, squeezing his brain. He adjusted his sunglasses as they left the hotel and walked to the rental car.

Chipper.

Why was she so chipper?

Then he realized she'd been talking but hadn't actually made eye contact with him.

Damn.

He'd hurt her feelings. That pent up pain would come back to bite both of them in the ass if he let it fester. He almost wished she would unleash her anger with him now and get it out of her system. Then her wrath wouldn't spring on him at some point when his defenses were down.

Who was he kidding? His defenses were already down.

He slouched in the passenger seat and let Raine drive them to the airport as she rambled about the prophecies, stopping her mono-logue only long enough to check traffic or sip her coffee. He would rest, hydrate, and then tackle a conversation with Raine about last night.

RAINE MET up with Will at the gate after deboarding the plane in Houston. Their seats hadn't been together on the plane, so Raine had used the time without her partner to review more of Noble's prophecies.

> *Rain bleeds*
> *Storm screams*
> *Sky shatters*

Until the pounding started.

Now, the headache had already spread behind her right eye. She needed dark, quiet solitude. She took her migraine prescription as soon as symptoms began, but those would only delay the inevitable.

"Why are you wearing sunglasses inside the airport?" Will asked.

They began walking down the terminal, carry-ons in tow.

"Headache. I get them sometimes." She focused on one foot in front of the other, trying to keep the glimpses of fluorescent lights overhead out of her direct line of sight. Crisscrossing pedestrians blurred in front of her.

"You look pale." Will gripped her elbow with one hand.

"It's a migraine, actually. I get them sometimes," she repeated. "They're agony until they pass." She didn't want Will to know she had a health ailment, but there would be no hiding her pain.

> *Hell's flames*
> *Hell's fury*
> *Hell's creations*

"How long does it take?"

They boarded the tram to the baggage claim and ground transportation terminal.

"Hours."

Sometimes days.

"Hours? You're hurting for hours?"

On the night of day
The battle of good versus evil
Hell's wrath unleashed

"The sooner I get to a dark, quiet place, the faster it resolves." A streak of light blinded one eye, like a flash of lightning, followed by gray storm clouds crowding the periphery of her vision. She pressed a hand to her temple.

"Okay. Let's do that," he said.

When the tram stopped, he led her toward the taxi depot.

"But, the rental car... " They'd already reserved a car.

"It will take at least an hour to get through the rental car line, get the keys, and get inside it. We'll take a taxi to your parent's house. I'll worry about the rental car and my hotel after you're tucked in."

"I'll be okay."

"You're a terrible liar." He led her outside to the taxi line. When an attendant assigned their ride, Will and the driver took care of placing the luggage in the trunk while Raine crawled into the back seat.

When he joined her in the back, he pulled her into his arms. She buried her face in his side where all light was blocked out, not carrying how much she was imposing on him.

Will had the driver turn off his country music. Soon, only the hum of the engine and the tires on concrete filled her ears as his scent of oak and mint soothed her. In the darkness and calm, the stabbing pain subsided to a dull throb.

•　•　•

Will paid the hefty cab sum for taking them out of the city before helping Raine out of the taxi. She'd kept her head buried against him for the duration of the trip. He suspected she'd even slept for part of it.

Two people, presumably her parents, bounded out of the house with whoops and cheers.

"We're so happy to have you home!" her mother cried. She spread her arms wide but cast Will a perplexed look when Raine didn't rush to her.

"Migraine," he said.

"Oh, dear, Wyatt, it's one of her migraines. You get the luggage. I'll go close the blinds in the guest room." Raine's mother was barefoot with yards and yards of flowing purple fabric fanning out around her as she walked. She had short, curly, white hair.

Her father, dressed in jeans and a Hawaiian shirt stretched around his abdomen, obediently went to the rear of the taxi.

Following her mother, Will walked with Raine through the two-story house, up a flight of stairs, and into a modest bedroom with a dresser and queen bed.

Her mother rushed to close the blinds. "I'm Ida. You must be Will. Sky told us about you." She kept her tone quieted for Raine's sake.

"Yes, ma'am." He recalled Raine mentioning her sister, Sky.

"Here, here." Ida folded the covers down. "Right into bed with her. We'll use this room since the curtains are darkest."

Raine lowered herself onto the bed, mumbling a 'sorry' to her mother as she slid under the covers.

"Hang on." Will untied and tugged off her boots.

When she buried her head under the pillow, he pulled the covers around her. She looked fragile, unlike he'd ever seen her. He wanted to lie beside her and stroke her head as he had in the taxi, but he feared the bedroom was too personal a space to hold her. He couldn't turn away and leave her alone with her pain, yet he had nothing to offer her for relief.

Ida tugged on Will's sleeve. "We'll let her rest a while."

"She'll be okay?"

"She'll be right as rain in a few hours." She chuckled at her own play on words. "Best to let her rest."

Ida led him out of the guest room and down the stairs where Raine's father situated their luggage at the bottom of the steps.

"Wyatt, this is Raine's partner, Will Decker."

They shook hands.

"Pleasure meeting you, Will. I appreciate you seeing to our daughter like that."

"No problem. She's always so strong. I didn't know she had a condition."

"Oh my." Ida placed a hand on her chest. "She'd be mortified if she heard you call it a *condition*. She's terribly embarrassed to have an Achille's heel like that. Those migraines don't come often, but when they do, they're doozies." She leaned closer to Will. "She told me once how they feel like something's bursting to get out. Like some part of her is caged but she doesn't have the key."

"Interesting."

"Isn't it? All my girls are so strong, yet they're all frustrated by their limitations. Limitations are a part of life, I always remind them. Now, Will, can I fix you anything? Coffee, iced tea, water? Though I'll warn you, I never took to Southern sweet tea, so you'll have to dose it yourself if that's how you like it."

"No, thank you. I should work on getting a rental car and check into my hotel room for the night. I just wanted to get Raine safely here."

"Nonsense," her father piped in. "We have a guest room. You can borrow the truck if you need to go anywhere. I'll fix up the room, and you go have a beverage with Ida."

Raine's father disappeared, and Will turned toward her mother. "Are you sure?"

He wondered if Raine would mind, but he was tired enough from travel that the offer the Thorens presented appealed. Also, he didn't want to be miles away from Raine when she was weakened, even though he couldn't make sense of the protective worry he felt for her. She had clearly managed her migraines and all the other danger in her life for many years without him.

"I don't mind. And if we keep you here, we get more time and meals with Raine." Ida winked. "She's always gone working, though at least she visits a few times a year. Our oldest... well, she's been gone in the wind for years. We have to track her through her online travel blog just to know where she's been. At least our youngest stays close. Sky has a natural remedy shop in town."

Ida cocked her head to one side before pouring a cup of coffee. "I'm going to guess coffee."

He smiled. "Sounds perfect." He was going to enjoy his time here, learning more about Raine and her adorable family. He only needed to sit back, listen, and be entertained.

CHAPTER

EIGHTEEN

Raine woke to the smell of bacon. Blinking her eyes open, she recognized her parents' guest bedroom, which had once been the room her two younger sisters had shared. Morning sunlight streamed through a set of sheer, cream-colored curtains. The heavier drapes had been pulled aside.

Home.

Should her childhood house still register as home when she was in her thirties? She supposed so given she'd never established her own space as an adult. She'd trained with Usha and traveled across the country on missions, from big cities to small town USA.

The blissful aroma of coffee filled the air. When she sat up, scrubbing her hands across her face, she noticed she was still wearing yesterday's clothes.

Right.

Migraine.

She remembered going directly to bed. Will had escorted her, genuine worry in his pinched brow and quiet tone.

She glanced at her suitcase by the door and her phone charging beside the bed. Probably all partners thoughtfully took care of each other this way. She needed to let him know she was ready to work.

She sent him a text, *I'm up. I'll be ready in forty-five minutes.*

Instead of a text back, he called her phone. "Feeling better?"

"Yes, much. Sorry about yesterday. We've got the Priddy interview today? I can meet you there." She could ride share to either Will's hotel or the next of kin's house.

"The interview is tomorrow. Why don't you come downstairs, have some breakfast, and take it easy today?"

"Uh. You're here?"

"Your parents insisted I sleep in the art room—apparently, that was your old bedroom. Your mom told me about all the boy band posters you had hanging in there. And the I LOVE RODGER doodles on college ruled notebook paper plastered behind your bedroom door."

"Ugh. High school crushes are so mortifying." She pulled a change of clothes out of her bag.

"Oh, I don't know. He was the quarterback, and you were a cheerleader. Seems logical."

"You mean stereotypical."

"And where is your knight in Spandex now? Married to the vale-dictorian and playing for the Cowboys?"

"I think he's a used car salesman, and I'm fighting ancient evil bloodlines. Clearly, high school has little bearing on the trajectories of our lives."

"Well said." Will chuckled. "The bed was comfortable, and I'm just going to pretend the entire room didn't smell like a joint."

His deep, teasing tone stirred something in her. She enjoyed hearing his voice first thing in the morning, especially talking about sleeping in her old bed. Something about that man in her space...

She shook her head. Her stirring desires weren't the topic of conversation.

"Call it medicinal," Raine said. Her mom liked to smoke while she painted. "She's manic without it. Well, less crazy with it, anyway. You wouldn't arrest her for it?" She chewed her lip.

"Cut me some slack. I come down on hardened criminals. Join us downstairs, and I'll have a plate of food and coffee ready for you."

"My hero. Be right down after a shower. Thanks." She turned off the phone and turned on the shower.

WILL OBSERVED Raine sitting across from him at the kitchen table nibbling on bacon. Her long hair was in damp ribbons over her shoulders. The bruised look of fatigue under her eyes from yesterday had disappeared.

She thanked him for the food but didn't look up at him, and he suspected her behavior had something to do with the novelty of him being in her parents' home. *For breakfast.*

My hero, she'd sighed over the phone.

Although the tone was playful, the words stirred something in him. The woman hardly needed a hero. She was her own force to be reckoned with, but perhaps she was missing someone to lean on, fix her coffee, or hold her through a migraine. Why did he have the desire to fulfill that role on a regular basis? That was food for thought for another time.

He held up the newspaper and continued to peruse the sports section. He'd been so fascinated to meet people who still read actual newspapers that he had to read it—at the kitchen table over a cup of coffee. Classic.

Raine's mother entered the kitchen carrying a handful of hand-picked flowers. "Oh, look at you two!"

She walked to Raine and gave her a peck on the cheek.

"Thanks for letting Will crash here."

"Of course, of course. Handsome man like that can't stay in a hotel like a stranger."

"Mom, Will is my work partner." Raine sipped her coffee.

The words stung slightly. He felt as though they were more than colleagues, but he hadn't made time to discuss his feelings with her. In any case, he knew how she felt about him after their debacle the other night—work partner. Was she expressing how she truly felt or thought she was supposed to feel?

My hero.

No. He was reading too much into her words.

Ida gave a tsk as she dropped the flowers into the empty vase on the table. "A mother can hope. Three daughters left home and not a one of them married."

Raine's cheeks reddened. "Will and I are solving crimes."

"And it's a crime to have no wed daughters. Everyone is so goal oriented these days that all of you forget to enjoy life."

"I second that," Will said. "Life is short. *Carpe diem.*" He raised his coffee mug in mock toast.

"Oh?" Ida batted her lashes. "Well, if you want to seize the day, we can fire up the hot tub for the two of you."

"Mom." Raine pushed her bacon aside.

"Only a suggestion." She took the vase to the sink and added water.

"How about a horseback ride?" Will suggested.

He wasn't opposed to a dip in the hot tub with Raine—clothing optional—but she obviously wasn't comfortable with the idea, at least not at her parents' place. And they still hadn't addressed the kiss from the other night. A serious conversation needed to precede their next bout of intimacy.

If, not *when*, they took the next step into a relationship, rules and boundaries needed to be established. He smiled, thinking of how Raine would tease him about creating more rules.

"I'm not quite recovered enough for physical activity like horse-back riding," Raine said. "I might do a little work on the case. I'd be up for a walk later though." She refilled her coffee, kissed her mom on the cheek, and disappeared up the stairs.

Ida chuckled. "I think I scared her off with the hot tub suggestion."

"I bet it would help her relax. She should do it without me there to make her uncomfortable." Will sipped his coffee.

"She wouldn't care if you didn't mean something to her."

Unprepared to discuss his feelings with Raine's mother, he squirmed slightly in the chair.

"Hellooo?" a light voice called from the patio door as it opened. A red-headed woman, mid-twenties, breezed into the kitchen wearing a mauve dress.

Definitely one of Ida's daughters, Will thought.

"Oh, hel-lo." She stopped at the sight of Will and arched a sculpted eyebrow.

He stood. "You must be Sky."

"Ah, and you must be Raine's uh—FBI partner." She smiled with a twinkle in her eye.

When he extended a hand, she shook it, and he wondered what Raine had said about him to have her sister appraising him the way she was.

"Oh, my." She giggled. "You actually do like her. Very much."

"Excuse me?"

She pulled her hand back and blushed. "Sorry. Sometimes I pick up on potent feelings people have."

"Interesting," he said with reserved uncertainty.

She grimaced. "Sometimes it is. Most people don't like it. Oh, uh." She glanced at the ring on his hand before tapping her index finger to it. "You should tell Raine about that." Holding up her hands, she stepped back. "Sorry. Sorry. None of my business."

Will gaped for a moment before recovering. He picked up his coffee and turned to leave. "I'm going to go take a walk."

RAINE EXITED the truck they had borrowed from her father and looked around at the wooded plot of land. She glanced at Will, whom she'd avoided most of yesterday. She was afraid more personal time together would enable him to see through her façade of indifference. She wanted to recreate the passion and kissing of the other night, but this time see where it would lead.

No, no. They had a job to do.

During the truck ride over, he'd thrown her for a loop when he'd said, "After we talk to Priddy, I'd like to grab lunch and talk about us." She hadn't known what to say other than, "Sure."

Which part of 'us' did he want to discuss? The sensational kisses, her hopes of intimacy, or their working relationship?

"This is not the cozy cabin I envision for myself," Will said as he closed the truck door.

The noise brought her thoughts back to the present. The isolated cabin rested on a cleared quarter acre surrounded by bulky pines crowded together so densely that sunlight only pierced in sporadic areas, creating a checkered pattern of light and shadow on the wooden roof of the house.

Together, they walked down the gravel driveway and approached the home. An old, faded green pickup truck rusted beneath a cattywampus carport which looked like a strong gust of wind might topple it.

"Don't take another step!" A man holding a shotgun stepped through a screen door and stood on the porch.

Raine and Will both froze.

Will raised his hand shoulder level high. "Easy, Mr. Priddy. I'm Will, and this is my partner, Raine. I'm a special agent with the FBI. We are trying to find your brother's killer, and we've come to ask you a few questions."

She suspected he would have had his badge out by now but didn't want the gun wielding Texan to think Will was reaching for his Glock.

As Will spoke, Raine edged closer to Will without nearing the cabin. She caught him sending her a quick glare. Was he angry that she moved? Or did he understand she was better positioning herself to protect him if the gunman fired?

"I'm gonna need to see some identification," Mr. Priddy said. "Take it out slow and throw it over here."

Will opened his jacket slowly with one hand and pulled out his cred pack. He tossed it at the man's feet. Mr. Priddy bent to pick it up, keeping the shotgun trained on the two of them. He wore rust-colored overalls and a plaid shirt with well-worn, thick-soled, brown work boots.

She scanned the surroundings again. With so many trees in proximity, she could ease toward them and vanish from the man's sight. Then she could creep around the side of the house for a sneak attack. If she was alone, that would've been her strategy. But she wouldn't take any action which might risk the safety of her partner. Also, Mr. Priddy wasn't the enemy. He was protecting himself and protecting his land. Those actions were hardly worthy of an offensive attack.

When the man finished inspecting Will's badge, he lowered his gun. "Can't be too careful, you understand?"

"I understand," Will answered.

"You can come inside, but I got nothin' new to tell you wasn't already said to the FBI."

"We appreciate any time you have to give us." His voice was sincere, and Will's ability to find compassion and see the hurt behind the barrel of a shotgun touched Raine.

He took his identification back and stuffed it into his pocket. She followed him and Mr. Priddy inside the cabin. He placed his shotgun, still presumably loaded, against the wall on a rack near the front door.

"I don't get much company. I've nothin' to offer guests but beer and sardines. And stale crackers."

"We're fine," Will assured him. "It's hospitality enough if you're willing to take a few minutes to talk about your brother."

Raine stood by a shelf of knickknacks while Will sat on the couch and Mr. Priddy plopped into a recliner.

"I didn't know if the case was still even being investigated," the man said. "You're not gonna catch him, you know."

"What do you know about Jörmungandr?" Raine asked as she looked at hand-carved wooden figurines and charcoal sketches decorating the wall and shelves near her.

"Nothing you'd believe," Mr. Priddy answered, his tone more defeated than derogatory.

"You might be surprised by what I would believe," Raine said, but she sensed she'd have to prove it to him, so she took a different tactic. "Are these your works of art or your brothers?"

The corners of Mr. Priddy's mouth drooped. "Those were Noah's."

"I'm going go out on a limb here and say he didn't like wolves despite his prolific artwork of wolves." All the black-haired animals frozen in his art wore snarling expressions with fangs bared. "Did your brother have nightmares about Fenrir?"

Mr. Priddy's eyes widened, and Raine continued, "Did your brother see things? Visions? Maybe he didn't know what they were, or maybe he suspected they were glimpses of the future."

"Yeah, he had visions."

She pressed on, "We think that's why he was targeted. We think that's why Jör murdered each of his victims. They all had the ability of foresight or premonition."

The man scratched stubble on his chin. "I never expected the FBI to figure out the supernatural explanation."

Raine felt a small jolt of alarm and she considered Mr. Priddy's knowledge of the situation, acceptance of the supernatural, and self-induced isolation. "Do you have the ability, too?" she asked. "That's why you're hiding here, isn't it? Off the grid with no electricity and no Internet access."

Will leaned forward, seeming to sense the nature of Raine's

worry. "Mr. Priddy, if that's true, we need to get you into protective custody."

The man scoffed. "You can't protect me from the people after us. They're not human. You're no match for them. I'll stick with my cabin and my shotgun."

When the wood creaked from outside, all three of them turned toward the front door. Raine's heart rate spiked as she drew her gun out of her holster.

CHAPTER

NINETEEN

Standing, Will withdrew his gun.

"Porch?" Raine mouthed the question to Will.

He nodded slowly in agreement as his heart rate spiked while all senses went on high alert. Raine slipped into the corner to disappear, all calm and quiet stealth. Mr. Priddy bolted for his shotgun by the front door.

"Wait!" Will cried.

The front door burst open, and Mr. Priddy stumbled backward before he could grasp his gun. A flash of reddish skin filled the threshold. The attacker looked as though he'd been baking in the sun for a week. Will could see Jör in better detail now compared to the dark, abandoned office building. The creature had wispy blonde hair with brittle locks matching his flaking, dry skin. He wore holey jeans and a white t-shirt.

Will took aim. "FBI, freeze!"

When the attacker launched at Mr. Priddy, Will fired. Jör's motions blurred as he changed directions, and Will's bullet hit the wall. Mr. Priddy retreated toward the corner where Raine hid.

Jör advanced toward Will. Despite firing multiple times, Will inexplicably kept missing a target that was so close.

The lithe red demon surged at Will with supernatural speed and ferocity. Will fired his weapon several more times, emptying his magazine, but with Jör's zigzag pattern and quick steps, Will missed the killer every time.

The glint of a silver blade came closer and closer. Will dodged a swipe as it came toward his head and tripped over the corner of the Ottoman. He stumbled backward, enabling him to avoid another slash of the knife.

Jör turned his attention to Mr. Priddy, who cowered back into the corner near Raine. She'd been very still, and Will understood she now had the element of surprise on Jör—until she moved.

The instant she raised her Glock, Jör saw her and his reaction was faster than catlike reflexes. He slashed at the gun, knocking it from her grip before she could fire.

He began his assault, slashing and sneering. Raine ducked and took one of the wolf paintings off the wall, using it as a shield for the fight. The knife clunked against the thick wooden frame. When she had the opportunity, she kicked or swung, never contacting Jör's slinking body.

Will thrust himself forward, vaulted off the coffee table, and landed on the assassin's back. He wrapped his arms around the scaly neck and squeezed.

Raine tried to grab the arm of his blade-wielding hand, but Jör sliced at her, cutting a gash down her arm. She let out a brief scream of pain, but didn't withdraw from the fight.

Jör crouched and then launched himself backward, throwing Will onto the coffee table on his back. Pain shot through Will's spine as the wind was knocked out of him. His grip on the attacker slackened.

Jör jabbed an elbow into the side of Will's rib cage and pushed away from him.

Will sucked in a breath as his eyes watered. He tried to push himself back up and quickly re-join the fight, but his body refused to cooperate.

Raine had stepped between Jör and Mr. Priddy, but the killer slashed at her defenses. Her arms were covered in a mess of blood. Fatigue clearly slowed her motions. With a quick pivot and thrust, his blade sunk into her abdomen.

As she fell, the red snake pulled the knife back out. "Valkyrie," he snarled. With icy contempt in his eyes, he kicked her in the face.

Pushing through his pain and terror, Will bent over and picked up Raine's gun. His motions felt slow and clumsy compared to what they were up against. In the time it took him to pick up the gun, aim, and fire, Jör had already cut Mr. Priddy's throat.

When the shot rang out, the serpent spun sideways from the impact of the bullet in his back. Red blood bloomed on his shirt, and Will gained some margin of satisfaction that he'd hurt the bastard.

Jör snarled as he dashed past Will and leaped over the couch before running out the door.

Will was in no condition to give chase, even knowing the creature was now wounded and this was their best opportunity. Furthermore, his partner was severely injured and needed his help.

He fell to his knees beside Raine. "Raine? Can you hear me?"

There was so much blood. When he placed fingers to her carotid, he felt a strong beating pulse. Blood trickled from her mouth and her cheek was already swelling from the blow to her face.

"Raine? I need to roll you over and see how bad your wounds are." He tried to ignore the squeezing sensation over his throat at the fear that she may not survive this time. What were the limits of her ability to heal? She had said she wasn't immortal.

As he gingerly rolled her, she stirred with eyes still closed. She helped him move her even as she sobbed at the pain.

She'd been unbelievably fast dodging Jör's knife, but she sustained cuts all over her hands and arms. He was most worried about the deeper, penetrating abdominal wound.

He stretched his torso and an arm toward the recliner to yank off the throw blanket. Using it, he applied direct pressure, causing her to cry out.

"I'm so sorry, Raine."

How long would she take to heal? They couldn't wait here, vulnerable to another attack if Jör returned.

He had another option.

He'd never transported with anyone. He focused on his ring and closed his eyes, trying to ignore the pain in his back and the worry in his heart. Rainbow colors danced before his eyes as his surroundings turned liquid. He couldn't take them to their hotel room, as the blood would be a disaster. Anywhere public was out of the question. He opted for his trailer in Virginia, knowing he would have to return to the cabin after reporting the incident to the local authorities and retrieve the truck they'd borrowed from Raine's dad.

Raine's eyes flickered open, then shut again. In under sixty seconds, he sat on the floor of his trailer in the living room, cradling Raine in his arms. He kept the blanket in place and waited as the minutes ticked by for her body to heal itself.

Silent tears streamed down his cheeks.

God help her, he cried. He couldn't lose her.

Forty-five minutes passed when he noticed her forearm cuts had healed. She was still unconscious, and he didn't know if that was from the shock of blood loss, the pain of the healing wounds, or an internal head injury from when Jör had kicked her.

At last, heart in his throat, Will dared take down the blanket and look at the injury to her abdomen. He felt sick to his stomach seeing so much blood and knowing it all belonged to her. But when he pulled up her shirt, he could see the wound had sealed. The skin was still discolored, yet it wasn't the gaping gash it had been. Relief swept over him.

He took a shaky breath and sniffed, wiping at his eyes with the back of his hand. She would survive.

Her face was still ashen, though no longer as swollen and discolored. He gently laid her back down on the floor and stood, wincing at the pain in his back. After fetching a pillow, he placed it under her head. Pulling out his phone, he dialed Catherine's number with shaking hands.

"Jör got away again. He ambushed us at Noah Priddy's brother's house during our interview with him." That one man had 'ambushed them' seemed ridiculous to announce out loud, but when the images of the fight came to mind, that was exactly what it was. An ambush. They hadn't stood a chance against him.

"And the civilian?" Caroline asked.

"Jör killed him. I need to notify local PD." Cradling the phone between his ear and shoulder, he went to his sink and scrubbed the blood off his hands. Raine's blood. He swallowed at the bile rising in the back of his throat.

"Goodness, Will. Are you hurt?"

"I'm still ambulatory. Mostly." Back throbbing, he hobbled into his bedroom and dug around his drawers for clothing. Raine needed a fresh shirt. And Will couldn't stand the sight of her blood. He'd seen plenty of blood in his lifetime, but seeing her injured nearly broke him in half.

"And your partner?"

"She's alive. Got the ever-living-shit beat out of her like me, but she's alive." Worse than him, he knew, but thank Heaven she could heal herself.

"Send me the address. I'll get PD and FBI on the scene," Caroline said. "Are you in any condition to stay there and debrief them?"

"Yeah, I'll stay here." By here, he meant the Priddys' household. Caroline didn't and would never know about his ability to travel.

The call disconnected. He deposited the phone back in his pocket.

Will found a gray t-shirt, plucked it out of the drawer, and set it beside Raine along with a large glass of water. He held the shirt and stared down at her. He didn't want to leave her here alone, but struggled to think of who could watch her in her current condition.

Sky.

An image of the jubilant redhead popped into his mind. She could watch Raine and maybe help her recover faster. Hadn't Raine said her sister owned a natural remedy shop?

But he couldn't take her to her sister's looking like she'd walked out of a scene from a *Friday the Thirteenth* movie. Will made quick work of removing Raine's blood-soaked shirt and pulling his t-shirt over her head. She didn't even blink an eye open.

After dressing, he cradled Raine and focused on Sky. He'd never travelled twice in one month, let alone one day. He'd kept his secret guarded. As an FBI agent, he needed paper trails for all of his travels. He couldn't simply globe hop and expect not to get caught.

Once he had been somewhere or met someone in more than a brief passing, he could travel to the location or person. But he rarely risked using his magic.

In his mind's eye, he could see Sky in a cozy shop, stocking shelves as she bobbed her head to "Fall Out Boys." Will was going to scare her half to death when he showed up with Raine unconscious.

He was also going to give away his transportation abilities, when he'd told no one. For Raine's sake, he would have to trust Sky—except, based on her behavior yesterday, maybe Sky already knew.

Raine's sister stopped moving, and the music quieted. "Bring her to me," he heard her say, even though he wasn't physically in the same room with her yet.

Will focused harder. He'd only once transported *to* someone, a serial killer he'd met and later learned of his crimes. Fear of discovery kept him from using his magic. Sky's shop materialized. He was on the floor, still cradling Raine.

"What happened?" Sky asked.

"Bad guy won this round," he said. "She's mostly healed, but I didn't know if there was anything else you could do for her. I need to get back to the scene of the crime."

"I can help her. Do what you need to do. Will you be coming back here?"

"Wherever she is, that's where I'll come back to."

"I have a couch in the back office. She'll be there."

Raine moved, and Sky helped her sit up.

"She'll need water," he told Sky. Last time, with one cut to the arm, she'd guzzled about two liters.

Sky went through a door behind the counter as Raine blinked her eyes open.

Raine turned to look around. "We're... but this is Sky's shop."

"I can explain," Will said. "But first I need to get back to the body." He didn't want to leave her, especially not rushing off like this, but he needed to beat authorities to the crime scene since he couldn't materialize there *after* they arrived.

She pressed a hand to her forehead. "Dammit," she swore. "We were no match for Jör."

"Just stay here and rest. You look like a ghost. Do you want me to help you to the couch in Sky's office?"

"Okay." But she didn't move, and Will suspected she lacked the strength. "*Son of a hellhound.* He was so fast." Raine stared with a wide, glazed look. "How are we even still alive?"

"I shot him." Will shook his head and scoffed. "Barely slowed the bastard down."

"How do we defeat something like that? We need help. I need to talk to the Council of Mjölnir."

"First, rest. I'll be back as soon as I can."

Sky returned with a bottle of water and handed it to Raine. She took a long swig before Will helped her stand. He struggled with her as his battered back protested the movement after sitting for several minutes.

Raine noticed him wince. "Sky, what do you have for him?"

"Contusions? I have a salt and herbal salve. Works best when combined with oral anti-inflammatories." She went to one shelf and pulled down a round container.

Raine took it. "Turn around."

Will didn't protest. His back felt like it had been hit with a battering ram, and he would welcome any relief. As he lifted his shirt, Raine smeared on the salve. It smelled like mint and eucalyptus. The warmth instantly soothed.

"Thanks."

He turned around and helped Raine to Sky's office. When they were alone, he placed a hand on her cheek, so grateful she was alive. He rubbed a thumb along her smooth skin, trying to find the words, but his throat seemed to close.

Pulling her into a tight hug, he relished the feel of her. Too soon, he took a step back and activated the ring, traveling back to the crime scene.

CHAPTER

TWENTY

Raine lay on Sky's office couch in her shop and slept. When she woke, she felt more restored but still drained. Walking to the front of the shop, she noticed the setting sun through the display windows.

Sky stood at the cashier's desk, emptying the register.

"You need a shower," Sky said.

Raine nodded, pulling her phone from her back pocket. "I'll let mom and dad know I'm working and won't be home tonight. I don't want to go there looking like this. Can I stay with you?"

"No problem." She wriggled a finger at her. "Provided there is a shower involved."

Raine looked down at Will's gray t-shirt. "I'm sorry to drop in half-dead."

"You scared me. I've never seen you look so bad, but at least you were already on the road to recovery."

"That was the worst defeat I've ever had." Raine felt as if she was Thor after fighting the Midgard serpent—which she guessed she kind of was. "We hardly slowed him down. I'm not fast or strong enough."

"I'm sorry."

"And apparently my partner can teleport. Didn't know that."

Sky placed a hand on her shoulder. "I don't think he's told anyone. Don't be too hard on him."

Raine nodded, though she wasn't sure she could promise that. She'd held nothing back from him, but apparently he'd kept important details about himself from her.

"Can we head back to your place so I can clean up?"

Sky reached under the counter and withdrew her purse. "Yup. Grab the salve. Will's going to need more of it. You should text him and let him know where you'll be. I'm going to send a text to cancel my date tonight."

"What? No, don't cancel your date."

"It's okay." Sky shrugged. "On our first date, we were enjoying a nice Italian dinner, but the only thing on his mind was Sunday night football."

"You have a terrible gift." Raine definitely would never want the ability to read people's minds, even if it was just glimpses and not a full-on assault.

Sky's mouth quirked. "Well, it means I don't waste any time on uninterested or uninteresting men."

RAINE SHOWERED AND HYDRATED MORE. Clean but still exhausted, she crawled into Sky's guest bed. She wished she could help Will, but she wasn't much use to him in her condition. He texted her an update at one point that he was still talking to local police.

She tried to stay awake for him, but television and social media couldn't hold her interest. Raine clicked off the phone and set it on the dresser as her eyes grew heavier and heavier until they closed altogether.

When she awoke again, Will stood above her. He smelled freshly washed and wore jeans and a t-shirt.

"Is there room enough for two?" He sounded exhausted, but she couldn't see his face clearly in the dark.

"Yes," she began groggily, rolling to make room for him.

"I thought we could stay the night here and go to your parents for things tomorrow."

"Did you drive here or...?"

"Cleaned up at my place, then took the truck from the Priddy house to here so we can return your father's vehicle to him tomorrow. I'll explain everything. I promise."

"Did you take something for pain?" she asked, noting how they were mere inches apart.

"Yeah. Sky gave me more cream, and I slugged a few ibuprofen."

"I'm glad we're both still alive." She bit her lip, uncertain what else to say. Her mind raced with mixed emotions—gratitude for saving her life, grief they hadn't saved an innocent man, pride she could call a man like Will Decker her partner, frustration he hadn't trusted her with his magic, and longing for him.

So much longing.

"You should have told me about your powers," her voice came out harsh.

"Yes, I should have. I thought about it several times, not that that abdicates me from wrong-doing. I had no idea it could be related to Norse mythology until I met you. Even then, I needed time to process it. If I'd told you, I still would have been reluctant to use it. It's not a subtle magic."

"No secrets, Will. That was one of your rules."

"I'm sorry I didn't tell you. I promise not to omit anything ever again."

She simultaneously wanted to lash out and be in his embrace, and the sensation was so much more than simple sexual desire. She wanted the comfort and unity she imagined she would find there.

All these warring emotions mixed with her fatigue told her one thing: she needed sleep and the return of rational thought.

Will's warm hand slid into hers, and soon his breathing became slow and steady.

THE NEXT MORNING, Will worked on his laptop at Sky's kitchen table after helping himself to a bowl of cereal. She'd left to run her shop, pushing more ibuprofen and salve at him. He gladly took them both, amazed at how much his injury had improved overnight.

Raine was still sleeping. It was just as well. His report to the FBI took him over an hour to type up. Every time he replayed the fight in his head, he had to refill his coffee so he could drink something warm in an attempt to ward off the cold that came over him when he thought of their brush with death.

Seventeen bullets at close range, and he'd missed Jör every time. Will had never seen anything like it. And if this is what the world was up against—an army of creatures this horrendous planning something so terrible they were killing off prophets—he didn't have much hope for the future. Raine wasn't the only one of them reading the Noble Prophecies.

> *Three by three*
> *Hell's wrath to free*
> *Wretched destiny*

Becky spelled it Hell but he suspected she meant Hel, as in Helen—goddess of death.

Wretched destiny was right. Even Raine's supernatural gifts hadn't been enough. Although Jör hadn't seen Raine, despite being three feet away, as soon as she'd moved his reflexes had been too fast for her stealth or combat.

Raine.

He'd thought he lost her. He was pretty sure his fear was deeper than losing just a partner. If she'd died, she would never know how he felt about her.

As he pondered those thoughts, he finished his coffee and packed his laptop case. He dressed for the day and brushed his teeth.

Standing over her still sleeping form, he glanced at the bedside clock—eleven a.m. He knew she needed rest after healing herself, but for his sanity, he needed to see one more time that she was well.

"Raine?"

She rolled over and blinked up at him—hair down and disheveled with rosy cheeks looking infinitely better compared to how pale she'd been yesterday. She pushed herself up in bed, looking around. The dark circles under her eyes were gone. Haloed by the light from the window behind her through the sheer curtain, she looked like the Asgardian descendant of supernatural beings she claimed to be.

Relief at seeing her healthy enabled him to take his first deep breath since the harrowing fight.

"How are you feeling?" he asked.

"Better," she said. "Food?"

He ran a hand through his hair. "Yeah, let's get you fed."

A few minutes later, she was seated at the table with a bowl of cereal dressed in a t-shirt and shorts he suspected she'd borrowed from her sister.

"So... teleportation?" she said between bites of food, a slight edge to her voice.

"Uh, yes." He took off the ring and set it on the table between them. "The ring enables me to travel. I can also sort of hover between two places for a few minutes—able to see and hear both areas without being physically present in either."

She picked it up and inspected it. Will had gazed upon it a thousand times since it came into his possession. When the light hit the black ring, rainbow shades of color shone deep within it.

"How does it work?" she asked.

"I focus on a person or place, and then I can teleport there."

She handed the ring back to him. "I'm willing to bet you have some alien bloodline. The ring for any hubble is probably just jewelry. Where did you get it?"

"Inheritance. My grandfather gave it to me in an old wooden box. It was mixed in with a broken compass, old baseball cards, and other odds and ends. I had no idea what it was. The first time I used it was entirely accidental." He slipped it back on his finger. "I wear it. Always wear it, but seldom use it. Mostly out of cowardice—I'm afraid of being discovered as someone with supernatural powers."

"You have a gift, Will."

"Yeah, I see that now. Now that you've taught me about this shadow war, I can see I have this for a reason. Still, it scares the hell out of me."

"You're not alone."

"Damn right I'm not. If I go down for being a freak, you're going with me."

She grinned, but he stopped short of telling her how he was in this for the long haul. Dark Elves and wildebeests and rodents of unusual size. Whatever came next, they would tackle it together.

AFTER BREAKFAST, Raine freshened up and stole jeans and a blouse from her sister. When she emerged, Will looked ready to go.

Ready to teleport, she marveled. She stared at him, wondering about his bloodline, but soon was distracted, noticing the angle of his jaw, the way his jeans hugged his body.

She walked to him. "How's your back?"

"Better. Unexpectedly much better." He moved closer to her, crowding her space, his voice dropping an octave. "I thought I'd lost you in the cabin."

She rubbed her arms. "I thought I'd lost me too. I've never been injured that badly. Never fought someone so utterly and completely superior to me."

"I can't lose you, Raine," his voice cracked. He laid his head down on her shoulder and stayed still, as if he wasn't sure what he wanted to do.

His vulnerability tore at her heart. She touched a hand to the back of his head before sinking her fingertips into his hair. He sucked in a breath as his teeth grazed her neck. In that instant, she had to have him.

She tugged his head up by the hair and pressed her lips to his. His warm, soft lips instantly lit a fire in her. Still kissing, she backed him into the counter.

"Not here," he said, voice husky.

Rainbow light shimmered around them for a full dazzling moment as he kissed her again until the bedroom of his trailer appeared. He pulled her onto the bed with him.

She crawled on top of him as they kissed. His body was warm and firm beneath her. The kiss deepened as mouths parted and tongues explored. Will's hands moved to her hips.

She pulled away to tug off her shirt.

His heated gaze looked ravenous. He swallowed. "Raine, we should talk."

"Oh, we will. But not right now."

She closed her mouth back over his, pressing skin on skin. He didn't look like he wanted to talk, and she sure as hell wouldn't ruin the moment sputtering about whether or not this was a one-night stand. In this moment, she didn't give a damn.

She'd nearly lost Will in that fight. The emotions were too much. She needed to be with him—lose herself in him. If she only ever had this one moment of ecstasy, so be it.

Will pulled off her blouse and groaned as Raine pressed her breasts against him. Their mouths reconnected, and Will's hand slid up to gently grasp one of her breasts.

She sucked in a breath as she frantically tugged his shirt up. Hunger and need rose, and they finished undressing in unison. At last, skin pressed to skin.

Their lips met again for several long minutes as fingers explored each other. He worked his way down her neck and to her breasts. The touch of his tongue sent shivers through her as his fingers explored between her thighs, drawing out long moans of delight. He kissed her stomach, over the perfectly healed skin where she'd been stabbed. The tender caresses of his lips touched her heart.

He kissed his way lower, but she couldn't wait any longer to have him.

"Now. Please," she said.

"Okay, okay." Chuckling, he reached into his bedside drawer, pulled out a condom, and slipped it on. She positioned herself back on top of him, this time with him sliding into her.

She gasped as she settled over him.

"You are so amazing," he said, moving his hips.

They synchronized, slow at first as she savored the sensation of him, the feel of him inside her as his hands cupped her butt and his tongue licked her nipples.

Their speed increased to delightful thrusts with each groaning encouragement to the other.

"Raine," he panted, desperate and needy.

Her orgasm struck like a bolt of lightning—hot and fast. As she rocked with Will's deep thrusts, his body shuddered in his own synchronous climax.

Electricity, white and bright, flashed before her eyes as she called out Will's name. Sublime incandescence. Images danced before her, a sky of fast-moving storm clouds, a streak of lightning slicing through the gray and illuminating an enormous tree above a raging river of slate-colored water.

As the bedroom came back into focus, Will pulled her down on top of him and clung tightly to her, whispering her name over and over.

CHAPTER
TWENTY-ONE

After several amazing hours in the bedroom with Will, she laid in bed thinking about her vision. Although she didn't know its significance, she knew it was significant—the lightning, the tree, and the river.

She grabbed her blouse off the floor and pulled it on as she crept out of the bedroom. She found her phone charging on the kitchen table and wondered when Will had done that. Quietly, she stepped outside the trailer and gingerly closed the door behind her. The cool autumn air and dew chilled her.

"Raine." Usha promptly answered her call. "How is your assignment coming along?"

"Not well. We caught up to Jör, and we both nearly died by his hand. I'm no match for him." She pinched the bridge of her nose as she paced, bare feet sinking into the cool grass. "I need to know how to defeat him. I think I know where the answers are, but not how to get there."

"Elaborate."

"I had a vision." Raine would omit the part where it flashed before her eyes during the most amazing orgasm of her life. "An enormous tree—Yggdrasil, I'm sure of it—was beneath a lightning storm and above a river. I see this storm when I have my migraines. Something inside of me will reveal itself at this tree beneath the storm, but I don't know how to find where the tree meets the river."

The tree had been destroyed during Ragnarok. It was beyond space and time. Unreachable.

"Ah." Usha's tone conveyed understanding. "You are being summoned. It's time for your dream walk."

"A dream walk? How do I do that?"

"It's a spiritual journey. I will guide you, but you must travel back here."

When Raine hung up the phone, she walked back into the room and watched Will sleep, weighing her options: leave now to get started on this mysterious dream walk or stay and be delayed as she gave Will an insufficient explanation for something even she didn't understand but was drawing her away immediately after their intimacy.

Leaving Will without at least a conversation didn't seem right. They were on this journey together, even if she didn't know what their relationship was. They may be undefined, but they had been intimate in the throes of danger and passion. She would trust that she could explain the need for a dream walk, and he would grant her the time and space needed to accomplish it. Unless this afternoon was her one-night stand and she was supposed to cut and run.

She pulled her shirt back off. If all she got was today and tonight, then she would make the most of it. Naked, she slid into bed beside Will and glided her hands along his smooth, warm skin.

He instantly groaned her name and turned to take her in his arms.

Will woke to an empty bed. Sun peeked through thick blinds, and his eyes adjusted. He stared at the space beside him.

Was Raine's absence because she wanted it that way or because she thought he did? He didn't. Was she afraid he would leave, so she left first? Regardless, she should have stayed and had the decency of a conversation with him. Especially after a night like that.

Last night wasn't a simple sex and release. He could only think of their activity as love-making, but even that didn't encompass the depth and splendor of what he'd felt with Raine in his arms.

A mechanical click sounded, followed by the door to the bedroom sliding back and Raine entering. She carried a cup of coffee in each hand and her long, blonde hair was back up in her business ponytail.

"I made coffee." She stopped. "What's wrong? Why are you staring at me?"

She handed him his cup, and he set it aside to take hold of her hand. With a perplexed look, she set her cup down beside his on the nightstand.

"Everything okay?" she asked.

He tugged her into the bed beside him, thrilled she hadn't left.

"Will!" she cried as she laughed.

"Everything's okay." He wrapped his arms around her.

She accepted the embrace before pulling away. "I didn't know if you were a snuggle-in-the-morning kind of guy, so I just thought I'd give you your space."

He ran a thumb along her bottom lip. "I don't know what kind of guy I am in a long-term relationship. But I certainly want to hold you the morning after. And I definitely would like to know if you're just stepping away for coffee or if I won't see you for days."

She bit her lip.

"What is it?" he asked.

"I do need to disappear for a few days, and not because of last night—which I hope to repeat when I come back."

"Where do you need to go?" He searched her expression but found no indication of regret or shame at their night of pleasure.

She propped herself up on one elbow. "There's something called a dream walk or spirit walk. I need to take mine. I can't explain it, but I feel like there's something to be learned there that will help me defeat Jör."

"I'll go with you. To Usha's," he added quickly, "obviously the dream walk sounds like something you have to do alone."

"You... you will?" She smiled.

"We're partners and... and whatever else this turns out to be. I don't pretend to understand all the supernatural, nine realms' bloodlines—and it's impossible not to believe at least some of it with the strange things I've seen since meeting you—but I unequivocally believe in you. So if you tell me a dream walk is what you need to do, I'll back you up."

She leaned forward and kissed him with fresh, minty breath. "I think that's the most amazing thing you've ever said to me."

Will grinned. Maybe he would do okay in a long-term relationship after all.

Raine's eyes saddened. "But I already have tickets, and my flight leaves in three hours."

Will opened his mouth to protest, but Raine continued, "I'll only be gone a few days. I'll be back before you know it. And you can use that time to finish all those FBI forms you're so fond of."

Damn. He did have a lot of paperwork to wade through. "You're sure? You don't need someone with you? I could take you."

Raine going alone felt wrong to him, but he wasn't sure if that was some newfound overprotectiveness he needed to squelch or a gut instinct he shouldn't ignore.

"Usha will be there to guide me. Besides, I didn't want to impose on your ability and assume you'd give me a lift. I know you want to ensure your abilities go undetected."

"Please, impose on me. I want you to ask me for things you need. This wasn't a one-night stand."

Raine looked so eager and yet torn, as if she didn't want to hurt Will's feelings but needed to get on the road to the airport. He suspected she would change her plans if he pushed, but he refused to be the pushy boyfriend who insisted on inserting himself into every aspect of her life.

Was he her boyfriend?

He swallowed and took her hand. "You and I. We're dating now, right? We're an exclusive couple?"

Her smile lit up the room. "Yeah. We are."

"I could join you in a few days. Meet your mentor."

She gave him a broad smile. "That sounds perfect."

"Great. I'll call right before I come. Next time, you don't need tickets. I'm your ticket."

She bent over and kissed his cheek. "Perfect."

"THE TARGET IS ELIMINATED, MY QUEEN."

"Well, done."

Swallowing, Jör added, "There were... further complications."

"Oh? Am I to be disappointed again?"

"I have been shot again, but I have taken the necessary steps to manage the wound." He omitted the part where it hurt like hell and he'd chugged a fifth of whisky just to take the edge off. "I'll need a little more time to heal before the next assignment."

"Two injures. That's unprecedented for you." The dissatisfaction in her voice knifed him.

"The opponent who has presented a challenge I believe is a Valkyrie."

"Myths and legends," Helen fired back, voice sharply irritable.

He cringed. "She has powers exceeding the abilities of normal humans. Invisibility, speed, strength."

"She still lives after your fight?"

"I don't know. I dealt her wounds no mortal human could have survived."

The blonde woman had simply appeared in his target's living room. The man had been a more dangerous adversary this time as well, making Jör wonder if he, too possessed something other-worldly. He decided not to burden his queen with too much troubling news in one day.

"If this woman has caught up with you twice now, I wonder if she knows your mission."

"I don't know, my queen."

"Do you have a name? Some way I can identify her?"

Helen had power and money. With a name, he'd known her to track down adversaries and dispatch them with a team of Dark Elves or shapeshifting wolves.

"No. I have nothing." He felt his failure sink into his bones as he spoke the words. There simply hadn't been time to stop and take her photo or lift her ID.

"When will you be functional again?"

"At least a week."

"Call me then."

TWENTY-TWO

After Raine left for her mysterious dream walk, taking a rideshare to the airport, Will showered, dressed, and started his paperwork. He worked on his laptop in his kitchenette.

Next, he walked outside and called Caroline to update her on the situation with Jör.

"You got nine lives, Will. Don't use them all up."

"What else can you tell me about Raine Thoren's organization?"

"Not enough," she admitted. "It's called the CoM, and they're some spin-off investigative group which somehow has more funding and often better intel than we do. The first time they inserted themselves into one of our investigations, I fought it and lost. Good thing I lost. They proved valuable and—being super-secretive—took no credit for the solved case. I can tell you they cut time and cost on cases while helping. Why do you ask? Is everything working well with Raine?"

"Yes. Everything is working well. I'm making more progress with her than I would have without her." He infused a begrudging tone in his voice he didn't feel. Anything cheerful might betray how much he liked Raine and liked working with her.

"Good. Play nice. And if I know you, you're berating yourself that Jör got away when you should be thankful you and your partner survived."

Will ran a hand through his hair. "Yeah."

"Any new leads?"

He had a lead—a supernatural one. He'd spent enough time in proximity to Jör during the fight that he was certain he could track him down using the power of the ring. The problem would be how to subdue Jör once he found him. Will needed to brainstorm with Raine before attempting it. Once upon a time, he would have run a solo mission. Not anymore.

"No leads," he lied. And he had no idea what he would write in his FBI case report when they did find him on how that had transpired without magic.

"Then back to work, Special Agent."

After Will said goodbye and ended the call, he stepped outside to pace in the brisk fall weather. He called Coup.

"Will, good to hear from you."

"Coup, how's the family?"

"All good here. How's your case coming?"

"Could be better." Could be worse—they were both still alive, after all.

"And Raine?"

"We hooked up."

"Is that a good thing?" Coup asked hesitantly.

Will had broken his no dating co-workers rule and had every intention of breaking his no long-term relationships rule.

"It's good. It's very good. It's so good I'm actually worried about screwing it up."

"She's still with you so far. The feelings must be mutual."

"Yeah. In a span of a few days I've met the parents. I'm going to meet her mentor."

"Nervous?"

"Yes."

"Respect her and don't crowd her. You'll do fine."

Will was about to ask if inviting himself on her trip was crowding her, but he could hear Coup's wife calling to him in the background.

"I gotta go," Coup cut in. "Call you later?"

"Yeah, sounds good."

Will continued to pace after Coup disconnected the call. He had work to do, but he wasn't finished with his desire to share his excitement about Raine. Walt was the only other person he shared details of his life with.

Will's call to Walt's mobile phone went to voicemail. As it was Saturday, he was not likely working, so there was no point in calling the office. Perhaps Walt was at their parent's house, he visited them often. He and Winston sometimes teased Walt that he'd never actually left home.

Will pressed the button to dial their parent's house.

"Hello?"

Will cringed. "Hello, Winston. Is Walt there? I tried his cell first, but it went to voicemail."

"I think he's on a jobsite. Dad and I just finished a round of eighteen. He beat me by two strokes. Two," he repeated with annoyed emphasis. "Everything okay?"

"Yeah. All's good." Will didn't want to discuss relationships with Winston, no matter how jubilant he was.

"How's the serial killer hunt going?"

Yeah, the assassin who almost killed us both. There was no point telling his brother about injuries he and his partner had sustained but had healed.

"We haven't caught him yet," Will responded politely.

"We? You and Raine?"

"Yeah, Raine." Will walked back inside his trailer.

"You sound upset. Is Raine okay?"

"She's fine. She's on a side assignment today."

"Look, Will, I'm sorry for the way I behaved the other night when the two of you came to Mom and Dad's house. The things your partner said about being a family resonated—she's right. You should bring her back for another dinner. Mom really misses you."

Will wondered how much of his and Raine's conversation Winston had overheard.

"Well, as of last night we are actually sleeping together, so it might be a bit more awkward."

"Oh."

"We've known each other for less than three weeks and already met the parents." Already faced life and death together. And boy, he would have died without her.

Will opened the small fridge in the trailer and eyed the beer. Maybe if he was busy drinking, he'd stop rambling to Winston, of all people.

Too early in the day for alcohol, he decided.

He poured a glass of water instead.

"Oh," Winston repeated.

Will flopped onto the couch.

"Well." His brother cleared his throat.

Will braced for some childish comment or moment of triumphant gloating by Winston.

"Are things moving too fast for you?"

Was that genuine concern in Winston's voice?

"Surprisingly, no," Will answered.

"You remember that time you ran outside because you knew Molly had been run off the road on her bike?"

"I do."

Molly, a girl in their neighborhood, had been eight and Will twelve. They'd known each other from their parents' get togethers. Will had been inside his house with his brothers when he knew she was hurt outside. A moving van had run her off the road.

"Or the time you called Walt as soon as he'd been in a fender bender, like you knew the instant it happened?"

Will took another sip of water. "Rather observant of you." He'd had gut feelings he'd trusted for as long as he could remember. They weren't premonitions, nothing like the Noble Prophecies. He sometimes knew in real-time what people were up to or where they were.

"My point," Winston continued, "is that you have good instincts. If your instincts tell you she's the one, then what does the pace matter?"

"Really?" Will was as shocked to be listening to advice from Winston as he was to realize the advice made sense. "Damn, Winston. I don't know if the chill I'm feeling is about this moment we're connecting or hell freezing over because of it." Will chuckled as he pushed to his feet.

"So long as you know I get gloating privileges if I'm right," Winston said.

"I'd expect nothing less."

He needed to retrieve his belongings from Raine's parent's house and finish his FBI electronic paperwork in order to be done in time to see her in a few days.

Days? That seemed entirely too long.

RAINE WALKED across the dry ground in the South Dakota Badlands. The surrounding peaks were horizontal stripes of tan, red, and orange. The landscape would have been cause for reverence if her lips weren't dry and cracked and her legs heavy. She'd been walking for twenty-six hours. Her canteen was empty, and she hadn't eaten in two days.

And to think she'd left Will for this. But he didn't understand her world, and the need to dream walk had clawed at her the way thirst now did.

After leaving Will at the hotel, she'd made her flight and reached Usha's land in Southern Montana. On Usha's instructions, Raine had driven her rental car to the Badlands and started her dream walk with nothing more than a canteen of water.

But this was no dream. This was facing dehydration and death in the wilderness. Several times she'd wanted to stop—to succumb to exhaustion and lie down. But images of the fight with Jör spurned her onward. His knife flashed like a sliver of moonlight as he sliced through skin.

The dry air and her weariness slowed her pace. She felt as though she was trying to walk through quicksand as her aching muscles threatened to cramp and seize with every step.

But somewhere out here were the answers she sought. Except the landscape was all wrong—there were no clouds streaming and no lightning flashing. The dry air didn't even hold the slightest threat of a thunderstorm. Nothing matched her recurrent dreams of flowing water and the tree of life.

Had Usha been wrong? The woman was never wrong.

Raine blinked at the blinding sun. At least it was fall and not summer. Was she going to die out here? Another failure—just like failing to apprehend Jör. But if she didn't find a way to defeat Jör, she would die anyway. Everyone would, according to the prophecies. The prophecies which someone was trying to silence.

Usha had said this dream walk was the key to Raine unlocking more power. She had to succeed.

Her legs involuntarily locked up, and she tipped forward. As the ground came closer, she closed her eyes, knowing the impact would be painfully jarring when she hit the dry dirt, but her arms lacked the strength to catch herself.

Instead of her face slamming into a wall of earth, she kept fall-ing. When she opened her eyes, she saw a column of water rush to meet her. Her body plunged into a river, engulfed in cool, flowing water.

As she tumbled through a robust current, she became disoriented as to where the surface was. She needed to find air soon. Struggling uselessly, her lungs burned for release.

Massive hands lifted her out of the water and set her beside the river. As she gasped for air, she patted her clothing, which was somehow instantly dry. Taking in her surroundings, the beauty and enormity of everything struck her. The crisp, flowing river was an arctic blue beneath a horizon of different colors. Half the sky was comprised of rolling gray clouds. The other half was a clear, starry night with dancing and shimmering purple waves like the Aurora Borealis.

The two sky halves converged above a gargantuan tree ten stories high. The intertwining branches filling the sky held a majestic beauty in their curves, as if they were a choreographed dance that left a trail of flowing wood. Four reddish stags with fierce branching antlers stretched up to feed on the tree.

Lightning flashed, brilliant and bright.

"Magnificent, isn't it?" a deep voice asked.

She looked up to see the man who'd pulled her out of the river. He was a tall figure, probably eight feet, looking down at her with a smile. His long, dirty blond hair seemed to merge and flow with the same colored beard. A braid ending in topaz beads trailed over one shoulder. He wore taupe-colored robes with his arms clasped under their folds.

"Yes, it is," Raine agreed. "I don't think I've ever seen anything more beautiful."

"Too bad it isn't real... anymore."

"I suspected as much."

The man arched an eyebrow at her.

"Well, it is called a *dream walk*." She grinned.

He nodded sagely. "And as such, you must be here for answers."

"Should we do introductions first?"

"You are Raine Thoren. A chosen Valkyrie and an Asgardian by blood."

"And you are Thor, son of Odin."

CHAPTER
TWENTY-THREE

hor chuckled. "Well done. That makes me a very distant relative of yours."

"Well, you don't look a day over forty."

"I am what your mind projects me to be."

"What do you know of the assassin, Jörmungandr?"

As Thor ambled along the riverside, Raine walked beside him.

"He is an agent of Hel."

"Agent of Hell?"

"Hel. Or Helen—ruler of the Underworld. Of Helheim. She's amassing power. She aims to bring an army of undead upon Midgard."

Raine thought of one of the Noble prophecies:

> *The end shall come*
> *Hell's will be done*
> *Blood flows until war's won.*

Thor continued, "In the meantime, she's purposefully breeding the most diabolical bloodlines to undo the dilution of time."

Raine knew vaguely of Helen but hadn't realized the woman's breeding scheme or plans for global destruction. Raine's stomach knotted. "She's making stronger beings and an army of undead? When will she strike?"

"There is time."

"Time to stop her?" Raine's mind spun. Her objective all this time had been to stop Jör, as she had stopped other evil beings. If he was only the puppet of something bigger, how much stronger was the woman in charge? And how many other agents of evil did Helen have who were equally as difficult to kill?

"Perhaps," Thor replied.

But Raine wasn't alone. She was part of a larger organization. She would need to see what the Council of Mjölnir knew of this woman. Meanwhile, Jör was killing Vanir who possessed the magic of prophecy.

"Helen's trying to hide something by killing prophets," Raine said.

Thor nodded. "She believes they pose a threat should their revelations unveil her plans."

She wondered if that was possible, given how nondescript the Noble Prophecies were.

"If Helheim was destroyed during Ragnarok like the other realms, how is Hel still in existence?" she asked.

"Just as you are descended from me, Helheim descendants also walk Midgard."

"So, she's mortal?"

"Mortal, yes. But her strength grows. And she is no less a formidable adversary by present day magical powers."

Raine considered this. She knew all magic of the Nine Realms had been diluted over time, so no one today was as powerful as gods of old, but by comparison to modern day mortality, some were very strong.

She blew out a breath. "Okay. One problem at a time. How do I defeat Jör?"

The burly Asgardian stopped and turned toward her. "You have the power within you."

"Oh-kay. Well, he bested me twice, so how do I access that power for our next encounter?"

"That, I can help with. In fact, things are already set in motion."

"What things?"

"Every Valkyrie needs three things: acceptance of her role in the battle against good and evil, a weapon equal to her in power in might, and love."

"I have acceptance, and I have a gun."

"You couldn't have made this trip if you didn't have love—love for family, love of a man, love of mankind. It can be any or all of these so long as it runs deep."

Raine thought of Will but also considered her family a source of deep love.

"And a weapon?" she asked, suspecting he must be referring to something other than her hubble-made device.

"There is a dwarf—Brok Waldorf—who lives in New Jersey. He is making you a weapon."

"I have a gun. I barely slowed the snake down with a bullet. Regardless of the type of weapon—gun, knife, ax, arrow—I still have the problem of being fast enough and strong enough."

"You already possess the skill and speed you need. This weapon will help you harness them."

Raine's eyes widened in realization. "Like Mjölnir did for you?"

Thor smiled. "Like my hammer. Except carrying a hammer around with you isn't exactly inconspicuous. It was not in my time and certainly is not in your time."

"What then?"

"Like I said, a weapon to harness the energy within you— tailored to your needs."

She narrowed her eyes at Thor. "You don't know what it is."

He shrugged. "No idea. But Brok possesses ingenuity. It will be what you need it to be." He raised a large hand and gestured to the river. "You may enter the river and return from whence you came."

"So, am I a Valkyrie now?"

Thor chuckled. "That is up to you, not me."

"What does that mean?"

"You have to be receptive to becoming one. You have to accept your destiny, embracing it as a gift."

"A life of fighting evil is a gift?" There was an edge to her voice when she considered everything she'd been through.

"Events, good and bad, in your life have happened *for* you, not *to* you. You need to see them for the person they have made you become, whether or not you perceive those events as good or bad. They are part of you, but they do not define you. You have to decide how you want to define yourself based on those experiences."

He gestured toward the river. "You can harden and stiffen in the river of experience and attempt to stand or swim against a current capable of cutting through rock over time. Or you can flex and bend and ride the river, letting all of the pain and hardship and love of life flow over you without crushing you."

His words and the truth behind them sent chills along her skin. He'd given her much to contemplate.

"I have more questions. I need to know about Helen."

"In time."

"What about Jör? How do I find him?"

"Speak to Will Decker about it. He has within him the power to find others. Just as his ring harnesses the Bifröst for travel, so too does he have a minor form of Heimdall's ability to *see*." Thor walked away from her, a curtain of thunderstorms ahead of him.

Will? A descendent of Heimdall? She thought of his ability to transport and how the colors of the rainbow shimmered around him. The Bifröst was depicted in literature and art as a rainbow bridge. Will was as much entwined in this supernatural future as she was.

"What if I need to find you again?" she asked Thor.

"Then find me again," he said matter-of-factly. "Be wary of the journey back," he added. "Take the middle of the three rivers, and you will arrive at the destination of your choosing."

She looked once again at the tree. She didn't want to half-starve and nearly dehydrate herself to death to find answers. Especially when the few answers she'd retrieved had bred more questions than a pair of mating rabbits.

Still, Thor had given her hope. She could defeat Jör—with the three components. Acceptance. A weapon. Love. For now, Helen would have to put on the 'evil beings to deal with later' list.

Raine leapt, plunging feet first into the current of cool water. It spun her like laundry in a washing machine, once again disorienting her to which way was up. She swam as her lungs burned for air.

She opened her eyes, searching the swirling waters and bubbles around her. Up ahead, the river forked in three directions. She was set on a course to the middle.

A destination of her choosing.

She would choose to be back with Will, but first, she needed to let Usha know she had succeeded. Back to her car and then back to the ranch house she would go.

"You will not stand in my path!" A woman's voice, raspy and jagged, cut into Raine's mind.

Something large swept through the water and collided with Raine, knocking her off course. She was thrown into the tributary on the left.

WILL STEPPED onto the porch and knocked. "Raine?" He had tried calling her, and when he got no answer, he tried transporting directly to her. He hadn't been able locate her, which he found more than a little disconcerting. His power was under-used and under-developed, so perhaps it was his own fault he couldn't find her, but he'd had no problem finding Sky the other day.

Instead, he used Raine's PO Box number to narrow the search and then looked for homes belonging to a woman whose first name was Usha, Raine's boss.

Boards creaked from within the house, accompanied by the sound of slow shuffling, until a woman opened the door. She was short and shriveled as a raisin.

"I'm Special Agent Will Decker with the FBI. I'm looking for Raine Thoren."

She craned her neck back to smile up at him. "I thought you might one day arrive on my porch. Come in. Come in." She threw the door wide.

The ranch-style house had a broad living room trimmed with beige and rust-colored decor of sunsets and wild prairies.

"I am Usha Bakshi."

"Is Raine here?"

She gestured for him to have a seat on the couch. When he did, she poured him a glass of lemonade from a pitcher on her coffee table. He accepted but didn't drink, waiting for her to answer.

Usha took an inordinate amount of time to sink into a recliner three-sizes too large for her. He wondered how she would get back out again.

"Raine is on a spiritual quest. She needs to connect with her ancestors so she can transition to become a true Valkyrie and have the power to defeat Jörmungandr."

"Why wait until now? She's faced him twice now and nearly died twice." Out of sorts because he hadn't been able to speak with or locate Raine, he wasn't his usual polite self to this woman he'd only just met.

"The heart and soul must be ready for the transition. She wasn't ready until now." At his scowl of confusion, Usha continued. "She was adrift until your partnership and this quest gave her purpose. And you, yours."

"Quest?" He felt edgy. The sensation wouldn't resolve until he saw Raine, which irritated him further at the irrationality of it. He didn't want to be clingy in a relationship.

"The quest to stop Jör. One of her many."

"I know my purpose. I've been with the Bureau for a decade."

"That is your job, not your purpose."

"My purpose then is—what?—to join this shadow league?"

"Shadow Guardians," she corrected mildly. "But no. You will remain FBI, and your partnership with Raine will help turn the tide of the war."

"What war?"

"All in good time."

But he knew the answer. Usha was referring to the same war to which the Noble Prophecies referred. Will's head was spinning at the magnitude of it all, but more pressing matters needed to be handled first. The longer he delayed finding Raine, the more this strange angst expanded within him.

"Where is Raine?"

"On her quest."

"I can't sense her. I need to know how to find her." His left hand reflexively went to his right ring finger.

"The spirit walk is not a place with time and space. You can use that trinket?" she asked.

"The ring? Yes."

"Then you are a descendent of Heimdall—all-seeing, all-hearing guardian of the Bifröst. Your ring was forged from the rainbow bridge itself. You can use it to travel, but within you is the ability to find people. Reach into your mind's-eye and your heart and find Raine."

Usha's words resonated to his very core. He'd always sensed a faint supernatural ability to find people. As a child, he'd always won hide-and-seek. As an adult, he'd always found his bad guy, though he'd chalked it up to intuition rather than being descended from a godlike entity. Even before he'd received the call from local PD about what building Jör had entered, Will had known in what city he was lurking.

Will had the sudden sensation like a ghost walked over his grave. He sucked in a breath as he gripped the edge of the couch with one hand. The lemonade in his other hand shook.

"What troubles you?" A flicker of alarm crossed Usha's wrinkled features.

"Raine. She's back. She's hurt."

With surprising speed, Usha pushed out of the chair and stood by his side. "Take us to her, now," she said sharply.

Setting down his drink, he nodded and stood as he placed one hand on her frail shoulder. "It takes me a moment to focus." He wasn't comfortable attempting to use his abilities in front of a woman he'd only just met, even if she seemed to know more about him than he knew about himself.

She nodded. "Find her now."

Will closed his eyes to focus on Raine as the gnawing at his insides turned into a burning sensation in his gut. Had something happened to Raine? He had to locate her.

Focus, Will. An image of her came to mind—Raine with wide, brown eyes, long golden hair, and a radiant smile. Then, instead of the vibrant woman he knew, he saw her lying unconscious on the ground. Her surroundings were barren but not desert. He looked around at the columns of earth and the red hue of the dirt. Badlands!

Heimdall. All-seeing.

On an exhale, he dug deeper within himself and transported to her.

Raine was in a heap on the ground, somehow soaking wet in the middle of a dry desert. Will removed his hand from Usha as he knelt to look at Raine. Pulling her into his arms, he brushed strands of hair out of her face.

Don't be dead, he prayed.

Her chest rose and fell in small breaths. Two fingers to her neck revealed a slow, wispy pulse. Once again, he felt like he was holding her in his arms while her life hung in the balance.

"Talk to me Raine." He held her close. "What the hell is this?" he demanded of Usha.

Her brows were wrinkled with worry. "I don't understand. No one has come close to death on a dream walk."

"You mean a *suicidal walk*."

"Guardians go forth and they return with knowledge. Usually dehydrated and hungry, but they return. I don't know how she didn't make it back to my ranch."

"Let's get her back. She feels hot and she needs fluids."

Usha rested a hand on his shoulder as he clutched Raine to him. Closing his eyes, he focused back on the ranch in Montana.

TWENTY-FOUR

Raine gasped for air and flailed.

"Raine. Raine."

She felt a hard surface around her and the sensation of shallow water. Blinking her eyes open, she saw a familiar face.

Worry etched Will's expression.

"Will?" She looked around, finding herself in Usha's ranch house bathroom. The 1980s pink floral wallpaper was an eyesore. "How did I get here?" She pushed herself up so she was sitting in the tub. She looked down at her soaked t-shirt and jeans.

Will released her and leaned back on his knees while crossing his arms. "Because I found you half dead, lying in the Badland's prairie. Are you okay?"

"How'd you find me?"

"The same way I found Sky."

"Your ring." She picked up a nearby hand towel and dried her face. "I did my dream walk."

"What the hell happened out there? Usha said no one has ever almost died from a dream walk. She was as shaken as I was to find you unconscious."

She drew back from him, confused by his raised voice. "I was knocked off course."

Will pushed to his feet and paced the room, running a hand through his hair and taking a ragged breath. When she stood up, he handed her a towel. As she dried off, she stepped out of the tub.

"You need a minute or can you tell me what happened?"

She wrapped the towel around her and took a steadying breath. "I need a minute. You look like you need five."

On an exhale, he sat on the closed toilet and put his head in his hands. "You were lying on the ground, and I thought you were dead. I'm trying not to be overprotective, but I thought I'd lost you. Again. I thought I didn't get to you fast enough. You were overheated, so I brought you to the tub and placed you in cool water. That's when you woke up."

His vulnerability melted her heart. She placed a hand on his hair and sunk her fingers into its soft thickness. "I'm sorry I worried you. That wasn't my intention. I got my answers. Safely. Until the trip back. I'm not sure what type of existential location I'd been at, but I was traveling back by way of a river when—Hel—Helen knocked me off course."

"Helen? Hel? The character from the Noble Prophecies?"

Raine nodded. "I didn't see her so much as *feel* her. She was furious and screamed about not letting me stand in her way. She's powerful, Will. I would have died of dehydration if you hadn't found me—because of her interference, not because of the dream walk itself."

"So, this is what we're up against."

Will stayed seated and wrapped his arms around Raine. Her color looked infinitely better compared to when he'd found her lying in the middle of nowhere. The pressure in his chest eased.

"I don't know how many more times I can stand to see you on death's door."

"I've been doing dangerous things alone for a long time. I've never been injured this badly in such short intervals, but I wouldn't have survived without you. I'm not giving up. I hope that you're not about to ask me to."

"No. Of course not. But can you understand that I care about you and even that scares the hell out of me? Can you understand I might be overprotective until I make sense of these feelings?"

"I can understand that."

She pressed his head into her chest, and he listened to the steady beat of her heart.

"I can tell you what I saw. What I found." She ran soothing fingers through his hair.

"Okay." He didn't let go of her for several beats longer.

Pulling away, he rubbed at the worried ache in his chest which hadn't yet dissolved since seeing her unconscious on the ground. Especially since he'd feared he wouldn't have the chance to tell her how he felt.

"There's a special weapon I need to collect," she said. "It's supposed to help me defeat Jör."

Will stood and looked into her big brown eyes as he rubbed her arms on the outside of the towel. There was more he could see that she had to tell him, but he wouldn't press her now. He'd already let her see his anger, and he'd never showed anger or possessiveness like this to a woman. Was he suffocating her? He needed to give her space and contain his emotions.

Will took a step back. "Let's get you some food and water."

"Will?" Raine took a step closer. "Thank you for coming to get me."

This time, when he looked at her oval face with rose-colored cheeks framed in strands of wet hair, something inside him shifted. In that instant, he understood he'd always come to get her—no matter where she traveled. His life of solitude had ended, giving way to something better, richer. She wouldn't face demons alone any longer. Jör was neither the first nor last foe Raine would challenge, but he was the last creature she would ever have to fight alone.

"We're partners," he said.

She looked down and nodded.

Touching fingers to her chin, he lifted her gaze to meet his eyes. "And I love you."

She gaped at him. Her surprised reaction made him smile. He hadn't planned on making a statement so bold—least of all in an atrociously pink bathroom after she'd nearly died—but perhaps the best confessions were the ones made spontaneously.

He dropped his hand and turned toward the bathroom door. "C'mon, Valkyrie, we've got a bad guy to catch. We can discuss the intricacies of having a relationship over a meal."

"By intricacies you mean more rules?" She gave a wry smile.

He turned and grinned. "Hell, yeah, we need more rules. I'm in uncharted territory here. Not only am I in love with a remarkable woman, but she's a kickass, son-of-Thor warrior with some sort of wicked destiny where Odin only knows will lead. And apparently I'm a descendent of Heimdall."

"Usha said that?"

"Yeah, but you don't look surprised."

"Thor told me. Well—dream Thor. He said you'd be able to find Jör."

"First, you fill me in on that dream walk, then we'll formulate a plan."

"First, I want water and sex."

He arched an eyebrow at her.

"You just spontaneously told me you love me. I need to be naked with you now."

He smiled and pulled her into his arms as he activated the Bifröst ring to take them back to his place. "Your wish is my command."

RAINE SET the table as Will cooked steaks and simmered vegetables. They moved around each other with ease, and she found the domestication of working in the kitchen together soothing. After lovemaking, they'd returned to Montana.

"A magic weapon?" Will asked.

She had relayed everything Thor had told her. "He didn't call it a magic weapon, but he said it would help me harness my power—allow me to become faster and stronger."

Will added garlic salt to the asparagus in the pan on the stove. "So, a magic weapon."

"Yeah, I guess so." She straightened the silverware on the cloth napkin.

He stirred the vegetables. "Once you have your weapon, I'll try to locate Jör. We then use the element of surprise. I'm thinking full body armor would be nice this time as well. We'll be slower, but at least no one has to worry about a brush with death."

"Perhaps." She uncorked a bottle of Pinot to let it breathe.

Usha entered the room and took a seat at the table. "Smells delightful."

"We were just discussing my dream walk. I'm supposed to get a weapon imbued with powers from a dwarf named Brok Waldorf." Raine poured the wine.

Usha nodded. "He's the only one in the country with uru."

"Uru?" Will asked, turning over the pieces of asparagus.

"We also call it Asgardian ore, though some say it didn't originate there either." Usha sipped her wine.

"I thought it was so strong it could only be molded by the power and energy of a star?" Raine placed water glasses on the table.

"Perhaps 'where there is a will there's a way,'" Usha said.

Will came over next with a steaming plate of the long, slender vegetable. Raine went to the air fryer and checked on the steaks. She pulled out the tray as the machine beeped. Cutting into the center, she could see they were a perfect temperature and the outside was nicely crisped with a layer of seasoning.

"Um. I'm going to need mine cooked a tad more." Will leaned over her.

"Really? These are divinely medium rare." She arranged them on a serving platter.

"You may be a transplant to Texas, but you clearly like red in your red meat. I don't like mine mooing." He plucked a steak off the plate and plopped it back into the air fryer.

"These are *medium* rare. Not rare. Wait. Do not tell me you like your steak well done. That could be a deal-breaker in our relationship."

"Medium." He started the timer.

"Whew." She grinned at him as he gave her a peck on the cheek.

A few minutes later, they fixed plates and sat down to eat.

"I'd like to know more about the war you mentioned," Will said to Usha. "The war from the Noble Prophecies."

She nodded as she chewed and swallowed. "There is the ongoing war now, in the shadows. And there is the coming war. In uncovering Becky Noble's work, you have found the first written documentation of the prophecies. The Council of Mjölnir will scour the text for clues." She took another bite, chewed, and swallowed. "Legend speaks of three sisters who battle Hel, fighting her to preserve mankind and mixed bloodlines alike."

Will glanced at Raine. "Three sisters?"

She shook her head at his unspoken suggestion. "Three chosen ones. Not three misfits. Storm and I can fight, but Sky can't. I can't even defeat one Midgard serpent, much less the forces of Hel. And I don't even know how to contact Storm. She just shows up when she wants to. The three of us aren't some force to be reckoned with, as described in the prophecies I've read."

Will looked unconvinced, which was flattering but not realistic.

After a bite of food, Raine said, "Let's talk next steps. Magical weapon. Practice with said weapon. Then find Jör."

TWENTY-FIVE

Raine held Will's hand as they stood on Usha's porch. They wore their matching agent outfits—navy suits.

"Ready?" he asked.

"Ready." She wanted to enjoy the experience of magic travel with Will again.

He smiled at her as the world around them shimmered into iridescent red, orange, yellow, green, blue, indigo, and violet. Slowly, a house materialized nearby.

"Amazing," she said, on an exhale.

"The travel? Yes. This place, not so much." He frowned as he looked around them.

Brok's house rested on a few acres of unkempt land. Several cars and trucks sat in disrepair on cinder blocks surrounded by untrimmed grass and overgrown bushes. A wooden workshop lay off to one side of the property.

They walked to the front door and knocked.

A short, burly man answered the door, a shaggy beard draping down his dingy overalls. "*Son of a Frost Giant*," he swore jovially in a thick Jersey accent. "You even look like you're the offspring of Thor." Apparently, he'd been expecting her.

Raine extended a hand. "Raine Thoren."

"Brok Waldorf." He shook her hand, smearing grease on her fair skin.

"This is Will Decker, my partner." The title seemed woefully inadequate for what Will was to her, but it suited them for a professional interaction.

Will nodded, but apparently noticing the man's dirty hands, opted not to offer a shake.

Raine wiped the smudges on her navy slacks.

"Let's go to my workshop." Brok nodded in the direction of a wooden building nearby, which was both larger and in better condition than his house appeared to be.

He spit brown liquid into the grass as he led the way. Will shot Raine a raised-eyebrow look, obviously questioning the validity of this man having created some fantastical weapon for her.

They followed Brok into his shop, or more accurately his forge, complete with an enormous fire, large bellows, and worn metallurgical tools. The temperature inside felt thirty degrees hotter than outside.

Brok adjusted the snuff tucked inside his lip with his tongue. "So, a Vanir came to me six months ago and said a Valkyrie would knock on my door. And that you'd be needing a weapon."

"Who did that?"

"Uh. Name was Darren Willis."

Raine blanched. He was one of Jör's victims. She glanced at Will, whose brow furrowed.

Brok continued, "I already had Asgardian iron from Avery and Jake. They've been keeping me in supply."

Raine nodded. She'd previously met the duo, Avery Swift and Jake Folkvar. She was a computer programmer and a raven shapeshifter, and he was a UK-based Shadow Guardian. Together, they had been working for the last year to find uru all over the world, albeit in small quantities.

"How do you form the Asgardian ore?"

"Melting temperature of steel is over twenty-five hundred degrees Fahrenheit, fourteen hundred Celsius. Titanium is over three thousand Fahrenheit and sixteen fifty Celsius. Uru is five thousand Fahrenheit."

"Wow."

"To achieve that, I have to add my special ingredient." He wriggled his bushy eyebrows at her.

"Special ingredient?"

"Power." He rested a meaty hand on a large telescope device so long that one end extended through the roof of the workshop and the other end taper down to a point over a hammering table. The tripod holding it up were two inch thick steel beams.

"Okay. Power." She suspected he meant some form of magic. "That looks like a telescope."

"Concentrates the power of the sun." Will guessed.

"You got it." Brok patted the apparatus affectionately. "I call her Sunna, after the Norse god of the sun."

Will leaned in inspecting the device.

"What did you come up with for my weapon?" she asked, gazing around the room at swords, knives, shields, arrow tips, metal sculptures of different animals, equine bridal bits, and more.

Brok picked up something and held out his hand.

Raine inspected the object and cocked her head to one side. He was obviously extremely talented, based on his work lining the walls, but she said, "It's a rod."

"It's more than a rod." With a flick of his wrist, Brok extended the telescoped pieces of metal to the weapon's full length. "Worn on your waist in its collapsed form, no one will suspect it's a weapon of this magnitude. Since it's made from Asgardian ore, it won't bend, break, or chip in a fight with ordinary weapons."

Raine grasped the extended weapon and felt the weight—sturdy enough it would make a good club, but not so heavy as to tire her arm in a fight. She practiced collapsing and extending it.

She frowned. "I feel like something is missing."

"Now that you've spoken and fondled it," Brok said with a chuckle, "its biosensors are activated to you. Say 'Gungnir.'"

"Gungnir."

A spear tip shot out of one end flanked on either side by two small triangular spikes.

"Whoa." She stared at the sharp blade.

"As soon as you collapse the weapon back down, the blades will retract. You can also mentally tell the weapon to deploy the spear tip rather than saying the name."

She collapsed the weapon back down, then flicked her wrist to extend it while thinking the name of Odin's famous spear: *Gungnir*.

Faithfully, the tip snapped out of the end.

"Amazing."

"It's very you," Will commented as he watched her.

"Oh?"

"Subtle. Not ostentatious. And no one will realize it's a formidable weapon until it's too late."

She smiled. "I like it."

"Good." Brok nodded. "Now, let me show you and your partner a little something extra." He led them through the workshop and into an adjacent shed. This room contained pants and blazers.

"You have your own clothing line?" Will asked.

"Sort of. I contract this work out, because a seamstress I am not. These are bullet-resistant. I use nanotechnology combined with some of the Asgardian ore. The effect is half the weight of Kevlar and twice as effective. To be clear, if you get shot, this material will keep the bullet from penetrating skin and whatnot, but you're still going to feel like you were slugged with a fast-pitch baseball in that spot, with the bruise to prove it."

"What about knives?" Raine asked.

"Resistant. You can literally use the blazer as a shield from slashes. Swords will be different though—they won't cut the material, but because they are carrying more weight and force, you'll still feel the blunt force trauma."

Swords. That would be a new type of adversary for her. She wondered which bloodlines preferred to wield swords.

"I'd like two," Raine said.

"Wonderful," Brok said. "Cash or credit?"

"Oh, right." She reappraised her selection. Specialty weapons and defense clothing wouldn't be cheap. She hoped the stipend from the Council of Mjölnir she saved every month would be enough to cover it.

He shifted his weight. "Look, I get that there's some enormous battle coming—good versus evil bloodlines. But I've still got bills to pay. I mean, you saw my house, right?"

"Credit."

"What about you?" Brok asked Will.

"What about me?"

"You're part of this. And you're wearing a Bifröst ring, so I'm guessing you've got some of your own supernatural abilities. You need a weapon? Armor?"

"My 9mm works fine, but I am considering the armor, especially since it looks like normal clothing and not some type of skintight superhero outfit."

Brok smirked. "Are you sure? I bet the tailor could make you something skintight if you want."

"No," Will said.

The short man turned and lifted a sword off the wall. The blade was sleek, ending in a sharp point. The handle glinted gold.

"Can I interest you in Hǫfuð? This is a replica of Heimdall's sword. Uru blade with a gold plated handle."

Will's jaw went slack as he took the sword and hefted the weight in his hand. His eyes sparkled dreamily as if he was staring at a million dollar jewel.

Raine chuckled. "Looks like love at first sight."

With a lopsided grin, he lowered the sword and looked at Raine. "This is completely impractical. When am I going to use a sword? Where would I put it?"

Brok rolled his eyes as he snatched it back. "Amateurs. Look here." He pointed to the quillon. In it was an oval stone the same iridescent multicolor shade of Will's ring. "Store it in the Bifröst where you can retrieve it at will." Brok snorted. "At will. See what I did there?"

"How do I store it?" Will asked.

Brok set the sword next to the spear. "Same way all this shit works, Special Agent. Magic. Figure it out. It's not like there's a manual for everything in life."

The dwarf began scribbling down something on a piece of paper. "Go to this address to get sized. Come back here in five days to get your clothing. You can pay half now and take the baton and sword with you. Pay for the rest when you return." He tore the paper off the pad and handed it to Raine.

"Thanks." She tucked the note in her jacket pocket.

"And you," Brok turned back to Will, "should consider an enchantment so you don't run out of bullets if you plan on continuing to use that thing."

"I rarely need to discharge my gun and actually shoot people."

Brok stuck a toothpick between his teeth. "Well, we aren't talking about normal people, are we? You come back and see me when you understand the war that's coming." He winked.

Raine and Will lay in bed in a tangled heap under the covers.

"I'll never tire of us together like this."

"I love you," she said, feeling the words lift off her heart like a weight suddenly raised by a hot air balloon.

He ran a hand over her hair and twirled a strand in his fingers. "Good. Because you're the only one for me."

"I'm glad you let Brok enchant your gun."

"Everyone's convinced me being your boyfriend means I'll need to keep my weapon loaded."

She chuckled.

"Somebody has to look out for you while you're looking out for everyone else."

"Thanks, partner."

"What's the worst creature you've faced?" Will asked.

"They say you never forget your first." She frowned. "I had my first kill order eight months into my service for the Council. You're not considered a Shadow Guardian until you've completed a successful mission." She stared up at the ceiling, telling him the story she'd told no one else. "I was so excited. I was going to make a difference. Battle evil. Avenge my sister's fiancé by taking down one bad guy at a time."

She sighed and shifted her weight, feeling Will tighten his body around her, a sign she took as protective comfort.

"All of my bravado failed me, and I second-guessed my mission. He was still a person. What if I'd allowed myself to be brainwashed by a group of people with their own diabolical agenda? This was just some guy staying at a motel. He could have been a traveling salesman for all I knew, with a wife and kids. So, instead of killing him at the motel like I should have, I followed him. He drove to a house in suburbia where a woman opened the door for him."

She gave a bitter laugh. "I thought, wow, I'm so glad I didn't shoot first and ask questions later. This guy just went home or went to his sister's house or a friend's house. But I didn't leave, because something was off. I'd noticed he had a strange skin hue, a sickly orange like the color of a rotting pumpkin. Finally, I worked up the gumption to get closer to the house. And I smelled smoke. I realized the skin color I'd seen was that of a Fire Giant. Descendent of Surtr from Muspelheim."

She shook her head at the memory of how she'd let him waltz right into the home of his next victim.

"Gun drawn, I rushed my entry through the back, breaking the sliding glass door and stepping through it. The Fire Giant plowed into me, knocking my weapon aside. I could barely see for the growing smoke from a fire in the kitchen, but I fought for my life. We tussled in the living room—hand to hand with whatever we could throw at each other—vases, mirrors, books. My best efforts pissed him off more than slowed him down. I toppled a shelf on him, followed by a boot to the jaw, stunning him enough to wrap the cord from the blinds around his neck. I pulled as hard as I could."

She took a steadying breath, remembering the choking smoke, the stench of burning plastic, and the glimpse of a person unconscious on the floor of the hallway leading away from the living room. Will listened quietly, stroking soothing fingers along her arm.

"When he died, his body spontaneously combusted." The pain from the burns had been agony. She had never smelled her own flesh burning before that day. "I had second and third-degree burns from him, but fought to stay conscious long enough to leave the burning house, somehow managing to drag the woman on the floor with me."

"That must have been terrifying."

"I passed out in the grass. When I woke in the ER, they told me the woman had died—pre-fire, as there was no sign of smoke inhalation. If I'd stopped him back at the motel, she'd still be alive today."

"You were being asked to kill someone in cold blood. You didn't take it lightly. You fought like a hero. You did your best, like a hero would have."

Since becoming a Shadow Guardian, Raine had endured whispers from people about whether or not she was one of the three Valkyrie sisters who would supposedly take on Hel herself. "I'm no chosen one. Can't you see that? I let someone die. I was a coward, not a hero."

"All I see is a hero. I'm sorry for coming down hard on you before about my no killing rule. I obviously didn't understand the forces at play, and now I do. I understand what you've been up against—what you've persevered through—as a Valkyrie. You did your best, Raine."

His unwavering belief in her melted away the cold sensation of the failure she'd felt for so long.

"Can you understand why I'd rather kill the demons before they act than let them hurt someone else? There is no rehabilitation when their darker phenotype manifests. Sending them to jail won't reform them."

"I get that. Reality and my agency training aren't exactly running on the same frequency since I met you. Maybe someday there will be options for the other bloodlines... some medical way to suppress their evil urges."

"That's a slippery slope. Hubbles could just as easily turn such a medication against me."

He kissed the top of her head. "So then we keep to the shadows."

"We keep to the shadows."

TWENTY-SIX

Will sat on a mat the floor of Usha's barn, as she stood over him. He held a timer in one hand. The space had hanging ropes and ladders on one side with weights and weapons on the other. He suspected this was where Raine had trained.

She was off running the range for cardiovascular exercise and hopefully not getting knocked off course by the hand of Helen again.

Even as he tried to focus on transporting himself via the Bifröst, his mind churned, still trying to process all the radical changes in his life.

Norse bloodlines.

An evil queen of Hel.

Magic and prophecies.

A long-term relationship with a woman.

Raine wasn't just any woman. She was a powerful Valkyrie. She was one of the chosen three. Maybe she couldn't see it or refused to believe it yet, but the truth was in the Noble Prophecies and in the way Usha regarded her—the expectant mentor waiting for her pupil to realize her full potential. Will wanted to help and be supportive of Raine.

He felt an excited angst at what the future held for them. He marveled at the amazing feats the two of them would accomplish while simultaneously fearing just how dangerous life would be for them until evil was dispatched.

"Focus," Usha snapped.

Usha had impressed upon him the importance of mastering the gift given to him—the one he'd avoided using since its discovery.

"Inhale," she commended. "Take a cleansing breath and feel the positive energy course through you."

Exhaling, he expelled negative thoughts and emotions. He pressed the button on the timer and focused on transporting.

Will opened his eyes to see the front of his home and looked at the timer in his hand.

Thirty-two seconds.

After clearing and restarting the timer, he focused on traveling back to the barn.

"How long?" Usha asked.

"Thirty-two seconds out. Twenty-eight seconds back."

"A lot can happen in the heat of battle in thirty seconds. You need to get faster."

He swallowed and nodded. Repeating the process, she continued to urge him faster until he was at the ten second mark and growing fatigued. Summoning the power wasn't quite at his fingertips the way he would like it to be. He scrubbed a hand over his face.

"It's a process," Usha assured him. "Like building muscle, learning more rapid transport would take strength training in the form of consistent use."

He was tempted to use the magic now to gain insight on Jör. What if Will could catch the creature unaware? What if Jör saw him and attacked? If Will had learned anything from these weeks with Raine, it was that they were a team now. No more solo acts for him.

They would succeed against the serpent with careful planning and teamwork.

"Thanks for your help. I'll keep working on it," he told Usha.

He would probably never transport as fast as a snap of his fingers. Perhaps he could minimize it to a few seconds, like from the time Captain Kirk requested a beam up to when he landed on the teleportation pad.

That would be awesome.

WILL'S PHONE RANG. When he groaned, Raine chuckled.

He untangled himself from her long, smooth body and plucked his phone off the dresser.

"Hello, Powell."

"Will, are you still in the Houston area?" his boss asked.

He glanced around at his trailer bedroom. "Yeah," he lied. He certainly couldn't explain how he'd been hopping around from Virginia to Montana to New Jersey to Texas in the last few days—fighting a Midgard serpent, conscripting a dwarf for weapons and clothes, rescuing a Valkyrie from a dream walk gone wonky, sparring with supernatural weapons, and making love to the most amazing woman in the world.

"I need you to drop by an address in Springville and check it out. Someone accessed an email account at that location linked to prior cybercrimes. You're the closest."

Will was puzzled. There were hundreds of FBI agents in Texas. Perhaps they were closest or perhaps Caroline was choosing them for a reason. "Yeah, we can do that," he agreed hesitantly.

"The person linked to that email is wanted by the FBI and CoM. I'll text you the address." Caroline disconnected the call.

Will rolled over and wrapped his arms around Raine as she

attempted to climb out of bed. She let out a surprised laugh as he pulled her back down.

"Will!"

He embraced her and nuzzled her neck.

"Work beckons."

"Fine," he grumbled, nibbling her ear. "Breakfast first."

"How about breakfast with my parents?"

"Done." He pressed his naked body against hers. "When can I get you in that hot tub of theirs?"

"Uh—" She squirmed nervously. "Maybe when they're not home and we don't have an assignment to complete?"

He let her go, feeling a pang of worry. When would they ever *not* have an assignment? With a war coming, probably never.

RAINE PARKED her father's truck on the patchy driveway of rock and dirt. Two trailers sat in an isolated stretch of land, barren but for the overgrown Bermuda grass. One trailer home was a long, beige doublewide. The second, a smaller silver trailer, the kind that people attached to trucks for cross-country vacations, sat askew to one side of the trailer home.

"Which one do we check first?" she asked, adjusting her Kevlar vest. After the incident at Priddy's they'd agreed to wear vest until their armor from Brok was ready.

Will stood listening a moment, so she followed his lead and looked for signs of movement—a curtain moving aside or door opening. A soft cry, perhaps part wail, sounded from the smaller, silver trailer.

Weapons drawn and on high alert, they approached the silver bullet. The door was secured from the outside with a padlock, but on inspection, it was unlocked. Did that mean whoever was whimpering on the inside was a kidnap victim? Or bait for a trap?

Raine extended a hand, indicating to Will she would open the door while he entered.

He nodded.

In a quick motion, she yanked the door handle down and swung it wide as she stepped out of his line of sight.

"This is the FBI. We have reports of unusual activity, and we're entering your trailer. Put your hands above your head!"

She barely suppressed an eye roll. She would've preferred to go in covertly, but she needed to accept that Will would always put his badge and civil liberties ahead of his own personal safety.

He advanced up the steps and into the trailer, Raine covering his back. The interior of the trailer had been completely gutted, leaving no kitchenette and no bed. There was a bathroom and a small fridge but nothing more.

On the floor lay a young man, perhaps twenty, with dark waxy looking skin. Long dreadlocks obscured his face. He wore blue jeans and a baggy, holey shirt. The room smelled sour like days' old body odor mixed with mildew, and Raine wondered how long this man had been trapped in here with a chain bolted to the floor around his leg.

Looking around, she saw no sign of a nearby weapon, so she holstered her gun and knelt beside him. "We're here to help. Are you hurt?" Raine lifted a hand and brushed the dreadlocks out of the man's face.

Will had reached for his phone and was now giving a 9-1-1 operator their location and a request for an ambulance.

The young man on the floor looked up at her with a pair of glazed eyes, and despite the sadness in them, he smiled. "You're an angel."

"What's your name?" she asked.

"Dune." His body flickered and morphed, causing Raine to jerk back in surprise. One moment he was human and the next he became a stag with dark, reddish fur and a pair of three-pronged branching antlers, while still lying on the floor.

Still shackled.

Will disconnected the call and gaped at Dune. "Are you seeing what I'm seeing?"

The young man flickered back into a human form.

"He's a shapeshifter," she said, marveling at the transformation.

"A what now?" Will asked.

"I didn't know there were stag shapeshifters. But it makes sense."

"How is that, exactly?"

"Fenrir descendants are wolf shapeshifters and the origins of fairytales involving werewolves. Stag shapeshifters could be the descendent of the four stags who ate at the branches of Yggdrasil. The dew runs off their horns and creates rivers. Their names were Dáinn, Dvalinn, Duneyrr and Duraþrór."

Will blinked at her. "Like you said. Makes perfect sense."

She smiled up at him. "We need to get Dune out of this chain."

Frowning, Will kicked a toe at where it was bolted to the floor.

Raine rocked back on her heels. "My father's truck probably has a crowbar or something we can use to pry it loose."

Will nodded. "Yeah, if we bust it free from the floor, we can worry about removing the rest later."

He turned and walked toward the trailer door when a gunshot rang out. Raine jerked her head up to see Will fly backward before collapsing to the floor.

She instantly had her gun out of her holster as a man entered the trailer wielding a shotgun. Raine fired, but the man dove back outside the door before her bullet could strike him. She glanced just enough of his bald head, wife-beater shirt, and inky gray skin to discern he was a Dark Elf.

Raine pivoted and shot out the shackling chain holding Dune. Spinning back around, she leveled her gun at the door, waiting for the intruder. Will lay unconscious on the floor, visibly vulnerable to whatever stood at the front door. She couldn't tell if he was still breathing or not. Heart hammering in her chest, she debated her next move.

Protect her partner or protect Dune?

She couldn't simultaneously do both. She would protect the defenseless civilian. After leaping onto the refrigerator, she balanced herself as she unlatched the hatch on the top of the trailer.

Another shot rang out, and the window shattered. Raine dropped to the floor and covered Dune with her body as shards of glass blew past and over them. The Dark Elf had shot out the rear window. His next move would probably be to shove the barrel through the end of the window and fire. It wouldn't have to be accurate, because the scatter from the shotgun would hit everyone inside.

She bent to one knee and linked her fingers. "Go, go, go! I'll hoist you up. Go through the top."

Thankfully, Dune didn't hesitate as he stepped barefoot onto her hand and thrust himself up while she gave him a shove. The end of his dangling chain smacked her in the forehead, but he shot up through the hatch and out of range of the shotgun. She decided she would also exit through the hatch, but circle around and try to get a clean shot of the Dǫkkálfar.

She stepped onto the water cooler again, but this time launched herself upward and through the hatch. When she pulled herself to her knees, she saw Dune looking like he was about to jump.

"Wait." She needed to clear the danger before he leaped into the path of gunfire.

He ignored her and was in mid sail when he transformed into the beautiful stag. He was almost to the ground when she glimpsed the Dark Elf taking aim with his shotgun.

She dove off of the trailer, firing in mid-leap as the creature swept the barrel her direction and pulled the trigger. Another deafening roar from the shotgun unleashed, but this time, pain followed.

She hit the ground hard, knocking the wind out of her. Her vision blurred, but not completely. She could still see the uninjured stag running away into the distance at a beautiful, unencumbered gallop. Maybe when the pain subsided, she would tell herself it was worth it.

Stunned, eyes watering from the impact, she turned her attention back to the villain who was now lying on the ground. Although she couldn't tell where her bullet had struck, the fact that he wasn't transforming into primordial goo indicated her shot hadn't been lethal.

His body twitched, then moved. He sat upright, broke open the shotgun, and loaded two more shells from his pants pocket. Chest heaving, he gulped breaths as crimson blood blossomed over the center of his upper abdomen. He probably wasn't long for this world, but if she didn't put another bullet in him quickly, he would have time to kill her before dying himself.

She could feel the weight of her gun in her right hand, but her arm didn't want to cooperate and refused to move on command.

He snapped the shotgun closed and raised to take aim, grimacing.

If only he would bleed faster.

A thunderclap roared, followed by the creature crumbling to the ground. Raine's gaze followed the sound of a gunshot to where Will stood. He'd shot the elf down like a rabid dog.

Kill shot to the head.

The body of the demon sizzled and decomposed into a black tarry liquid.

Will walked over and stared down at what was left of the corpse. "Do they all melt like the Wicked Witch of the West?"

"Dark Elves? Yes, they do that." She opted not to point out how he seemed to have surrendered his no killing rule.

Will holstered his weapon as he approached Raine. He knelt beside her. "You're a hot mess." Although his words came out jokingly, his expression betrayed how worried he was about her. He lowered his voice, "Anything I can do to help?"

She scanned him, seeing the ragged-looking front of his Kevlar and grateful their vests had protected them both from lethal shots.

"You're hazardous to my health, special agent," she told him. "I've never been stabbed and shot more than I have working with you. Just give me a minute."

"Feeling's mutual. I'm glad he had buckshot and not a slug. I hope Brok's suit is everything he claims it will be. Judging by what we're up against," he glanced at the black goo formally known as the Dark Elf who'd got the drop on him and back to Raine, "we're going to need it."

TWENTY-SEVEN

Will's chest ached with every deep breath. By the time the ambulance arrived, Raine was sitting on a tree stump and plucking pellets out of her arms before the wounds healed closed. He'd been in some dicey situations and even shot at before, but the last two weeks were unparalleled.

Although his life had never been in danger so many times as it had been around her, he'd also never felt his calling so strongly until he met her.

Usha claimed they would make an outstanding team and together could turn the tide of the shadow war. Maybe Raine couldn't see her valor and maybe she wasn't sprouting Valkyrie wings—*was that even a thing?*—but he could see she was a chosen one. If she was, if that was her calling, then he would do everything he could to support her destiny.

Dune came slinking back to the trailers in human form with dreadlocks half covering his face and his hands stuffed in his pockets. The chain still trailed behind him.

"Let the ambulance check you out," Raine said.

"Thank you. Thank both of you for saving me."

"Why was he holding you hostage?" Raine asked.

"I don't know. Every few days he'd take a blood sample."

Will and Raine exchanged glances. Somebody wanted samples from a stag shapeshifter, and Will wanted to know why.

The kid sauntered off to the ambulance, and Will pulled out his phone as he followed him. He talked the paramedic into giving Will a bottle of water bottle for Raine. After he passed it off to her, he called Caroline.

"Powell."

"That was an unpleasant surprise. The man was armed and dangerous and had a kidnapped victim in his trailer."

"Did you get them?"

Will debated how best to answer that question. *I put a bullet in his head, but I can't prove it to you because the Dark Elf turned into plant food.*

"I shot him," he said. "Probably lethal, but I couldn't chase him down since he shot Raine."

"Lordy. The two of you see more action than a Die Hard movie. She okay?"

"Yeah. Vest stopped the shotgun pellets. Caroline, we make a superb team. When we bring down the serial killer, I want your promise that Raine and I will still work together. Give us the next most bizarre case you have. We'll take it."

A long silence stretched out on the other end of the line.

"Ma'am?"

"Funny you should ask that, agent. I just got a request from the CoM asking me to farm you out to them. Tit for tat since they loaned us Raine. I was expecting to brace for a fight upon telling you, but that doesn't seem to be the case."

"I don't have any objections to helping them if the FBI approves."

"I have to be honest with you, Will. I can loan you out, but I don't know how much this is going to hurt or help your career. When dealing with a secret organization like this, you won't gain any visibility when you break a case. They don't want publicity, which means you won't get recognition."

He turned and looked at Raine, who'd finished her bottle of water and was standing, dusting off her suit pants. Her once neat ponytail was now a mess of loose strands with grass sticking out. She rocked his world and showed him all the things he was missing, including his own abilities. She'd shown him his flaws, limitations, and short-sightedness. He would still need to be careful when and where he used his powers, but he had freedom knowing he could use them for all the right reasons. She was the love of his life and they had a war to win.

"Turns out I don't care so much about recognition anymore. I just want to stop the bad guys."

As Raine walked onto a large, cushioned mat on the grass in front of Will's trailer to spar with him, his phone buzzed.

"Caroline?" she asked.

"No. It's Winston. We're invited to Thanksgiving." He started to text back and hesitated. "I know I'm new to dating, but I'm pretty sure I should ask you before accepting invitations for family gatherings."

"Yes, you should. I appreciate that. Let's do your family Thursday and my family Friday."

His thumbs moved across the screen. "Done." He pocketed his phone.

"You seem to be excited to see them," Raine said.

"We're mending. I had a good chat with Winston. We've been texting more."

"I'm glad to hear it."

"Ready?"

They wore their respective nanotechnology enhanced clothing as they circled each other. She twirled her baton in her hand. If they were going to take on this serial killer with her holding a baton-spear-thingy, she'd damn well better know how to use it.

"I wish you'd gotten the blazer instead of the vest," Will said.

"I tried the blazer. The arms were too restricting. I need free range of motion for fighting." She rolled her shoulders and flicked the baton to extend it to its full length without deploying the blades. "Besides, Brok made me forearm protection shields." She adjusted her vest and vambraces. "I'm glad Brok accepts credit cards. And I hope the Council reimburses me for this body armor. It is pretty awesome, though."

"I don't like any part of you being exposed to sharp objects in a fight." Will gripped his stick, representing a knife. He'd covered it in chalk so that each contact on her body would be marked to assess if she'd taken deadly cuts.

"Let's do this." He lunged at her with the stick, holding it like a knife and swiping left, right, up, and down.

She blocked, but he didn't give her the chance to gloat at being ready for his surprise attack. When he attacked again, she parried and swung at him in return.

They sparred, the baton clashing against the dull thud of the stick, but neither landed a blow to flesh for the first five minutes.

"You're holding back," Will said with sudden realization.

"I feel stronger since my meeting with Thor. I don't want to hurt you." She paused and stepped back from him.

"We both need to know what you're capable of. You need to practice like your life depends on it. Because it does, Raine. My life depends on it too."

Her eyes widened when he lunged at her. She pivoted and swung faster this time. He blocked but couldn't keep pace with her. Her motions felt smooth and all senses tuned to the fight.

After a few more exchanges, he was down to one knee, sweating and panting, while she felt lively and full of energy.

She brought her baton at his head, stopping a mere inch from cracking against his skull.

His mouth opened in awe and his throat bobbed in a swallow. "I'd say you're ready," he panted out the words, "but you don't need me to tell you that. By the way, can you teach me how to fight with a sword?"

She dropped to her knees and let her baton fall. She grasped his face in her hands. "I don't like fighting you that hard."

He set his imitation knife down. "We have to be ready for him. And for whoever or whatever follows after him."

"We're a team, right?" She was over him now, practically crawling into his lap.

"More than a team. Now and always."

She eased him back onto the grass, straddling him as she buried her face in his neck. He smelled of sweat, oak, and a hint of cinnamon. Her lips found his, kissing and exploring.

She had found everything she needed to take the next plunge, unlock the next level of her ability. Her destiny was to help people and stop the tidal wave of evil. She would do that with her power, Gungnir, and Will's support and love.

The kiss began slow and languid, like they were two lovers with all the time in the world and no war looming over them. When she drew back, Will's hands reached up to undo the buttons of her vest.

She slid out of it and her shirt.

Will licked his lips and he pressed his hands against her bare skin. "I've died and gone to Valhalla."

"Not on my watch. But we're going to take a little trip to heaven and back."

His caressing hands had her ready for more. She undid the buttons of his jacket, needing to touch his firm skin. They kissed again, slow and teasing, coaxing moans out of each other. She'd never made love outside under an autumn sun, and she would make sure to relish every moment of this.

The realization he was letting her set the pace thrilled her. Whatever she wanted was hers for the taking. She wanted all of him... a thousand times over.

When she moved away and finished undressing, he mirrored her moves, then she crawled back on top of him, kissing her way along his chest until their lips met again. After another deep kiss, he hooked his arms around her and rolled her onto her back on the mat. He nudged her thighs apart gently with his knees before moving his body lower.

His mouth kissed, licked, and sucked its way lower until he was making love to her with his tongue and fingers. He brought her to the edge of ecstasy, where she reached for him and begged him to take her.

When he plunged inside of her, she raised her hips to meet him. Her eyes locked on his, loving his honed focus on her.

He gave her a devious grin as he activated his Bifröst ring, just enough so their immediate surroundings became a dance of brilliant colors.

"I love it," she said.

"I love you."

"More." She dug her fingers into his hips in encouragement.

He gave all of himself, his love and climax pouring into her as her orgasm rocketed through her, made all the more dazzling by the rainbow around them. They finished the last sublime thrust with bodies tight together and mouths locked in a hard kiss.

CHAPTER

TWENTY-EIGHT

Raine stood beside Will, holding his hand as he concentrated. "I see him," he said. "I can see him! He's walking through the woods as if he's stalking someone."

"Can you see who?"

"I can kind of back away and take in an aerial view, but there are so many trees. There's a clearing. Shit! Oh, shit! There's a family at a picnic table. Jör is closing in on them. We need to go now."

"I'm ready. When we arrive, you get the family out of there." She didn't want a repeat of Noah Priddy.

"Okay. I'll get them to safety. Time to shine."

Will began shimmering—glistening and watery rainbow colors. His beauty stole her breath. Around them, the trailer room faded and trees came into view. Tall pines loomed over the picnic table. Walking trails spread like tendrils out from the clearing.

Loud gasps emitted from the family seated at the table at the sudden appearance of two people arriving via rainbow.

"It's okay," the woman said to the man and two children. "It's them. They're here to help."

One of the kids, a girl of about six, whimpered softly as the father drew them nearer.

Raine pulled out her collapsed baton but not her gun, since she didn't want to panic the family and cause them to flee in terror from the two people there to save them.

To her right, the underbrush ruffled. "Will!"

"On it." He released her hand and stood near the table, addressing the woman. "We need to get you and your family to safety."

"I know," the woman said. "Everybody hold hands," she instructed her family.

Raine turned her attention to the rustling leaves-and flashes of reddish skin approaching. She extended the baton to its full length and braced for a fight.

Will placed a hand on the man's shoulder whom he suspected was the father. The mother evidently possessed the visions, as she was the calm voice of reason and surprisingly not stupefied by the magical appearance of two people at their picnic. He was still learning about the supernatural world, but even those with powers might be leery of magic they hadn't yet seen.

Usually, Will would introduce himself as an FBI agent and instantly earn the trust, respect, and cooperation of civilians. But this family probably didn't give a flip about his government credentials; he was wanted for his supernatural abilities.

"We're going somewhere safe. You'll see rainbow colors. Doesn't hurt at all." With that, he focused on taking them to Usha's farm. It occurred to him that if they were going to be rescuing people as part of this supernatural cold war, they would need to come up with a better plan for accommodations.

Colors shimmered around them as Will fought to keep his focus. He couldn't let worry over Raine distract him—even when he could hear the metal scrape of a blade against her baton. He trusted she could handle herself for a few minutes without him. She was stronger and faster than him, but abandoning his partner—however briefly—felt wrong... which was a reflection of his own insecurities.

The overcast sky drizzled a light snow flurry onto the grass and barn.

"You're in Montana. There's a very nice lady in that house who has hot chocolate and cookies. I have to go help my partner. When I return, I'll take you back home."

"Thank you. Thank you." The woman shook his hand vigorously. "I knew you'd come. Knew you'd save us. I had a vision. That creature—he isn't normal."

"Part Midgard serpent," Will said, as if that explained anything.

But she nodded and took a step back. "Thank you."

Will backed away until he was inside the barn. Stepping onto the mat, he pulled out his gun, knelt, and drew a breath in to focus.

BEHIND RAINE, Will and the family huddled together. She turned her senses forward, listening and watching with baton extended and ready in one hand and gun now in the other.

A hiss preceded a lightning-fast strike. Jör's blade sliced through the air. She blocked three strikes before the creature tried to sail over her. As he sprang into the air like an uncoiling snake, she struck his kneecap with her baton.

The impact gave a satisfactory crunch, indicating the snapping of bone or ligaments.

Jör cried out, hitting the ground in a crumpled heap. Before Raine could strike again, he was back on his feet, though unsteady on one leg. His eyes darted from the vanishing rainbow of his target to Raine.

He jerked right, making a clear move to pursue Will and the family. Raine didn't know if uninvited guests could simply tag along with one of Will's shimmers, but she wouldn't find out today.

She fired her gun. The loud shot reverberated through the forest as Jör's body spun away from the picnic table when the bullet hit his left shoulder.

The creature screamed as Will and the family fully vanished. Angry blood-shot eyes focused on Raine. Blood trickled down his left arm as he limped toward her, hissing and wheezing.

"Valkyrie," he sneered.

His next attack seemed only minisculy slower in spite of his injuries, but Raine felt her own power pumping through her veins, making her fast and agile. Even better, when his blade skimmed her suit, Brok's body armor protected her.

They did a sort of dance—swinging, blocking, and parrying—as the scent of moss and pine filled the air from their contact with the ground and low branches.

She felt quick and smooth with the honed focus of years of practice and experience in combat combined with the new power. As Thor had suggested, she had accepted her destiny, wielded a magical weapon, and possessed love. Perhaps she was a Valkyrie. Perhaps she was ready to accept the title.

And yet, with his quick motions—thrust, slice, retreat—she couldn't get a solid shot into him. She wasted five bullets. And despite striking his limbs with her baton, she couldn't land a debilitating blow.

Finally, her baton struck his forearm with enough force he dropped his blade. She moved to aim the Glock, but he high kicked into her shoulder.

She stumbled back on a rotting log, falling backward and losing hold of the gun. She took the fall into a roll and disappeared beneath the underbrush.

Rising slowly, she worked to steady her breathing as she melted into a tree trunk. Quietly, she watched Jör bend and retrieve his knife as he scanned his surroundings. His heavy breathing and perspiration reminded her he was mortal. She could win this.

Her gun was gone—hidden in the underbrush—but she had Gungnir.

To her surprise, Will dropped out of the sky, landing directly on Jör. His gun fired a split second before the serpent spun and flung him away. Crimson blossomed on Jör's shirt where Will's bullet had struck his shoulder.

Jör hissed before launching himself at Will, who was pushing to his feet.

Raine shoved off the tree, springing forward while thrusting the spear and commanding the blade to jut forth. She sunk it to the hilt into Jör's skull, and he crumpled to the ground.

"Are you okay?" Will asked.

She pulled her spear back out and kicked the knife away from Jör. "I'm okay. Your distraction was timed perfectly."

"You were amazing." Will bent over the body, placing two fingers on the creature's neck. "I could see the two of you fighting from an aerial view and timed my drop. No pulse." He jerked his hand back. "And suddenly hot as a fire poker."

He stood, brushed dirt off his pants, and looked warily at the corpse. "I need to get faster at teleporting, though."

"You were perfect."

"You were, once again, kickass."

"The family's okay?"

"A little freaked out but, yeah, okay."

She looked down at Jör's body with a frown as she collapsed and stored her baton. The red skin bubbled and sizzled as steam streaked skyward. The flesh curved in on itself like a coiling snake before melting into the ground, disintegrating his clothing along with it.

Will holstered his gun. "Right. Apparently checking for a pulse was superfluous."

"This is the first Midgard serpent I've faced. Fire Giants spontaneously combust and Dark Elves turn into a primordial ooze with a little sizzle of their own—as you already saw."

"Wonderful," he deadpanned.

"It's impossible to get the goo out of clothing." She rummaged around the underbrush for her gun, found it, and holstered it.

They walked side-by-side back to the picnic table.

"Let's see what we can salvage here for the family, so maybe they don't have to come back here except for their vehicle." Will said.

Raine began packing the food back in coolers.

WILL and Raine traveled back to the Southern Montana ranch, retrieved the family, and brought them back to their vehicle.

"Your family is safe now," Raine told them.

The mother clasped Raine's hands, expression overjoyed with gratitude. "Thank you for saving us. Thank you for everything you're doing for the cause."

Will was puzzled. "If you knew Jör would come for you here, why take a picnic?"

She gave him a pitying look, as though he was one of her sweet yet simple children. "I can't run from fate any more than you can."

Her face slackened and her gaze turned distant.

> *"Three fierce sisters*
> *Asgard guardians*
> *On battleground of fire and ice."*

She blinked and took a step back. "I'm sorry about that. I unnerve most people when I have a vision. It came on so strong when I touched you." She patted Raine's hand, who stared at her in shock. "You have time. There's still time to wrap your head around everything. Thank you again." She stepped back and motioned for her family to get into the vehicle.

Will and Raine watched them drive away.

"Wow. Prophets are a little creepy," Will said.

"A little? Did you see her eyes?"

"Yeah, like she was looking right through you." He shoved his hands in his pockets. "So, three sisters, huh?"

She cast a side-long glance at him. "Yeah, yeah. Everybody thinks we're the chosen ones to fight some future battle. I get that, but I'm also going to need time to wrap my head around it, as the prophet said. I've imagined how my work is protecting my family. The thought of dragging Sky into the fray is sickening. And Storm? How do I pin her down?" She shook her head. She hadn't seen Storm since a beach vacation which Sky had managed to wrangle all three of them to a few years ago.

"You're not alone." Will stepped forward and took her hand. "I know we have an uphill challenge, but today was a win for the good guys."

She stepped into him and wrapped her arms around him. "You're right. I'm so grateful for you."

EPILOGUE

The scent of turkey, pumpkin pie, cinnamon, and nutmeg filled the air as Will entered his family's home. He held Raine's hand while they crossed the threshold, having opened the door without knocking.

Will and Raine both wore blue jeans. He sported a long-sleeve green cotton shirt Raine had told him matched his eyes, and Raine had on a blue sweater, which reminded him of the baby blue scarf she'd been wearing the first time they'd met.

"Hello?" he called jovially.

"Oh, Will's here," his mother's voice rang from the kitchen.

Walt came bounding down the hall with a cheery smile. "Happy Thanksgiving!" His eyes drifted down where Will's fingers were entwined with Raine's, and his smile widened.

"Happy Thanksgiving." Will started with a handshake and then pulled Walt into a hug.

"Raine, how are you?" Walt asked. "Good to see you again." He looked like he didn't know if he was allowed to hug her so she stepped forward and opened her arms.

"I'm good. Really, really good." She returned the hug and patted his back a few times before breaking the embrace.

Will followed Walt into the dining area where Tom was carving the turkey. "Son, so good to have you here for the holiday. Can you help Winston fetch a few more logs for the fireplace?"

"Sure, Dad." He gave Raine a peck on the cheek before walking toward the back door to find Winston. As he left, he heard his father welcoming Raine and thanking her for coming to the family event.

When Will went outside, Winston was approaching the deck stairs with a wagon of wood. He wore blue jeans, a brown sweater, and thick leather gloves stained with smears from bark and ash.

"I'll lift this side," Will told him.

"Thanks."

After getting a load onto the porch, they continued into the house where they stacked the wood on the stone slate in the fireplace. Will carried the empty wagon back outside to refill it, and Winston followed after him. "It's good to see Raine here."

"Yeah." Will left out all the things he could've said about her to his brother, not really knowing how his feelings would come across. She was the most amazing woman he'd ever met. She was strong in the face of the physical and emotional trauma, and not just because she could heal herself. She was a better, faster fighter than him, and he was okay with that. And despite all of her monumental strength, she could tell him she needed him during her most vulnerable and tender moments.

"You seem... better with her," Winston began hesitantly when they reached the woodpile outdoors. He began loading logs with Will.

"What are you trying to tell me? She completes me?" Will tried to make light of the situation because he wasn't sure he was ready for anyone to know the depths of the feelings he felt for his Valkyrie.

"I don't know anything about that. But you're lighter. Better," he repeated. "I'm glad of it. I'm not sure how an outsider seemed to bring our family back together, but we're healing because of her."

"That's good to hear. I'm not saying I'm ready for marriage, but I see her as a permanent part of my life."

In the distance thunder and darkness rolled across the horizon. Will wondered if the nimbostratus clouds were bringing snow or rain. And what about the storm the future held? Whatever they were, whatever hurtles fate dealt them, Raine and he would take them on side-by-side.

RAINE GAPED at the feast her parents had prepared. Wyatt had cooked a massive lasagna, which was accompanied by a bowl overflowing with broccoli. On the opposite side of the table was a platter heaped up with slices of garlic bread. The countertop was littered with bowls of chopped vegetables and lettuce as a make-your-own salad bar with a half dozen varieties of dressing in bottles, including Ida's homemade ranch. The scent of Italian seasonings percolated the room—basil, oregano, thyme, and garlic. Heavenly garlic.

"This looks amazing," Raine told her parents. "You know you only have three guests, though, right?"

Ida beamed. "Three of my most important guests. Besides, I was half hoping Sky would bring a man."

Sky, who was standing near a countertop pouring glasses of Merlot, rolled her eyes. "If I could keep one longer than a few weeks, maybe I would."

"Oh." Ida waved a hand with a giggle. "Raine brought a man home. We'll just celebrate that."

Raine had told her mother she and Will were officially dating now. In her mother's eyes, that seemed to suggest they were practically married. Ida was already fussing over him and treating him like family.

The evening was vastly different from Will and Raine's second visit to the somewhat more subdued Decker household. They had visited yesterday on Walt's invitation. Walt and Tom had been infinitely more civilized and even engaging enough to ask Raine about her family background. Ilene was especially relieved to hear they'd "caught" the "serial killer." Will and Raine had exchanged a look, knowing they would never share with their families exactly what they were up against.

Ida handed Raine a spatula. "Do the honors of dishing out the lasagna?"

Raine kissed Will's cheek as she walked past him while he placed filled wine glasses around the table.

"I'd be delighted," she said.

<<<THE END>>>

******BRIEF NOTE FROM THE AUTHOR******

I HOPE you enjoyed Book 1 of The Shadow Guardians Trilogy. You can sign up for my newsletter and get Raven's Flight, a prequel novella for FREE at www.cbsamet.com. In my newsletter, you'll learn about me, special discounts, and new releases. Keep reading for the exclusive novella in the paperback version of Book 1.

Raine Down, Book 1

Rosalyn's Run, novella

Storm Surge, Book 2 (releases 2.22.23)

Anka's Orb, novella

Sky Fall, Book 3 (releases May 2023)

ROSALYN'S RUN

BONUS NOVELLA

CHAPTER

ONE

Rosalyn's spy mission transformed into a rescue mission the moment she spotted the prisoner in the cage. Whoever he was, he was important enough to be locked in a plexiglass enclosure with a guard posted on the outside.

Only one guard. A man dressed in a red suit with white buttons paced the exterior in a loop around the cell. Perched on a platform off to one side, Rosalyn pondered why the room was so large yet so sparse—it could have held a dozen cubical cages, but there was only one.

One cage. One prisoner. One guard.

Something smelled fishy.

Literally.

The room had a fish odor like the docks of Belfast without the ocean breeze.

Not one to rush headlong into danger, Rosalyn watched the scene before her. The prisoner was of medium build, dressed in white scrubs, with bare feet on a poured concrete floor under laminate. The cell contained a bed, a lounge chair, a toilet with a sliding privacy curtain, and a treadmill. The set-up reminded her of a gerbil cage, only cleaner.

The man sat in the lounge chair, reading a book as if he was relaxing on a beach rather than solitary confinement. She would've gone crazy trapped in a room so small with no view of the outside world. How long had he been in there?

From a distance and with robust facial hair, she couldn't tell his age. Only that he was desperately in need of a haircut. How valuable was he to be under guard in solitary confinement in a place like this?

She watched him for several more minutes, knowing she would rescue him but wondering if he would resist. Any information he could share about Helen's operation would be invaluable to Rosalyn's organization. What if he'd been here so long he wouldn't leave? What if he slowed down her escape? What if rescuing him was a trap?

Except no one knew Rosalyn was here. Helen hadn't expected anyone to successfully infiltrate her laboratory.

Rosalyn bit her lip and grimaced. She would risk her life to free this man, hoping he wouldn't screw up her plan and get them both killed.

"All hope abandon, *ye who enter here.*"

Apollo closed his book and stared at the ceiling, through his flat glass cage roof and into the gray rafters and overhead piping. The same view he'd stared at for two years. Dante's words ought to be inscribed on a sign at this facility. Hell, maybe they were. Apollo had never actually seen the outside of this place.

Glancing at his small stack of books, his only link to sanity, he considered for the millionth time how life in a box was no life at all. Two years of no technology, of no contact with the outside world. Two years of reading the same ten books. Two years of helping his captor with her genetic misfits.

Two years and he hadn't devised an escape plan. Well, at least not a viable one. The best route was through the enormous ventilation ducts. The problem was not being incinerated by his guard on his way to or once inside those ducts. After he escaped the compound, then what? This facility could be in the middle of the desert like an oasis or the middle of an ocean like an oil rig. He had no idea.

He suspected, based on the German accents and language, that he was, in fact, in Germany. His interactions with the people and creatures, though, were his only proof.

Commotion outside his door had him sitting upright. A woman dressed in all black with a head of white hair was fighting Nid, his guard.

She came out of nowhere with a flying kick. The sneak attack sent Nid stumbling backward.

Recovering, he started swinging in choreographed motions, suggesting he had martial arts training, though Apollo didn't know which type. The woman blocked, parried, and struck with obvious superiority in skill and strength.

In under sixty seconds, she had him incapacitated with a blow to his larynx, followed by a kick to his head. She snatched the key card off his belt clip and swiped it. With a beep and click, the door to Apollo's cage unlocked.

He pushed to his feet and gaped as the mysterious woman swung it open and motioned for him to leave.

"Hop to it." Her voice was chipper, with an Irish accent, a stark contrast to the harsh German tones he'd heard for the last two years. "Are you coming?" she asked, brushing hair from her brow with impatience.

He was awestruck when he noticed her beautiful face. She had strong cheekbones and large, round eyes so pale blue they were practically gray. She rolled her r's delightfully when she talked, and "you" sounded more like "ya."

"*Sprichst du Deutsch?*" she asked when he only stared.

"No. I'm American," he stammered.

"Then get a move on. We've not got all day."

THE SHOCKED CAPTIVE followed Rosalyn out the door. She scrutinized him while walking. He was agile and with nothing in his movements to suggest he might slow them down. Good. She needed no more delays.

This close to him, she glimpsed vibrant green eyes staring at her. Judging by just a few wrinkles at the edges of those eyes, he was probably around her age, in his early thirties.

"You've no shoes?" she asked.

"I think I was lucky they clothed me."

They started toward the stairs when a low growl caught her attention. The entire room seemed to rumble and shake.

"About that…" the man's voice trailed.

When Rosalyn turned around, she saw the guard, to whom she'd most thoroughly handed an ass-whipping, replaced by an enormous, fifty-foot-long, red dragon.

Her mouth fell open. She knew about shapeshifters, hell she was one, but she hadn't known dragon shifters existed. "Jaysus, Mary, and Joseph," the swear tumbled out of her.

Ponder how dragon shifters were possible later, she decided.

She tapped her Bluetooth earpiece to wake it out of sleep mode and said, "Call Raine." Fortunately, the phone registered her command despite the shake in her voice.

The giant beast unleashed a deafening roar that echoed off the walls. When he reared his head back, Rosalyn was certain she was about to be incinerated by the first dragon she'd ever met. Instead, he hacked and coughed.

Grateful she'd struck his larynx earlier, she turned and ushered the bearded man in white up the stairs.

"Go, go, go!"

"Hello? Rosalyn?" Raine's voice came through her earpiece.

"I'm at the German Ginnungagap facility. Requesting back up."

"Do you need an extraction?"

"Depends." She gasped for breath. "If you're feeling spunky, you can take on a dragon. If not, you can zap us out of here."

"Did you say dragon? And who is *us*?"

"Yes. Fill you in on the rest later." With a faint beep, Rosalyn hung up the phone just as they reached the top of the stairs.

The dragon below snapped at them, but his muzzle was too large to reach between the handrails. He croaked again, but this time he managed to spew a streak of fire—bright red and orange and as hot as the sun.

Rosalyn screamed as the agonizing pain of something like a hot poker dove into her leg. The dragon clawed its way across the floor, closer. His blood-red scales shimmered under the fluorescent lights above.

She pulled her Sig Sauer and fired, but the bullet barely made a dent. She fired again, aiming at a different part of his body. Avoiding the use of a firearm to keep her presence quiet was a moot point after the roar of a dragon from the basement probably alerted the entire building of an intruder.

She dared a look at her charred ankle. With second and third-degree burns, she had no escape plan. She would have to stay and fight. Maybe she could hit the creature in the eye, but her aim was questionable with her hands shaking from the pain.

When she fired a third time, she hit the underside of the claw that was raking its way toward her. The dragon shrieked and drew back his limb. She made a mental note that while the scales were tough enough to resist bullets, the underside of him was not.

Another hand of claws swiped at her, but this time she wouldn't be able to avoid its wrath.

Strong hands gripped her underarms and moved her out of the path of the dragon's raking grasp. Metal screeched as his talons dug into the platform where she'd been moments ago.

A burst of rainbow light appeared in the room. Fellow Shadow

Guardian Raine Thoren and her partner, Will Decker, shimmered into the room under the beam of light.

The dragon turned angry eyes toward them.

"What in the name of Asgard?" Raine looked down at the baton in her hand as if acknowledging the weapon was woefully inadequate for the adversary she faced.

"No rocket launcher?" Rosalyn asked.

"I left it in my other trousers," Raine quipped, never taking her eyes off the enormous beast.

"*Sonofafrostgiant,*" Will swore. Gun already drawn, he pulled the trigger and saw for himself just how impenetrable those scales were.

"Underbelly!" Rosalyn called out. "And watch out for the—"

The beast unleashed another spout of flames. Raine and Will dove in separate directions, dodging the molten heat.

Strong arms dragged Rosalyn to her feet.

"Can you make it to the duct?" the man asked.

She glanced at the door she'd initially come through and saw it steaming from a spray of fire. The AC vent he referred to was fifty feet away.

"Aye, with a little help." She holstered her gun, useless as it was.

He slung her arm over his shoulder and wrapped one of his around her waist to support her. She had to hop on one leg, unable to tolerate the pain of trying to sustain weight on her injured foot, but with his help, they reached the vent.

"I've studied the ductwork. I know how to escape through it." He let her lean against the wall as he set to work, tearing the vent open.

"Then why've you not escaped?"

"Because I didn't want to be burned alive on my way to the vent."

"Fair point."

He wrenched the vent free and tossed it to the side. Climbing in, he disappeared from view.

Lowering herself and fitting inside on her hands and knees, she swore, not liking the plot twist kinking her mission—she was supposed to be rescuing him, not having to trust a stranger for her exit strategy.

At least she could manage this crawl, even if it gave her time to dwell on the devastating injury she had. She might never walk again. She might never run again. If that was the case, somebody might as well put her down.

"What's your name?" she asked. If she was going to stare at his ass in a confined, dark space while escaping a fortified research lab, they ought to at least be acquainted.

"Apollo. You?"

"Rosalyn."

She considered how they were leaving Raine and Will to defend themselves, but they were a pair of warriors—Raine was a Valkyrie and Will a descendent of Heimdall with the ability to transport. Rosalyn didn't know if they could handle themselves with a dragon, but Will could teleport them out if they couldn't.

"Let me know if you need to slow down and we'll take a break, otherwise I'll keep booking it to get us out of here. We probably shouldn't talk much, because our voices will reverberate and carry. Some of these stretches of duct run through populated areas in the facility, so tug on my pant leg if you need to signal me."

She wiped sweat from her brow before it could drip down and sting her eyes. "Unless there's a place along the way to stop for morphine and mimosas, never slow down."

CHAPTER

TWO

Heart jack hammering, Apollo moved swiftly, stopping every few minutes to let Rosalyn catch up. By her panting and grimacing, he was pushing her hard, but this was their one chance at freedom. At life.

At last, they reached the spinning turbine before the air intake vent that led outside.

Rosalyn caught up, and they were suddenly crammed very close together. Her hair was matted from sweat, and her skin was pale from pain.

"Catch your breath a minute," he told her in a quieted voice.

"This exit'll set off the alarms when we breach it," she panted between every few words. "I investigated it as an entry point for my infiltration... and decided against it."

"Then we need to be ready to run when we hit the ground."

She glanced at her burned ankle. "I think my running days are a thing of the past." Her voice held a sad, defeated tone.

"There's a reason Helen kept me captive."

"That so?" She eyed him warily.

"I can heal. If you let me, I'll heal your burns."

She blinked at him. "I'll be able to walk? To run?"

"Like new."

"G'way outta that! Why'd you not offer sooner?"

"We've been a little busy crawling away from a dragon. And there's a tradeoff."

She cocked her head to one side. "G'wan. I'm listening."

"Healing drains me. So, while you will be able to run, I won't. It might be better if I carry you to safety and wait to heal you until then."

She snorted. "You've been trapped in a cage for I don't know how long, and I'm no lightweight. You'll not be able to carry me through the forest. Heal me, and I'll give it a lash." When he blinked at her, she clarified, "I'll get us to safety."

He opened his mouth to protest but closed it at her determined glare. Although he'd been caged for two years, he'd stayed fit—the treadmill, pushups, sit-ups, and crunches. In fact, all he had to pass the time was reading, meditating, and his fitness routine. He would have to heal her and hope he had the strength to push through and escape. Also, she clearly had friends who could drop in at a moment's notice, so perhaps sacrificing his strength for hers was a wiser move.

He hovered his hand an inch above her wounded ankle and concentrated. Energy flowed from his hand to her wound in a soft, golden light. He watched as the tissue repaired itself.

Rosalyn gasped and lashed out a hand, fisting his shirt. He hadn't used his talents to help someone other than Helen and her genetic mutations in so long, he'd forgotten to warn the patient about the rush of sensation—itching and burning, followed by a quick crescendo of pain and rapid resolution.

"Sorry about the pain," he murmured.

As the magic concluded, he went lightheaded and dizzy before slumping forward, where Rosalyn caught his torso in her arms. They rested there for several minutes with his head on her shoulder, each recovering from the experience.

She rubbed her healed skin beneath the tattered and singed pant leg. "Fair play," she said in a dazzled voice.

Apollo didn't get the direct translation, but her tone sounded like a compliment.

"Oh, god, you smell amazing." The words were out of his mouth before he could think straight. Her scent was a musky lilac.

"Uh. Thanks. Um. Your beard is really, really scratchy. Think you can sit up, fella?"

Dreamily, he leaned back, noting her cheeks were rosy and her energy looked rejuvenated. "You are so damn beautiful." He clamped his mouth shut.

Was he drunk? He felt woozy, like he'd been drinking. That healing had done a number on him.

Before he attempted a coherent explanation for his words, Rosalyn was taking off her shoes. She wore pink socks covered in white horses, a stark contrast to the black outfit and warrior motif. Nid the dragon had been bested by a white-haired beauty with pink socks. Apollo resisted the urge to laugh. They weren't free and away from danger yet.

In a quick motion, she shoved one of her shoes into the turbine, followed by the second, bringing the spinning blades to a halt.

"Brilliant," he said.

"Make haste, Apollo. The cavalry doth descend upon us soon." She squeezed through first, followed by him.

He clumsily banged his head on the dull blade, adjusted, and wiggled through. When he was out, he stumbled, bumped the blade, and dislodged a shoe. The fan spun again, and Rosalyn's shoes were slung in different directions.

He groaned. "Oh, crap, I'm sorry."

She'd said they would be traveling through a forest, which meant she would need shoes for traveling. His thick soles would tolerate most any terrain, but her sock-covered feet...

She tugged on his beard, drawing his attention back to the grate separating them from freedom. "Be a dear and kick that out, will you?"

"Yeah, of course." He shook his head, trying to loosen the magical haze of cobwebs that had formed there. Bracing his hand on one wall, he reared back and kicked at the top of the vent. After two more blows, it gave way, swinging out and down with a loud racket of metal hitting brick. His feet throbbed from the impact.

Rosalyn wasted no time agilely dropping to the ground, and Apollo scrambled toward the ledge.

"Wait." She held up a hand, halting him. She pointed up. "We've company."

She stared at him a beat, as if struggling with a tough decision. "Right. When I change forms, ride me."

Ride me?

No, he surely hadn't heard her correctly.

Before his eyes, she morphed into a beautiful gray mare with a long silver main and tail.

"Stars above," he marveled. His senses were still hazy. Perhaps he'd only imagined her transformation.

She gave a snort and pawed impatiently at the ground.

"Right. Ride you." He eased out of the vent and dropped onto the back of Rosalyn's horse form, gripping her with his thighs for dear life, arms around her neck. "I've never ridden a horse before."

Like a racehorse out of the gate, she bolted as soon as shouts from above them erupted. Gun shots rang out.

Every impact of hooves on the ground jarred him and sent clumps of dirt flying behind them. If the bullets didn't kill him, this woman would.

The air was a crisp and vegetation ripe with the first sprigs of spring in the grass and on trees.

They reached the safety of the trees, tall pines, spruce, oak, ash, and maple, but she kept at a gallop, ducking limbs and jumping logs.

At last, she finally slowed to a walk. Between his thighs, her rib cage expanded and retracted in great heaving breaths. Apollo sat up and leaned back, also catching his breath, heart thudding.

"Oh, glorious fresh air." Sunlight through the trees threatened to blind him, and he embraced the beams as if heaven itself was shining down on him. "I'm indebted to you, Rosalyn. I haven't seen daylight in two years. I don't even know if you understand me, but I'm so grateful to you. Give me a sign, and I'll dismount."

She eyed him before turning her head forward as she continued to walk. Her ears moved like an adjusting satellite dish—in tune to their surroundings.

"You're still beautiful," he said, running a hand down her silky mane.

This time, she glanced back with what appeared to be annoyance. Because she didn't like him stroking her or because she did?

He smiled, knowing he was probably ridiculously imprinting on the first creature that had saved him. He knew nothing about her personal or professional life, but she had been willing to risk her life to save him, which meant he knew her character. That and her grit were enough to indulge the attraction he felt. For now.

AFTER TEN MINUTES OF WALKING, Rosalyn lowered her front torso and knelt down on one knee. She'd caught her breath, and they seemed to have left the flying bullets behind them.

"Ah, I'm guessing that's the dismount signal." Apollo slid off of her, noticeably more steady on his feet now.

She transformed back into her human form. "You grand?" She kept her words clipped, annoyed by how much she'd liked the feel of his legs gripping her as she ran. She wasn't attracted to scraggly men with who knew what enormous baggage from having been a captive of the goddess of the Underworld, even if they called her beautiful and had healing powers.

He stretched out his legs as he walked beside her. "I'm good, not sure about grand."

She pulled out her phone to call Raine. "Are you outta the building?"

"Yeah. That was a nasty surprise."

"Didn't you hear me? I said the word dragon."

"I know, but I thought maybe it was a metaphor for something. I didn't know those existed," Raine said.

"I don't think they do, naturally. I think that facility was the equivalent of Frankenstein's lab."

"What did you find?" Raine asked.

"I'll fill you in later. Can you give us a lift?"

"Lift where?" Apollo was stepping away from her, looking concerned.

"Um, Raine, hold that thought. Let me call you back." She hung up the phone, realizing she needed to deal with this man's sudden fear before he bolted. She could force him to go with her, but that would make her no better than his last captors.

"I want to take you into protective custody. I work for a group called the Council of Mjölnir. We're fighting Helen's forces." She kept her voice calm, as if talking to a frightened horse. "You were a prisoner of that poxy she-demon, Helen, right? So, you can help us."

He didn't look convinced, but she wasn't about to lose their best breakthrough in the shadow war because he ran in fear of her.

He shook his head. "You want me to jump from one cage into the next? Not just no, but hell no."

"My people are good people. You saw them in action today, risking their lives to save us."

"I want to go home to my family. My country. The US of A. I've been missing, probably presumed dead, for two years."

"Apollo," she softened her tone, but the hint of pity only amplified his look of disbelief. "Just hear me out. You go home and you've to answer for your absence. You can't expect normal humans to reasonably understand you've been locked in a dungeon in Germany guarded by a dragon for yonks. There were probably tax dollars spent looking for you, which means authorities will demand answers. Maybe you make up a story, but nothing you can substantiate under scrutiny."

"You're a bundle of good news," he said bitterly.

She sighed, hoping he could feel the sympathy in her voice. "I'm trying to set expectations for a banjaxed situation."

"A scenario which conveniently fits your agenda."

"That's a bit harsh." She pursed her lips.

He wasn't wrong, though. Her agenda was to win the war. If Apollo could help shed light on Helen's secret laboratory work, perhaps it would give the Shadow Guardians an edge they needed. Hence, she had to convince him to cooperate.

Apollo scratched his wiry beard. "I trust you. Just not your people."

She couldn't drag him along unwillingly, and telling him he had no other options was probably not how to win his friendship. Trusting her was at least a good starting point. She could work with that.

"Right. Let's start small. We'll have Will take you anywhere you want go. A weekend of getting re-acclimated to the world. Room service. A sports game. A greasy American cheeseburger with minerals and a side of spuds. Twenty-four hours of reality TV. You name it. After that, you agree to talk to the council about what you know about Helen and that facility. We can arrange it as a video chat on a secure line if you don't want to feel like a captive somewhere."

"Your word?"

She placed a hand over her heart. "My word."

"Then you'll be with me the whole time?"

"Um." She hadn't considered she would need to stay with him, but if he only trusted her, she would need to remain by his side. If keeping his trust and earning his cooperation meant staying with him during these early stages of his release from captivity, she would do it.

"Aye. The whole time until you're reacclimatized to life outside of walls."

CHAPTER

THREE

Apollo watched as Rosalyn's friends arrived in the forest through a shimmer of rainbow light. Traveling via rainbow wasn't a magic Apollo was familiar with, but he admired it. As far as he knew, no one on the side of the dark possessed traveling abilities.

Does Helen? he wondered with alarm.

He'd never seen her outside the compound, but as a descendent of Loki, perhaps she could. If she possessed such magic, could she use it to find him?

"This is Special Agent Will Decker of the FBI and Raine Thoren. She's a Shadow Guardian like me," Rosalyn said, her words disrupting Apollo's worried contemplation.

Apollo shook both of their hands. "FBI, huh?"

Will nodded, wiping moist, dark locks of hair off his forehead before shaking hands with Apollo. "One of the few who knows about the existence of the different Norse bloodlines. What about that creature holding you captive down there? That's a new one to me."

"One of Helen's many pets," Apollo explained, jaw ticking. "Nid. Descendent of the dragon who used to guard Hel's gates. If I had your transporting abilities, my life would be very different right now. How does it work?"

"Magic and the Bifröst. I can go anywhere with coordinates or I can home in on people."

Home in on people?

The thought of Helen locating him sickened him. She hoped she had no Bifröst magic.

"Is Nid dead?" Apollo asked.

Raine cleared her throat. "No. Turns out trying to fight a fire-breathing mammal, or reptile—whatever—in a confined space with no windows is like trying to do calisthenics in a super-heated sauna." She smoothed back blonde flyaway strands from her face and toward the lopsided ponytail on the back of her head.

"Yeah," Will agreed. "We didn't last long in there."

"Blimey, is that new?" Rosalyn asked as she reached for Raine's hand. She inspected the diamond on the left ring finger.

"Yes. We had a very nice dinner with Will's family, and he proposed."

Rosalyn beamed. "Congratulations! I'm happy as Larry for you. We need to celebrate over a pint."

Who's Larry? Apollo wondered.

Will turned to him. "Why were you being held prisoner there?"

Rosalyn dropped her conversation with Raine and cut in. "Apollo's been through an ordeal for the last two years. How about we give him time to decompress before a game of a hundred questions? I'm sure he'd fancy a hot shower, an enjoyable meal, comfortable clothes, and, hopefully, a shave."

Will took a retreating step back with an amused arch of his eyebrow. "Okay."

Apollo shot her a look of relief and gratitude, though he noted her mention of a shave. And she'd brought up his facial hair before. Did she dislike all beards or just his?

He hadn't given it much thought since he'd been busy surviving, but prior to captivity, he rarely grew a beard. Shaving it might be a nice beginning to his new freedom. Maybe altering his appearance would help him stay hidden.

"I can see how decompressing should be the first order of business," Raine said.

Will shrugged. "Not sure what we can get on short notice for a hotel stay. But I'll take you wherever you want—New York, Paris, maybe a spa resort out in Phoenix. Could do Las Vegas, if you're looking for entertainment."

Apollo didn't want a five-star hotel in a major metropolitan city. In fact, he wasn't sure he could handle sizeable crowds and all that stimulus after two years of solitude. "There's a bed-and-breakfast in Wilmington, North Carolina my parents went to one time. A quiet retreat on the beach would be nice."

"No problem. I can take you there and check back in a few days," Will offered.

Raine turned toward Will. "Can you take Rosalyn and I to Usha's after we get Apollo tucked in? We need to debrief about that facility."

"I need to stay with Apollo," Rosalyn said. At Raine's arched eyebrow, she added, "You can understand how a person who's been held captive in an evil lair for two years might have wee trust issues. I can't leave him with anyone else," she shot him a sidelong glance, "and I don't think he should be alone right now."

Apollo suspected there was an undercurrent to her meaning— that perhaps she considered him a flight risk and so he would be in her custody as opposed to just her safekeeping. The notion didn't bother him. He liked the idea of spending time with her, regardless of how she justified it to herself and her friends.

WILL DROPPED them at a car rental dealership about an hour away from the bed-and-breakfast where Apollo wanted to stay. Rosalyn would take time out to help Apollo get acclimated to a world without cages, but she wouldn't be confined to some sleepy house on the beach without wheels to leave when she wanted.

"Can you drive on the right side of the road?" Apollo asked when they climbed into the car.

She arched an eyebrow. "Aye, fella. If by right you mean wrong. You trusted me to get you out of that compound but not drive to the beach?"

He pulled on his seatbelt. "Just asking."

"I've traveled to sixteen different countries killing Helen's pets. I can handle a drive in the—what'd you call it?—US of A for a mere hour."

They headed south on I-40. When they hopped off the interstate, Apollo insisted on the windows being rolled down. He stuck his head out to enjoy the breeze. With all his shaggy hair flapping in the wind, the only thing missing was his tongue hanging out. Rosalyn shook her head but couldn't help smiling at his enthusiasm and pleasure in the simple joys in life.

"Oh! There's a Starbucks!" Apollo pointed. "Can we stop?"

She glanced at him and saw to her surprise that he was serious. Normally extremely task oriented, she considered this a deviation from their intended schedule to reach the bed-and-breakfast, but there wasn't any harm in indulging him. Perhaps this was one of life's little enrichments he needed to help him readjust.

She pulled into the lot and then the drive-through line.

"Can we go inside? It's so much better inside where all the aromas surround you."

She eyed him skeptically. "I'm inclined to think it'd be problematic. You've quite the resemblance to a homeless person." After she spoke the words, she grimaced, waiting for him to take offense at her lack of sensitivity.

He laughed, the rumbling sound of amusement filling the car. She startled, not remembering the last time she was around someone so filled with buoyancy. His personality was an attractive feature.

"Okay. Maybe next time," he said.

"Ah, dash it." She pulled out of line and into a parking spot. She couldn't deny him something as simple as a trip to the coffee shop. Although he looked like a Wookie in white scrubs, he was clean with a surprisingly sparkling set of teeth.

"Really?" He grinned.

"Come on, Chewbacca." She got out of the car and closed the door with Apollo scrambling after her like a kid on his way to a candy shop.

When they reached the entrance, Apollo hesitated. She couldn't tell if this was an emotional moment for him or he was afraid of walking into a room full of people. As she opened the door, she looped her elbow through his. His throat bobbed in a swallow, but the gesture seemed to give him the strength to come with her.

He took a deep breath, obviously savoring the surrounding scents.

After waiting in line, he ordered a caramel latte. She ordered a small green tea. Fortunately, no one seemed to notice his absence of shoes or her one burnt pantleg.

As they walked to the car, he held his small paper cup as if it was the Holy Grail. Eyes lit with anticipation, he raised it to his lips and took a drink. Coughing and sputtering, he stared down at the cup with a look of absolute disgust.

"Too hot?" she asked.

He rolled his tongue around as he squinted. "It's so sickeningly sweet. It's awful. I haven't had sugar in two years. I don't know if I can ever have sugar again."

"Think of the bright side. You just saved yourself five dollars from a daily latte for the rest of your life. Here, swap with me. Green tea, no sugar, to soothe your soul."

He accepted the cup. "Thanks," he said. The gratitude in his voice seemed disproportionate to the favor.

"It's just tea."

He walked over to her and hugged her. "No one has given me anything out of kindness in a long time."

Rosalyn stood stiffly in surprise, careful not to spill hot coffee on either of them. No one ever spontaneously hugged her. His body was warm and firmly muscular and invading her space. Wow, he felt good against her.

"Boundaries," she said, voice cracking. "And the scratchy beard thing."

He jerked back. "Right. Sorry. I just thought... well, I rode you, so what's a hug?"

She arched an eyebrow at him.

His eyes went wide and a blush was evident even under his beard. "Oh, god. Not rode you like... I didn't mean..."

She took a sip of the caramel latte, trying to mask her amusement at his discomfort. "Relax, Chewy. Back in the car with you."

APOLLO STARED OUT THE WINDOW, mesmerized by the trees and hills and the magnificent beauty of it all. Soon, he would smell the ocean breeze.

Freedom.

His first beverage of freedom was green tea, given to him by the woman who rescued him. It might just be his new favorite drink. His liquid consumption for the last year had consisted of water and some god-awful protein shakes that tasted like liquefied chalk—unless it was chocolate-flavored, in which case it tasted like liquefied charcoal.

"The path to paradise begins in hell."

Maybe Dante was right. Apollo had left hell and sprinted directly into paradise.

He took a sip of his tea, glancing toward Rosalyn and then back to the road. She drove relaxed and smooth, but her mind was clearly somewhere else. She probably wanted to be anywhere but babysitting someone recently released from captivity. He was grateful she'd agreed to the task. Watching over him wasn't the high stakes adrenaline rush of escaping a dragon, but he at least seemed to provide her with some amusement through his antics. He was so thrilled to be free that there was no point in trying to contain his joy and new chance at a life.

However, he might have to curb his inclination to hug her every time he got excited. She was apparently unaccustomed to displays of affection, whereas he'd grown up in the South—hugs were passed out at every greeting like candy at Halloween. Her discomfort, coupled with his near arousal at their last embrace, was probably a sufficient sign he should keep his hands off her. He would settle for conversation. Her Irish accent, though fast and sometimes a little tricky to decipher, had a melodic rhythm like chimes in a breeze.

He didn't know if his attraction to her stemmed from her being the first woman he'd spent any time with in the last two years, the fact she had risked her life and saved him, or if the sparks were genuine.

He smiled. Although she seemed entertained by some of his behavior, he didn't sense the attraction was mutual. She'd told him he was a hairy homeless man, which was accurate. She didn't have to like him back. He was satisfied knowing she was the most generous person he knew, and he adored her for it, even if all the affection was one-sided.

"What're you grinning about?" Rosalyn asked.

"I'm planning out my day. I get to *plan out my day*. Shower and then cheeseburger for dinner. Can I have a cheeseburger? I am actually a homeless man, you realize. I'm also broke. I used to have a nice savings account, a prudent six months of my salary, but I don't know if it still exists or if after a certain amount of time as a missing person your family just gets the money. In any case, I can't access it."

"Oh, for the love of all that's holy, yes," she hissed out the words, surprising him. "What the Frigg? Of course I will buy you a cheese-burger." She wrung the steering wheel with her left hand.

He frowned. "I didn't mean to upset you."

"I'm not pissed at you. I'm pissed at Helen for holding you hostage. I'm pissed you seem like a decent person, and you haven't had a bloody cheeseburger in two years. I hate that for you."

He stared at her. "You're mad for me, not at me?"

"Damn right I am. It makes me wish I'd planted C4 throughout that entire facility and wrecked the goff."

"Wrecked the goff?"

"Destroyed the place. Blown it to hell."

He laughed, startling her. He seemed to surprise her whenever he laughed, making him wonder if she was missing out on laughter in her life. "Remind me never to piss you off." How delightful he felt to have someone enraged on his behalf.

He composed himself. "You can do that? Do you know how to plant C4, as you say, and blow the hell out of something?"

"Yeah, I do." Her voice turned small and hollow. "I'm part of the Shadow Guardians. We try to protect Vanir bloodlines and the other bloodlines of the light. We fight Helen's forces in a war the rest of the world knows nothing about."

She held the wheel with her left hand as her right hand gripped her thigh, fingers curled into it. "We aim to stop and prevent exactly what you've gone through in the last two years. Obviously, I don't know what all your misery involved, but captivity in that facility guarded by a dragon encompasses everything we stand against. It sickens me."

He reached over and took her right hand to prevent her nails from digging further through her pants and into her thigh. When she glanced at him, he caught sight of those glacier pale-blue eyes.

He smiled. "Okay, but as far as I'm concerned, today was a win for the good guys. Instead of being angry at finding me there and somehow thinking anyone should have done something sooner, enjoy your success. You gave me a new life, Rosalyn. I owe you in a way that can never be repaid."

"Don't say that," she whispered, staring straight ahead.

"Why?"

"Because you make me want to use that debt to coerce you into helping us. Helping the Shadow Guardians. And I know it's too soon for you. You've to decide to want to help, not because you feel a sense of obligation." She pulled her hand back and gripped the wheel before giving him soft, heart-felt smile. "Let's focus on you getting some enjoyment out of life for a few days."

CHAPTER

FOUR

When they took the interstate exit, Apollo's mouth watered as Rosalyn pulled around a Wendy's drive through and ordered a double cheeseburger meal for him and a baked potato for herself. After she picked up the food, she drove to a clothing store beside a pharmacy in a nearby strip mall.

"Sit tight and enjoy your meal. I'll grab us some clothes and toiletries."

Apollo was already peeling the foil away with eyes only for his burger. "Sounds good. I'd love razors and scissors."

When he bit in, his mouth exploded with the flavor of the patties, cheese, bacon, and catsup. He ate slowly, savoring every bite. And God bless that woman, she'd bought him the full meal with fries. Halfway through the burger, he had to stop. He was unaccustomed to the rich, greasy food. He sensed if he ate too much, he'd upset his stomach.

Reclining his seat, he closed his eyes to relax and enjoy the sensation of a full stomach. Images of captivity flashed through his mind.

Helen's lab.

Her unrelenting demands and threats.

Her insatiable desire to inflict pain—hot wax, raking nails, gnashing teeth.

She was a beautiful woman with a dark heart and demon blood. He'd hated being her plaything for so interminably long. His own personal hell.

A cold sweat poured over him.

He must have dozed, because he jerked awake when Rosalyn dumped a cheap looking overstuffed beach bag in the back seat before settling in the driver's seat.

"I bought us both some outfits, bathing suits, pajamas, and undergarments, hazarding a guess at what size you might be. I also got toiletries."

"Thank you for everything," he said, shaking off the chill from his catnap visions.

"Was the burger all you remember it being?" She eyed him as if noticing his fading distress.

"Yes, thank you." He smiled. "Do you want me to drive while you eat?"

"Um. I'll keep driving."

"I haven't forgotten how to drive, Rosalyn. In fact, I used to work as a paramedic, and I was an excellent driver."

"Yeah, well, the rental is under my name, and you've not got a license. Why don't we make driving one of those pleasures we ease you back into? Like lattes." She patronizingly patted his leg.

"Funny," he deadpanned, though he enjoyed her sense of humor. Settling back into his seat, he didn't close his eyes this time.

ROSALYN PULLED INTO THE BED-AND-BREAKFAST, a cozy three-story house with a wide porch and plenty of shade from river birches and sycamores. A swinging love seat hung under the shade of a red maple.

"Looks like a fine place for some rest and relaxation." She put the car in park and hopped out.

"You say those words like you're not even sure what they mean. How long have you been fighting this war?" Apollo climbed out of the car.

"Donkey years." At his puzzled expression, she clarified, "Too long." She glanced down at his bare feet on the gravel lot leading up to the front porch. "Doesn't hurt?" She reached in the back seat and pulled out the bag of goodies she'd purchased earlier.

"I haven't owned a pair of shoes in two years. Makes for tough soles."

Rosalyn suspected he had more than durable padding on his feet after two year's as Helen's captive, but she wouldn't pry, despite a strange urge to offer a sympathetic ear.

They climbed the steps together, and Rosalyn knocked on the front door.

A plump woman in her sixties with a broad smile opened the door. Her expression went a little wide-eyed when she took in the sight of Apollo, but she maintained her smile.

"Afternoon. I'm Rosalyn Capall. We called ahead and prepaid."

"Of course, of course. Two bedrooms. I have you on the third floor."

"This place looks wonderful," Apollo said.

"Oh, thank you. We try our best. Come on in. My name is Nancy." Sweeping her arms from side to side, she gave them a tour, showing them where morning breakfast would be served. She handed them a brochure with directions to local hiking trails, antique shops, fruit stands, and nearby diners, then led them up the stairs. "We have two other couples staying currently. They are on the second floor."

The top of the stairs led to a hallway with the two bedrooms at opposite ends and a shared bathroom in the middle.

"I'll let you two get settled." She retreated down the stairs.

Apollo was surveying the floor, grinning with delight as if he was staying in Dunluce Castle.

"Right." Rosalyn lifted the bag of clothes and toiletries. "Here's your paraphernalia. You can have the bathroom first while I eat my spud."

"You're amazing, you know that?"

She stepped back, giving a wary look. "You'll not hug me again, will you?" She refused to admit how part of her liked his body wrapped around her. Even the handholding in the car had sent an unfamiliar warmth through her.

She was here to protect him, not indulge romantic fantasies.

AFTER EATING HER MEAL, Rosalyn paced her room, restless in the small space. It was neatly furnished with a mauve montage among the dressers, bed canopy, and colorful metal wall decor of crabs and fish. The lovely, cozy room was certainly nicer than any place she'd stayed at in her travels on a budget.

Still, she struggled to enjoy the ambience and couldn't shrug off the nagging feeling she should be planning for the next mission. She should be scheming how to destroy that facility. Except that wasn't so simple. Now that Rosalyn had infiltrated the place, stolen Helen's pet healer, and angered a dragon, Helen would know the location of her scientific lair had been exposed. Before Rosalyn would even have a chance to coordinate a strike against it, Helen would probably relocate her diabolical lab. The only thing for Rosalyn to do was to settle in, ensure Apollo's every comfort, and hope he would agree to a debriefing with the Council of Mjölnir.

After she ate her baked potato, she contemplated taking a walk to shake off some of her excess energy. Maybe on an isolated section of beach she could even transform into her four-legged variant and gallop for a stretch.

If she left for, say, an hour, did she have to worry about Apollo? What if he ran off? What if the magnitude of his freedom struck him in a sudden panic attack and she wasn't here for him? No, she couldn't leave and risk giving him the impression she'd abandoned him.

She could take a relaxing, hot shower. Maybe that would help. When she walked out of her bedroom, she saw that the bathroom door was closed. She checked her watch and noted Apollo had been in there for thirty minutes.

After moseying back into her room, she flopped onto the bed and stared up at the mauve canopy, strumming her fingers on her abdomen. Ten minutes later, she got back up, paced again, and checked the bathroom again. Still occupied.

Back in her room, she texted Raine and let her know they'd arrived safely at the bed-and-breakfast, and Rosalyn would keep her updated on Apollo's status.

A few minutes later, she peaked back out into the hallway to see the bathroom door still closed. She checked her watch again. He'd now been in there an hour now. She wondered if she needed to be worried about him or frustrated he was taking his sweet time.

Setting her resolve, she marched down the hall and prepared to raise her hand to knock on the door. Before her knuckles could make contact, the door swung open. A man, glistening and gorgeous, wearing nothing but a towel, stood before her. Sinewy muscles ran beneath pale skin from lack of sun. His now short brown hair was wavy down to his ears and almost dry. He had a square, cleanly shaven jaw and thick, full lips.

"Oh, hey." Apollo gave her a lopsided grin. "I hope Nancy doesn't mind that her trash can is full of hair."

"Um…" Rosalyn knew she was staring, but she couldn't help herself. "You…"

He had well-formed peck muscles and a six-pack she could run her tongue along. Speaking of tongue, why did hers feel swollen and useless in her mouth?

"I… check on you." She felt the heat of embarrassment and mortification creep up her neck and into her cheeks. That body had hugged her earlier. That body had ridden on her back when she sprinted into the woods. That body had no business being paired with a man of his sweet disposition.

He ran a hand over his jaw, the same jaw she wanted to run her lips over. "I don't think I missed any spots."

She pursed her lips and shook her head, not trusting herself to attempt speech again.

His grin widened into a smile. "Okay, well, I will relinquish the bathroom to you."

When she didn't–couldn't–move, he eased around her, one hand still holding the towel around his waist. She turned to watch the back side of him walk away, half-hoping the towel might slip lower, because she knew there must be an amazing ass under there.

A HOT SHOWER. A long shave. Clean clothes.

Life for Apollo was bliss.

He had the rest of his life to figure out, but that novelty could wait until after he'd relaxed on the beach. Images of sand and waves conjured Rosalyn walking beside him, enjoying the view and enjoying a view of him in swim trunks. Had a woman ever been so lusty-eyed and tongue-tied around him? Not that he recalled.

He smiled to himself, thinking of how she wouldn't be calling him Chewy or hairy or homeless-looking anymore. He would have liked to stand there and let her look as long as she wanted, but her heated gaze had been affecting his body. If her eyes had trailed lower, she would have noticed the tenting towel.

If he could recreate the moment during a sunset walk on the beach, maybe he could chance offering her a kiss. Then again, he considered how she'd taken down Nid in hand-to-hand combat in under sixty seconds. Maybe he should let Rosalyn make the first move. He didn't want his first post-freedom kiss to end in a throat punch.

A knock sounded at his door. He swung his legs off the bed and stood. When he opened it, Rosalyn stood before him in nothing but a towel, long wet hair draped over her shoulders. Her skin glowed soft and clean by the hallway light. She smelled like the ocean breeze mixed with citrus.

Her presentation was much more sudden than anything he'd hoped for, and he was a little hesitant to seize the opportunity. He'd imagined there would be at least a little courting before they fell into bed together. That being said, he wouldn't make the mistake of offending her by asking to slow things down.

When he smiled and took a step forward, she stopped him with a firm hand to his chest. "You've the bag with our clean clothes. I need my clothes."

Mortification washed over him as he realized he'd badly misread the situation. "Oh, of course." He leaned back and spun, eager to find the bag in hopes she'd forget the way he'd practically lunged at her while she wore nothing but a bath towel.

He thrust it toward her.

She glanced inside without taking it. "Why don't you take out all your things so we aren't constantly back and forth in each other's space?"

He tossed out his swimsuit, change of clothes, and flip-flops before handing the bag to her. Before she could take it, he said, "For the record, I like you in my space."

Expression hiding behind glistening gray strands of hair, she took the bag, turned, and walked back down the hall.

CHAPTER

FIVE

When Rosalyn finally slept, she slept hard. She suspected the adjustment was in part to having been in a European time zone and now suddenly in US Eastern time. That and fleeing for her life from a dragon. The exhaustion certainly couldn't be related to the way Apollo jumbled her up on the insides.

Waking, she tossed off the covers and looked out the window at the beach. Frothy waves rolled onto white sand in front of a horizon of dark blue sparkling water. The sun would soon rise, filling the gray sky with a burst of orange.

A man in swim trunks weaved in and out of the surf. Apollo appeared to be enjoying himself. Intermittently, he would bend and inspect seashells in the sand, the wind whipping through his hair.

He'd been about to kiss her yesterday when she'd shown up to get her change of clothes. She couldn't let that happen. Could she? Apollo was her responsibility and probably vulnerable, fresh out of captivity. He was also a full-grown man with manly desires matching her own yearnings. Was there some moral code about physical entanglement in a situation like this?

In any case, this was entirely too much deep thinking before a cup of coffee. She dressed and crept down the stairs to the kitchen, where she spotted Nancy.

"Good morning, Rosalyn."

"Morning, Nancy."

"No need to be stealthy, though it's very thoughtful of you. The other couples left this morning on a bike tour. You and your friend have the place to yourselves. Coffee?"

"Yes, thank you."

"Of course, dear. Cream's in the fridge." She handed her a cup. "Did you sleep well last night?"

"Very well. The ocean sounds lulled me into oblivion." She set to work fixing a cup of coffee for herself, black, and one for Apollo. She took a guess and added a splash of cream to his.

Moving around in a homey kitchen around an older woman had a lump forming in Rosalyn's throat and the sudden need for air. As soon as the steaming cups were ready, she stepped onto the back porch, grateful for the breeze.

Apollo was coming up the steps with disheveled hair and a broad smile. When he saw her, his smile faltered. "Are you okay?"

She held the cup up for him and nodded. Swallowing, she shook her head. "Just a sentimental moment in the kitchen with Nancy. Flashbacks of my ma."

He blew on his coffee but kept his eyes on her. "Something happened to her?"

Rosalyn nodded. To her dismay, a tear slipped out of one eye. She wiped at it. "Ugh. I hate crying."

"I don't mind it." He plucked the drink from her hand and set both of them on the porch railing. "These need to cool down anyway. Walk with me on the beach." He extended his hand to her as he walked toward the steps. "If you feel like talking, talk. If not, we'll just walk."

She took his hand, and they descended the steps down to the beach. Cool sand sank between her toes and her hair stirred in the breeze. She let go of his hand in order to quickly braid her hair and keep the strands from flying in her face.

"I grew up in a little town called Adare. Ma was an accountant, and Da was a writer. Life was simple, happy. They protected my secret of what I am and promised me I'd find others like me one day. I was a surprise baby, so Ma was in her late fifties and Da was late sixties by the time I was a cagey teenager. With Ma's health not so good, we didn't travel. I was barely eighteen and taking a gap year when they were killed in Dublin. Robbers, the authorities said. I learned later it was a gang of Fire Demons."

She looked down to see Apollo's hand in hers again. Had she done that or him? Regardless, she squeezed in appreciation.

"After the funeral, a Shadow Guardian recruited me. I've been doing missions ever since."

He stopped walking. "Since age eighteen?"

"Six years."

"I'm hugging you now. Just take it. If you don't need it, I do."

He wrapped his arms around her. She accepted him and returned the embrace. They held each other in silence, listening to the sound of the surf.

She sniffed and took a step back. "I usually do reconnaissance or demolition. You're my first rescue, but we didn't even know Helen had captives in that facility."

Because she didn't want his compassionate gaze melting her into a puddle of tears, she turned and kept walking. She hadn't chosen an easy life, but she had purpose. Her role in helping the shadow war kept her going each day.

"You mentioned you used to be a paramedic," she said, needing a shift in conversation.

"Yes, I loved my job. I had one-on-one patient contact. I could heal people in the back of the truck and no one knew it was magic, not modern medicine. The shift work was simple, and I made enough money as a single guy to feed my hobby—dirt bike racing."

She gaped at him. "You rode dirt bikes but you were terrified riding a horse?"

He held up a finger. "Intimidated. Not terrified. Besides, I control the speed and direction of travel on a dirt bike. It's entirely different from riding a wild animal."

She scoffed. "I am not a wild animal."

He chuckled. "When I met you, you kicked Nid's butt and faced down a dragon with an excruciating wound like it was just another day at the office. Then you transformed into a horse. You looked like a wild animal to me."

She shook her head with a grin. Looking up and down the beach, she noted only a smattering of people in the distance on either side.

"You want to ride now?"

His eyebrows lifted. "On the beach?"

"I've always wanted to run through the surf," she said.

"Far be it from me to deprive you of a dream."

"This time. Sit back. Use your thighs to squeeze and hold on. You can grab my mane if you need to, but you'll keep your balance better if you rely mostly on your legs."

"Legs. Got it."

With one last glance around, Rosalyn transformed. She'd done it so many times that the process was seamless. Clothes, or anything she was holding, morphed with her and changed back to its original form when she did.

Apollo beamed at her. "That's amazing. I'll never tire of seeing that." He took two bounding steps, leaped, and swung a leg over before pulling himself upright.

He stroked her neck, creating a soothing sensation she'd never felt before since she rarely shared her horse form with anyone. Most of the world contained normal humans, unaware of the supernatural world around them. She couldn't share her gift with just anyone. Others like her hid their abilities out of fear of discovery. Those putting them to good use were fighting the shadow war.

He whispered, "Okay, gorgeous. Show me what you've got."

She sprang into a gallop, hooves digging into the moist sand. When the small waves washed under her, her powerful legs sent sea spray into the air. She paced herself, loping without an all-out sprint.

He kept his balance in the center of her back. "This is wonderful!"

She took them about two miles, passing the occasional jogger or family who gaped with surprised delight.

At last, she slowed to a walk and turned back the way they'd come.

Apollo leaned close, hugging her neck. "Absolutely incredible." He slid off her back, leaving her coat bare and cool in the spot. "Don't change back yet. You have an audience."

The few scattered people lounging on the beach or on their condo porches were pointing at the pair of them. They walked side by side, Apollo resting one hand gently on her neck. His touch eased her angst at having so many eyes on her.

WHEN THEY WERE on a more isolated stretch of beach, Apollo watched Rosalyn change back into human form.

"Your magic," he began, "it's breathtaking."

Truthfully, so was she. Her long, white braid had come loose in areas, causing little strands to dance around her head. Her cheeks were flushed and eyes bright.

"You can heal people. That's pretty fantastic. For a homeless person," she added with a wink.

He extended a hand and gently gripped hers. "This okay?"

"Yeah," her voice was slightly hoarse.

Did she understand the implication? This time, he wasn't offering to hold hands for emotional support. This was something more intimate. He rubbed his thumb up and down her hand as he held it. Little sparks of delight danced along his skin anywhere they touched.

Chemistry.

They turned toward the porch of the bed-and-breakfast where Nancy came out to greet them. "Breakfast is on the table. Get it while it's hot."

As they climbed the steps, he lifted his nose into the air. "Do I smell bacon? I've died and gone to heaven."

Rosalyn chuckled. "You're so unabashedly American."

He raised the hand he held and pressed his lips to the back of it before releasing it all together so they could wash hands before eating and he could put on a shirt.

A few minutes later, they sat at the table before a helping of scrambled eggs and hash browns. Rosalyn had retrieved their coffee cups and replaced the cooled drinks with hot ones. Apollo had several pieces of bacon, but Rosalyn skipped it. They each had a glass of orange juice.

Apollo dug in, profusely thanking Nancy for the excellent meal as she passed through the dining area.

Rosalyn ate slowly, staring at him in amusement. "I've never seen someone so thoroughly enjoy a simple breakfast."

"Stick around and you'll see me enjoy all the simple pleasures in life."

"Okay. What's next? Kayaking? Beach lounging? I spotted a rental place for little four wheelers you can drive around town. That may feel a little like dirt bike riding."

He blinked at her. Damn, she was thoughtful. "I'd like that... provided they don't need to see a driver's license first."

They chatted for several more minutes about other activities before Apollo declared himself full. Standing, he carried both their plates to the kitchen sink.

"Oh, never mind that," Nancy said. "I'll take care of the cleanup."

Turning back to Rosalyn, he said, "Shall we clean up and then take a stroll down to the ATV rentals?"

They walked up the stairs together, hands bumping into each other.

"Sounds rollicking."

At the top of the stairs, before they could split apart, he took her hand again. He stared at the delicate bone structure and trimmed bare nails. Practical for her line of work. He rubbed a finger along the smooth skin, not making eye contact as his heart kicked faster.

He raised his eyes to hers, leaning closer and terrified she might jerk away from him in disgust. Would she hate him for wanting to kiss her so badly when they'd only recently met? When he reached one hand up to cup the side of her face and she didn't move away, hope filled him.

He bent lower, and she threw her arms around his neck, pulling him down for a searing kiss. Her mouth was warm, soft, and yet another part of her that was magical. He slid hands around her waist, drawing her closer and deepening the kiss. Her curvy body fit against him perfectly.

After a full minute of tongues colliding, she pulled away from her. Wide eyes with dilated pupils stared up at him as she licked her lips.

"That was nice," he said.

She nodded, touching a hand to her lips.

Clearing her throat, she said. "Aye. Nice. Meet you downstairs in ten?"

"Yeah."

CHAPTER
SIX

Rosalyn made her mission for the day to fill Apollo's cup with activities he'd missed out on for the last two years. He could forget the horrors of his captivity, and perhaps she could even forget about the war and her role as a soldier for the next twenty-four hours.

Could time and compassion dispel the haunted look in his eyes he gained every once in a while when there was a pause in conversation? The title of goddess of the underworld wasn't bestowed on someone who would serve tea and crumpets. She had a reputation for torturing her victims. Apollo had been her prisoner for two years, and she'd probably done any number of unspeakable things to him. With his ability to heal, he would only ever have internal scars.

They walked along the beach, played a round of putt-putt golf, drove race golf carts around the track, and ate ice cream after lunch. They talked about him growing up in Georgia and his work as a paramedic. This was as close to 'normal' as even she could remember her life in years. Fighting a shadow war didn't have built-in vacation time.

"I'd like to help your cause," Apollo said as he nibbled his ice cream. He took small bites, and Rosalyn wondered if the desert was too sweet—like the latte.

"We could certainly use the inside information you have on Helen," she said cautiously since his offer to 'help' sounded suspiciously like 'join.'

He leaned over the railing on the dock, looking out at the ocean as his scoop melted and dripped onto wooden planks. "I don't mean just inside information. I want to help the cause."

She shook her head, a flare of protectiveness toward him surprising her. "You don't know us, Apollo. You need more information before you make a decision to change your life, like joining us."

His mouth quirked. "It's not like I can research your company on the Better Business Bureau or check out if your health insurance plan is up to snuff. I've seen what you and Raine and Will are capable of, and that's enough for me to pick a side. '*The hottest places in hell are reserved for those who, in times of great moral crisis, maintain their neutrality.*'"

She tossed her half-eaten cone into the trash. "Is that so?"

"Dante and I spent a lot of time together these last two years."

She sighed. "Frigg knows we need someone like you. We don't have a healer, but I also don't want you to feel like you've moved from one cage to the next."

He chucked his ice cream after hers, and wiped his hands with a napkin. "So don't put me in a cage." His voice had an edge to it she hadn't heard before now.

"You wouldn't be in a cage per se, but you wouldn't have a normal life either."

He gave a bitter chuckle. "I haven't seen normal in a long time. I don't get to see my family again—not if I want to keep them safe. Not until Helen is dealt with. In the meantime, anything I can do to undermine Helen will give me satisfaction."

They resumed walking along the boardwalk, fingers entwining. Holding his hand felt blissful natural, like they'd been doing if for weeks.

"Then I'll put in a grand word for you," she said. "Please understand how there may be some hesitancy on their part. The four of us know the circumstances under which you've been in captivity and how we barely escaped with our lives. But the Council is entrusted with thousands of lives and is always worried about spies. They'll probably want to keep a close eye on you for some time, including any forms of communication."

Apollo squeezed her hand. "They trust you?"

She snorted. "As much as I've done for the cause, I certainly hope so."

"Then you could be my guardian in my probationary period."

"I've feelings for you. I'm sure that'll be seen as a compromise in judgment."

He spun her sideways and into him, wrapping his arms around her. "You have feelings for me?"

She laughed and smiled. "Uh. I think that's obvious."

He pressed his lips to hers for a brief kiss. "I like kissing you. I like feeling you against me like this."

"I like it too." She relished the feel of him. "There's no guarantee we'll be assigned to work together if you join."

"If I'm their only healer, then I'll use that leverage. You need to be part of the package. I trust you. I know you." His voice was soft, not like he was staking his claim but filled with a hope of more time together.

She was flattered by his affection but shook her head. "You've known me for only two days, Apollo. That's not a lot of time for trust." She wanted so much more time with this man and liked the idea of working together. She also wanted to protect him and wasn't sure she could do both.

"It is to me. Let's go rent that ATV."

AFTER THE ATV RIDE, Apollo parked the vehicle at the bed and breakfast so they could use it again the next day. He'd loved driving with Rosalyn hugging his back. He pocketed the key as they made their way into Nancy's house. Dusk settled over the beach behind them.

As they climbed the stairs to the third floor, fingers entwined, he offered sincerely, "Thank you for everything, Rosalyn."

"Day one. We'll have more fun tomorrow," she said.

He pulled her into his arms at the top of the stairs. "I'm not ready to say goodbye yet." Leaning down, he pressed his lips to hers, and she opened to him, mouth and body pressed against him as her arms snaked around to hold him.

He'd intended only a chaste kiss, but her touch and her tongue were driving him wild. Locked together, they backed toward her bedroom. He couldn't think straight with her breasts against his chest and the moans escaping her lips. Suddenly, they were on her bed with the door closed.

"Rosalyn, Rosalyn." He didn't even recognize his own panting, rasping voice. "I want you more than I want my next breath."

She smiled, sliding her shirt up and over her head, revealing large, plump breasts beneath her bra.

His breath hitched, but he held himself back. "It's important that you know one time with you won't be enough. I like you. I like everything about you—your work, your compassion, your magic. I want this moment with you, but I want so much more. I want to give you so much more." He kissed her soft, exposed flesh.

"I'd like that. While we're being honest, you need to know this is me wanting you and not some attempt to manipulate you into helping the Shadow Guardians."

"No, I don't think that at all." His lips moved over her neck, loving the soft moans he drew out of her. "You need to know that parts of me are broken."

"Everyone has broken parts, Apollo. No one travels this world unscathed. We can work through our issues together."

She ran a hand through his hair, arching her back as he kissed her delicate skin. "I'm clean."

"Me too." Perhaps that went without saying given his healing abilities, but he wanted her to know she was safe with him.

He leaned back to look her in the eyes. "You are so beautiful." He slid a hand lower, under the elastic waistband of her fitted pants. "And I won't last long, so let me take care of you first."

He worked his fingers as he alternated kissing her mouth and breasts, drinking in her moans and gasps as she clawed at the bedsheets. She finished undressing, giving him full access to her body. He stroked again and didn't stop until she quivered, shook, and stilled.

Rosalyn was certain she'd melted into a puddle on the bed. No man had brought such euphoria with just his hands and mouth.

Their intimacy was the definition of too much too soon, but she wanted to give him pleasure, loved watching the way his expression glowed every time something brought him joy.

She'd been so busy with this never-ending war that she'd forgotten to enjoy all those little moments—cheeseburgers, walks on the beach, and the feel of a man's hands on her.

He shifted his weight, and the warmth of his bare skin touched hers. She blinked open her eyes to see him hovering over her. Muscular biceps held up a long, lean torso. He held still, pressed against her, but rushing nothing.

"Are you sure—"

Before he could finish that statement, she adjusted her hips and moved them up to let him slide into her.

"Rosalyn," he bit out the word, and his voice on the edge of control had her aroused all over again.

She wrapped her arms and legs around him. "Take me. Take what you need."

He took, but he also gave. She rode the wave of pleasure with him, faster and harder, until they reached the peak together and dove headlong over it and into sweet oblivion.

Their bodies lay entwined in a heap, Rosalyn loving the feel of his weight on her. Joy, plain and simple, filled her heart and had her smiling.

He nuzzled her neck. "I don't have words for how incredible that was. Not too rough?"

"No. And I believe the word is phenomenal."

"Yes."

Silence settled for a moment.

He stroked a thumb over her lips. "'My course is set for an uncharted sea.'"

"Dante?"

"Yes."

"I'll help you chart it," she offered.

"There are nine circles of hell in Dante's Inferno: Limbo, Lust, Gluttony, Greed, Anger, Heresy, Violence, Fraud, and Treachery. Bickering, fighting, flaming crypts, rings of blood and fire, trenches, and frozen wastelands. I felt like I visited them all over the last two years." He held her tighter. "I want to wrap my life in good memories with you so the nightmare of Germany will fade all the sooner."

Her heart broke for him. "What did Helen want with a healer? With you?" she asked.

"She's genetically engineering creatures of different Norse bloodlines." He adjusted his weight off of her but stayed close, one arm resting on her hip.

"To what end? Is she trying to make them stronger? We've heard rumors she's trying to breed out human DNA."

"I think that was some of her earlier work, but it was too slow. After mounds of genetic research, when she and her scientists got it wrong, she was back to the drawing board. I think she realized she didn't have that kind of time if she was going to have an army to win the war for her. Nobody knows when or where the battle the prophets declared will take place, but the general consensus seems to be within the next several years. She can't grow an army of evil adversaries in that amount of time. So, she's creating her genetic monstrosities and speeding up their growth."

"That's an atrocity. Is it working? Hell, it must be working. She owns a pet dragon for Pete's sake."

"Yes, and no. That's why she needed me. The genetic stitching, growth hormones, and steroid performance enhances only go so far. She was using me to heal them on a molecular level. I repaired her creatures as they rapidly grew, which seemed to keep them alive."

"Can you tell all this to the council? What creatures and how many? Any information could end up saving lives. I need to go back and destroy that facility."

"Yeah, I can do that."

"Shite, I'm sorry. I'm asking all of this after sex when I told you I wasn't sleeping with you for information. I'll stop. Are there other activities you want to do first? What about seeing your family?"

He shook his head. "I do, but there's too much at stake. Even if I did figure out a way to explain my absence, there's still Nid."

"What do you mean?"

"I reflected on a few things last night. I am an integral part of Helen growing her army. She won't simply chalk up my escape as an acceptable loss. She doesn't have a replacement. Nid is a dragon and has been my personal guard for the last two years. He knows exactly what I smell like. There was a Vanir prophet that escaped once, and Helen put Nid on her scent. He hunted her down and ate her for dinner. They will probably suspect I'd want to go back to my family. That'll be one of the first places Nid goes, and if he finds my scent there, he'll kill them all. Helen assured me that if I ever escaped or if I ever disobeyed, she would end all of them."

"Do we need to put protection on them now?" Rosalyn squeezed his arm.

He shook his head. "She would only hurt them after she got ahold of me. If she never finds me, they're safe. She wouldn't risk hurting them first and not having them as leverage to force my cooperation."

"You're in a terrible predicament. I'm sorry. We'll find a way to reunite you with them. Perhaps when the war's won."

"Perhaps." He wriggled closer to her and leaned in for a slow, succulent kiss. "For now, I just want to think about you and me and our time together."

"More ATV tomorrow?"

He pressed his lips to her clavicle. "Maybe. Or maybe we take another walk on the beach. I enjoy learning about you. But first, I want seconds."

"Seconds?" she asked, breathless.

He nibbled her ear, sending little waves of anticipation through her.

"Seconds," he repeated, his hot breathing spilling over her neck as one hand cupped her backside to pull her body flush with his.

Her body tingled with warmth. "I like the sound of seconds."

CHAPTER

SEVEN

The morning sun hadn't yet risen, and a gray horizon spread before them out the large window in her room. They had both woken in the early hours after a splendid night of passion. Rosalyn marveled at how quickly this man had endeared himself to her. She feared getting too attached. The future was as unpredictable as the weather in Ireland.

Apollo would help them—help the cause. His intel would be critical, and his healing abilities as well. At some point, perhaps he could be free of Helen for good and see his family again.

"What should we do today?" she asked him, not ready to discuss reality yet. She ran a hand along the muscles on his back, delighting in the feel of muscle and smooth skin. She would never tire of touching this man.

"Kayak."

"What's this?" Rosalyn asked, her fingers feeling a smooth lump under the skin of his lower back.

"I don't know. What does it feel like?"

She pressed down with her fingers to find the outline of a firm, oval-shaped object. "It feels like one of those big encapsulated pills people take for an infection. But what's it doing under your skin?"

She sat straighter as she continued to feel. "*Odin and Frigg!*" she swore.

"What's wrong?"

"I think it's a tracking device."

"Oh shit. Cut it out of me, Rosalyn. You have to get it out of me. I can't go back there." His voice rose in a terror she'd never heard from him.

After shoving up from the bed, she found her panties, bra, and a t-shirt and hastily dressed.

From off the nightstand, she pulled her pocketknife. "It's not sterile."

"I can heal myself. I won't get an infection. Cut it out." He lay with his back bare, hands fisting a pillow under him with a white-knuckle grip.

She hesitated, swallowing. "This'll hurt."

"It's going to hurt a lot less than whatever Helen will to do to me when she gets her hands on me. Cut it out." Gone was his chipper personality, replaced by commands and borderline panic.

"Right. Right." She snatched a towel out of the bathroom, opened the knife, and bent over Apollo. The only people she'd ever used a blade on were enemies. She'd never cut on a friend. A lover.

The damn thing wasn't shallow. If she was slow and hesitant, she would hurt him more. She would have to commit and be quick about it.

How had Helen secretly implanted a device? She must've drugged him.

"Here goes." With two fingers, Rosalyn spread the skin taught over the implant before slicing with her knife. She cut through the skin layer by layer. She wished her blade was sharper, more scalpel-like rather than just an average pocketknife.

Apollo buried his face in the pillow and unleashed muffled screams. She didn't slow down.

Slice, slice, slice.

Sticky blood coated her fingers and oozed out onto the towel. When the blade struck a solid object, she reached in with her left hand and used the fingernail of her index finger to torque it free.

"It's out." She pressed the towel to the wound.

Apollo stilled as a light golden glow emitted from his body. When she pulled the towel back, she watched the wound seal. She'd seen Raine heal herself, but this was different. Raine didn't glow, didn't have to focus on healing, and couldn't heal others.

Rosalyn stared at the blood coated tracking device, small and metallic. But what to do with it? She couldn't leave it here or they would track it to Nancy's. And if she destroyed it at this location, they would still track the last signal to the bed-and-breakfast. Perhaps she could get it somewhere in the ocean, away from condos, hotels, and homes.

"Can you move?"

He rolled over, face as pale as Lady Isobel's ghost at Ballygally Castle. "I can move," he croaked.

"Pack up. We've to go," she told him.

Shaky and sweating, Apollo pushed himself up. "Yeah, you're right."

APOLLO THREW what little belongings he had—toothbrush and swim trunks—into a plastic bag before joining Rosalyn on the stairs. He wore the same jeans he had yesterday and a fresh t-shirt from the three-pack Rosalyn had bought him.

When he joined her in the hallway between their rooms, her eyes flashed with caution. She held a finger up to her lips. She wore black jeans and a t-shirt they'd bought yesterday that said 'Beachy Babe.'

Apollo stilled, heart pounding at the look of concern in Rosalyn's eyes.

She tilted her head back and sniffed the air while simultaneously drawing her gun into her right hand. He sucked in a breath and smelled the fishy odor mixed with the scent of smoke.

Nid.

The bottom stairs creaked, and Apollo's stomach leaped into his throat. His hand holding the bag of belongings trembled

"In the middle of the journey of our life I found myself within a dark woods where the straight way was lost."

He tried to grasp at Dante's words and focus his sheer terror on something that would release him from immobilizing panic. He looked into Rosalyn's eyes—worried but with a controlled sort of calm.

"Get the others out and call Raine for help." She passed her phone to him as she whispered the order. She told him the four-digit passcode to her phone.

"Shouldn't I be the one to fight him? I can heal."

She cocked her head to one side with a smirk, as if thinking his suggestion was so absurd it was cute. He agreed. She was the experienced fighter and the one with a gun.

He nodded before heading down the stairs beside her. He exited at the second level, making his way toward the other guests' doors.

Rosalyn spotted Nid as she wound around the stairs from the second floor to the first. He wore the same red uniform with square shoulders and white buttons—as if he were a guard for the Queen of England or a Beatles singer in Sgt. Pepper's Lonely Hearts Club Band.

When she took aim to fire, he jerked right. The loud shot rang out, but she knew she'd only clipped him as he spun away from her. She fired two more shots, trying to trail her bullets after him.

Behind her, Apollo's voice boomed as he banged on doors. "There's a fire! Everybody out of the house!"

She could smell the smoke more heavily now. When she pivoted around one wall, the kitchen and living room came into view. Before her eyes, Nid was transforming into his dragon form. Red scales fanned out, filling the room and blocking the view of the sliding glass door that lead to the porch and out to the surf.

She fired again, but Nid spun and the bullets harmlessly skimmed off his thick scales, spinning off into walls and shattering the glass behind him. She needed to get him out of the house before he started spewing fire and incinerated the occupants.

She sprinted at him, half-man, half dragon, as he was turning back toward her. Ramming into his still human torso, she wrapped her arms around his chest, her momentum carrying them out onto the porch.

Nid let out a grunt, stumbled, and tried to catch his balance as he fell down the stairs. He flung her aside using thickening, meaty limbs with such force it launched her over the dunes between beach and house.

She tumbled into the sand, the wind knocked out of her. Gasping, she pushed herself up to her feet, her mouth tasting of blood and sand, gripping her side as she sucked in air.

When her vision cleared, she watched in horror as the great red dragon spewed flames, coating Nancy's bed-and-breakfast. Even knowing she wouldn't cause any damage, Rosalyn fired her Sig at Nid's back in a desperate attempt to turn his focus to her to buy the house guests a little more time to escape.

Nancy's home erupted in flames, great billowing and bloated clouds of black rolling into the sky. Odin willing, no one was still in there.

Nid turned slowly to regard her with cool disdain, the way one might a fly buzzing around the house. The boards of the porch splintered beneath his enormous weight. Springing upward, he flapped his gargantuan wings to take flight.

She could appreciate his full glory as his body blocked out the sky. Four powerful, muscular legs, which meant twenty razor-sharp claws, were tucked close to his body. Large nostrils flared above a mouth full of predatory teeth made for ripping flesh. He had a crown of bone beneath the scales on his head, and Rosalyn imagined he could plow through a brick wall with a skull that sturdy.

She had his full attention now. Glancing up and down the beach, she only saw a few lone walkers and joggers were in the distance at this early hour. No one was close enough to be injured during her battle with a dragon.

"Come and get me." She glared at Nid, ignoring the quivering in her legs.

Turning, she ran. In mid-stride, she transformed into her horse form. Hooves digging into the ground, she bolted at a full gallop. Her lungs burned and a stabbing pain bore into her right side, but she didn't slow.

She would have one opportunity when he swooped down on her to take him out. Timing would be everything. If she failed, she would die and Apollo would return to the ninth circle of hell in Dante's *Inferno*.

EIGHT

Apollo herded the guests and Nancy to the front door and into the gravel parking lot. With the amount of smoke, everyone had given their instant cooperation, despite their gasps of surprise and whimpering protests at leaving their belongings behind.

Gunshots rang out, but he had to continue to move the group away from danger, ushering them to the farthest edge of the parking lot.

Behind them, the house burst into flame. Nancy fell to the ground weeping, but Apollo didn't have time to comfort her. Fortunately, two of the patrons stooped to attend to her.

With hands shaking, Apollo entered the passcode on Rosalyn's phone and found Raine's name under favorites.

"Hi, Rosalyn."

"No, this is Apollo. The dragon found us. Nid found us."

From around the flames of the house, Apollo glimpsed the tip of a red wing. Forgetting the call, he stuffed the phone in his jeans pocket and moved around the house to get a better view. In the distance, Rosalyn stood on the beach. His heart soared, but just as quickly constricted at the sight of the dragon's focus locked on her.

Could Apollo get to her before he did? Nid would destroy her, but he wouldn't harm Apollo. He was too valuable to Helen. Apollo needed to put himself between Rosalyn and the dragon.

He remembered the ATV. Dropping his bag of clothes, he felt in his jean pockets. Key.

Dashing over to the four-wheeler, he fired it up and headed down the road toward the small inlet beach access.

He swerved around bikers and a few cars, but there wasn't much activity at this time of the morning. Jerking the handlebars left, he jolted onto the narrow access road to the beach. He was sweating now, desperate to reach Rosalyn before Nid killed her.

On the narrow wooden path over the dune, not designed for four-wheelers, he bumped the edges with the wheels as he fought to keep the vehicle straight. When he reached the beach, icicles of fear coursed along his spine at the sight of Rosalyn in her beautiful equine form, running for her life with the crimson dragon bearing down on her. In the distance, beach pedestrians gawked.

Apollo gunned the engine. Just as the dragon dove toward her, claws first, Rosalyn shape shifted back into a human form while spinning in midair.

A gunshot rang out.

The dragon roared, but the bullet to his chest wouldn't slow him down enough to prevent him from colliding with Rosalyn. She would be crushed in a mound of flesh and scales.

Apollo jumped off the ATV seconds before he sent it careening into Nid's body. The four-wheeler slammed into the dragon's torso, sending him off course and toward the waves.

Apollo hit the sand hard, tendons tearing and joints dislocating as he tumbled. Coming to a stop in a heap in the sand, broken and useless, he watched helplessly as the dragon shook off momentarily being stunned and moved once again toward Rosalyn.

· · ·

ROSALYN WAS OUT OF BULLETS. She'd fired her last one, proudly dead center of his chest, but it hadn't been enough to kill the beast. The four-wheeler crashing into it might have broken a few ribs, but the dragon was still coming for her. Nid crept closer, pain in his movements slowing him down but anger in his eyes driving him onward.

She wondered what he would do to her. Did he like his meals raw or char-grilled?

What's waiting on the other side? she wondered.

Valhalla? Heaven? Nothingness? Her parents?

At least she'd had Apollo. She could focus on their moments of happiness and maybe just disconnect from the reality of what was about to happen to her.

Sadly, she had failed him—failed to keep him safe. When Nid finished with her, he would take Apollo back to the goddess of the Underworld. Rosalyn should've known something so valuable to Helen would've been marked, tracked. She was a fool to not have considered it sooner

The feel of hot breath and the smell of putrid sulfur told her the end was near.

Vibrant colors danced behind the dragon's enormous red head, illuminating him. Did he always glow like My Little Pony when he was about to kill, or was this how death greeted everyone?

With alarm, Rosalyn realized what those rainbow colors meant. She rolled old out of the way just as a metal spear plunged through the dragon's neck. Blood, dark and tarry, spilled onto the sand as Nid crumpled onto the shore.

Raine pulled Gungnir back out of Nid's neck just as Will swung his sword over his head like an ax and decapitated the creature.

Strong arms pulled Rosalyn close as the warmth of Apollo's magic filled her and healed her. She closed her eyes, her breath heaving in and out, both from the Irish Derby she'd just run and the fear of almost dying.

. . .

APOLLO HELD Rosalyn as he healed both of them. His head spun with the effort and the horizon took on a watery glow like a Van Gogh painting.

In the surf, Nid's form sank like a deflating bouncy house. The vast outline of him in red scales floated on the surface of the water before the brisk ocean breeze whisked it away.

Ashes to ashes. Dust to dust.

Apollo thought of Dante's words, "*Hope not ever to see Heaven. I have come to lead you to the other shore; into eternal darkness; into fire and into ice.*"

Raine and Will sheathed their weapons as they walked over to check on Rosalyn.

"Sleeping on the job?" Raine asked, a teasing tone in her voice.

Rosalyn blinked her eyes open. Apollo moved the hair out of her face, careful not to drop sand on it. She had saved him again. She and her friends.

After two years under Helen's oppression, he hadn't thought anyone stood a chance against her, but seeing this group in action changed his mind.

"I'd be perfectly content never to see a shape-shifting dragon for the rest of my days," Rosalyn said.

Apollo didn't have the heart to tell her right now that he knew Helen had one more just such a pet. He knew because he'd helped mend the creature's faulty genetic composition and strained development because of growth hormones.

"From Germany to the East Coast of the US. How did that thing even find you?" Will asked.

"Bloody tracking device," Rosalyn grit her teeth as she said the words. "Rookie mistake on my part."

"Just rest," Apollo told her.

"We need to get you two out of public view. It's sparse out here, but there are bound to be a few people who will have seen a big red dragon," Raine said.

"Do you have anything you can't leave behind?" Will asked.

Only this woman, Apollo thought.

"No," he said, "but there is the rental car in the lot and the four-wheeler in the ocean."

"We'll deal with those later."

Around them, rainbow light rippled, and the beach faded from view.

CHAPTER

NINE

Apollo swayed to the music as he danced with Rosalyn in his arms. He marveled at how they had become an inseparable unit in just three months. They were a team. She'd been teaching him to shoot and fight in between information-gathering missions.

Together, with Will and Raine's help, they had returned to the facility in Germany and let Apollo press the detonation button. Although the facility had been abandoned, blowing his prison to smithereens had given Apollo some closure to the nightmare he'd faced as Helen's captive.

"Twas a lovely wedding," Rosalyn said, drawing his attention back to the present.

Raine and Will had a simple outdoor wedding with fifty guests, half of whom were armed to the teeth should any demon intruders try to spoil the joyous occasion.

"Yes, it's nice to see romance and love blossoming in spite of the chaos around us. Breaks up this never ending war. Do you think we'll see the end of it in our lifetime?"

"Aye. The Council of Mjölnir is investigating the premonition of prophets. Apparently, three sisters and their mates will fight Helen in a battle to end it all. We certainly hope to be on the winning side, though my understanding is that the prophecies don't specify the winner."

"Three sisters?" Apollo glanced at Raine, who looked regal in her white dress, twirling with her new husband, whose adoring eyes watched her in his arms.

"Three Valkyrie to be precise," Rosalyn said.

"Doesn't Raine have two other sisters?"

Rosalyn snorted. "Raine is powerful. And we all consider her a Valkyrie, but let's have a look at the other two, shall we?" She angled him so he could see a woman standing off to one side scowling at the festivities. She had long dark hair and wore one of the bridesmaids' purple dresses. "That is Storm. I've never met her, and this is the first time I've even seen her. From what I understand, she doesn't spend much time around her family because she's too busy writing her travel blog."

Travel blog? Apollo mused.

"Raine doesn't speak about her much, owing to something painful in their past. Or so I've been told."

Rosalyn turned him again, where he could see the dance floor opposite where Raine and Will danced. "That carefree redhead who has a different partner for every song is Sky. She owns a wellness shop selling herbal remedies in Texas. She's away with fairies, that one."

"Fairies?" Apollo asked, still learning all of Rosalyn's Irish sayings.

"In her own bubble," she explained.

"She definitely doesn't look like a hardened warrior. So, does the Council of Mjölnir know who the three saviors are?"

Rosalyn shrugged. "If they do, they've not shared it with us."

And so, we wait, Apollo thought, *using the time to fight demons and trying to make the world a safer place.*

Rosalyn laid her head on his shoulder. He'd adored her when

he'd first met her, but that had morphed into love in a short time. Someday he hoped to see his family again, and introduce Rosalyn to them, perhaps as more than just a girlfriend.

For now, their life was one of travel and danger until the day three mysterious sisters came forward to fight the goddess of darkness. He hoped they would win the battle and end the shadow war.

******<<<<<<~~~~~>>>>>>******

Storm Surge, Book 2 (releases 2.22.23)

CHARACTER LIST - BOOK ONE

Leads

- Raine Thoren - Shadow Guardian and Valkyrie
- Will Decker - Special Agent of the FBI and descendent of Heimdall

Valkyrie Adversaries

- Jörmungandr (AKA Jör) - assassin and agent of Helen
- Helen ógn (Hel) - descendent of the ruler of Helheim

Shadow Guardians Supportive Team

- Usha Bakshi - US representative on the Council of Mjölnir
- Caroline Powell - Assistant Director, Criminal Investigation Division of the FBI

- Brok Waldorf - dwarf and weapon's maker
- Becky Noble - author of the Noble Prophecies
- Avery Swift - raven shapeshifter
- Jake Folkvar - Vanir and UK based Shadow Guardian

Main Characters' Family Members

- Wyatt Thoren - Father of the three Thoren sisters
- Ida Thoren - Mother of the three Thoren sisters
- Winston Decker - Older brother to Will Decker
- Walt Decker - Younger brother to Will Decker
- Ilene Decker - Will's mother
- Tom Decker - Will's father
- Storm Thoren - Raine's sister
- Sky Thoren - Raine's sister

NORSE NAMES

Mjölnir - Thor's hammer
Yggdrasil - Norse tree of knowledge
Gungnir - the Spear of Odin

Niflheim (Old Norse: "Niðavellir") - realm of frost and mist. This was the darkest and coldest realms and contained the spring Hvergelmir protected by the dragon Nidhug (Old Norse: Níðhöggr). The spring was the source of Élivágar, the seven rivers.

Muspelheim (Old Norse: "Múspellsheimr") - land of fire. Fraught with lava, flames, and smoke. Surtr reined over this land where Fire Giants and fire demons lived.

Asgard (Old Norse: "Ásgarðr") - home of the gods and goddesses (Aesir) and ruled by Odin. He was married to Frigg and possibly also Freya (some scholars postulate they may be the same woman).

Midgard (Old Norse: "Miðgarðr") - Earth. Midgard and Asgard were connected by the Bifröst, or Rainbow Bridge.

Jotunheim (Old Norse: "Jötunheimr") - realm of wilderness, forests, and snowy mountains. This is home of the Frost Giants (Jotun) who were the sworn enemies of the Asgardians. Utgard, the king, lived in a fortress of ice and snow.

Vanaheim (Old Norse: "Vanaheimr") - home of Vanir gods. Vanir were masters of sorcery, magic, and prophecy.

Alfheim (Old Norse: "Álfheimr or Ljósálfheimr") - home of the Light Elves. These minor gods of nature and fertility were known for having inspired poetry, art, and music.

Svartalfheim (Old Norse: "Niðavellir or Svartálfaheimr") - home of the Dwarves. Known for their master craftsmanship, these dwarves lived under rocks, in caves, and underground.

Helheim - home of the dishonorable dead. This realm was grim, cold, and devoid of happiness. Hel (daughter of Loki by some legends and daughter of Odin by others) ruled Helheim with her wolf, Fenrir, by her side.

DEAR READER

As I mentioned before, I would love to have you join my mailing list. I promise I won't spam you. I only send an email when I have a new book released, giveaways, or special discounts. And I'll never sell your information. You can also unsubscribe at any time.

You can also follow me on any of these social media platforms. Check out my Etsy page for signed paperbacks.

Also, as an independent author, I rely heavily on readers to spread the word about books they've read. If you enjoyed this story, kindly let others know by posing a brief comment on social media or leave a review where you purchased it.

Thank you for reading,

www.cbsamet.com

facebook.com/authorcbsamet

instagram.com/cbsametauthor

bookbub.com/authors/cb-samet

tiktok.com/@cbsametauthor

OTHER BOOKS BY CB SAMET

The Rider Files Suspense Novels

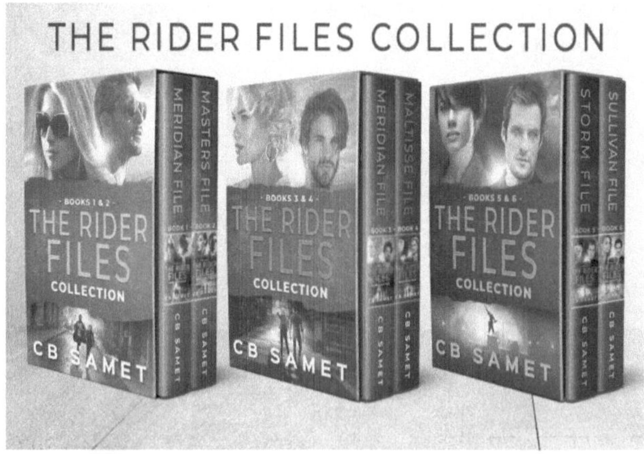

Join the Rider File protection team as they guard and defend their clients from deadly villains. Using their unique skillset and wits, they serve and protect

Meridian File / Masters File / Box Set 1

McMillan File / Maltisse File / Box Set 2

Storm File / Sullivan File / Box Set 3

<<<<<~~~~~*****~~~~~>>>>>

The Dr. Whyte Adventure Novels

Black Gold

Whyte Knight

Gray Horizon

<<<<<~~~~~*****~~~~~>>>>>

Sweet Romantic Suspense Novellas

IN BOXED SETS

<<<<<~~~~~*****~~~~~>>>>>

Love action/adventure and strong female leads in a fantasy world?

Check out my other genre:

The Avant Champion Fantasy Series

The Avant Champion: Rising

Malakai: An Avant Champion Origin of Malos Story (prequel)

The Avant Champion: Honor

The Avant Champion: Ashes

Brothers' Bond: An Avant Champion Malakai Story

The Avant Champion: Conquest

Isabel: An Avant Champion novelette

The Avant Champion: Redeem

www.ingramcontent.com/pod-product-compliance
Lightning Source LLC
Chambersburg PA
CBHW060909190726
48286CB00002B/426